SARA'S JOURNEY

THE BESS AND PAUL SIGEL

HEBREW ACADEMY
OF GREATER HARTFORD

In Honor of
Miriam Klau's
Bat Mitzvah
from
Mom and Dad

February 2007
Shevat 5767

*Publication of this book
is made possible by gifts from*

Betty Brudnick,

Mickey Cail,

and

David Gordis

and is dedicated to the memory of

Irving S. Brudnick,

who never stopped learning and teaching

SARA'S JOURNEY

David L. Shapiro

THE JEWISH PUBLICATION SOCIETY
Philadelphia
2005 • 5766

The Jewish Publication Society
2100 Arch Street, 2nd floor
Philadelphia, PA 19103

Design and Composition by Book Design Studio II

Manufactured in the United States of America

05 06 07 08 09 10   10 9 8 7 6 5 4 3 2 1

Library of Congress Cataloging-in-Publication Data

Shapiro, David L.
Sara's journey / by David L. Shapiro.
    p. cm.
Summary: Tells the story of Sara, an orphaned Jewish twelve-year-old in 1919 Russia, and her daring journey to Poland, Budapest, and eventually Palestine, interspersed with chapters narrated by Sara's daughter, a Zionist in Palestine in the days just before Israel becomes a nation.
ISBN 0-8276-0776-8 (alk. paper)
    1. Jews--History--20th century--Juvenile fiction. [1. Jews--History--20th century--Fiction. 2. Orphans--Fiction. 3. Antisemitism--Fiction. 4. Zionism--History--Fiction. 5. Israel--History--1948-1967--Fiction.] I. Title.
PZ7.S52944Sar 2005
[Fic]--dc22
                                    2005013351

To my wife, Nat,
for an irrepressible and steadfast love
that never wavered, even when I stole away
to spend midnight hours with Sara

To our son, Stephen Shapiro,
and our daughter, Nancy Duke,
for encouragement and discussions along the way

To our grandchildren,
Jonathan, Aimee, and Matthew Shapiro,
for they inherit the future

And to our parents, Samuel and Anna Shapiro,
and Mike and Sydelle Adelsdorfer,
who instilled, by example, the power of selfless love

I am blessed to have such a family.

ACKNOWLEDGMENTS

Thanks to Diane Bryan, Mark Jacoby, and Donald Silverman for criticism and support; to Dr. Ellen Frankel, CEO and Editor-in-Chief of the JPS, whose early observations and patience helped make Sara a reality; to Janet Greenstein Potter for meticulous copyediting and guidance.

1

DRESKA, RUSSIA. WINTER 1919.

"One last favor, Peter Fedorovich. Save me from those Cossacks one more time!" The older man held out his hands in supplication. "Please, do it yourself—before they get here!"

Young Count Fedorovich shook his head. "How can I shoot my dearest friend? You are still my Jew, Ilya. I order you to run before I leave." Reaching across the table, he gripped Ilya's arm. "Sara is barely 12. Will you rob her of her only parent?"

Ilya ran his hand across the scar on his face. "I have prepared her for this day. What difference how it happens— by a Cossack's sword or the cough and fever I cannot cure? Either way, the end is near. Do it, my friend, and help me cheat them of this final victory."

"No, Ilya. You will get better. The czar is gone, and Mother Russia needs you and all the rest of her Jews. You know, as the landowner's son I must ride with the Cossacks out of the barracks. But when they make the turn for Dreska, I will continue straight ahead. I cannot return tonight."

Dying embers sparked in the fireplace as they left the table together. Ilya placed his arm around the nobleman's waist. "No more running, my friend. I am tired. These legs will not carry me where I wish to go." He slipped the count's pistol from the holster and pressed the young man's unwilling fingers around it. "It is settled, Peter. I'd rather die at the hand of my old friend than under a Cossack sword."

"This is insane. Sara would never forgive me. Where is she now?"

"Safe in Odenko, with a friend . . . unless Cossacks ride there as well?"

The count's eyes narrowed. "The colonel said only Dreska tonight. I'm sorry I could not send word sooner, but he insisted on another drink with my father and me. One sweep and back to the barracks, he said. But I'm afraid the taste of blood will surely make them partners with the drunken peasants who follow. Have all your people left?"

"The few who are quick. Others are still leaving, but I refuse to run another step. I gave Shmuel a letter for Sara." He buttoned the top of his best, white Sabbath shirt. "In your heart, Peter, you know I have reached the end. It will be a blessing." He threw his arms around his friend in a bear hug.

There was a time when Ilya could match the young count's strength, but that was long ago. The count's fine woolen jacket felt warm and smooth against his cheek, but it did not stem the cold emptiness spreading within him. He took one last look around the dilapidated hut that would soon go up in flames. He had tried so hard to shut out the evil world around them, but none of his prayers had ever made it better. "Come, my friend. It is time." Ilya buttoned his shirt at the collar, noticing for the first time how loosely it hung since he became ill.

Opening the door, he limped into the darkness. Memories flooded his mind. Only a few blinking stars, just like that night long ago when the Cossack's horse knocked him to the ground.

"Let him be. He's my Jew!" Count Peter had shouted, parrying the Cossack's saber. Ilya thought angels sent the young man, for he had never met him before. Tended by the count's personal physician, he was excused from working the fields until his legs healed.

Ever since, the young nobleman had watched over him and Sara and personally warned the tiny shtetl in advance of Cossack raids.

Ilya felt uncomfortably warm. He loosened the collar of his shirt as the moon suddenly slid into view, bathing the field in pale light. He turned to face his friend, still struck by the silent beauty of the Russian sky. How was it possible he could love this cursed land that tortured his people with such vengeance?

"Do it now!" he shouted.

Ilya heard the hammer click. How lucky he was to have such a friend. For the first time in his life he felt at peace. The count leveled his arm. Ilya raised his in farewell.

Was that Sara in the distance, running toward them, waving her arms? She cupped her hands around her mouth. What was she yelling? The crack of a pistol thundered in the still night. Ilya sank to one knee.

Sara vanished. She must have been an illusion. He lowered himself gently to the crusted snow. Warm and inviting, it enveloped him like the goose-down comforter in his grandmother's house when he was a boy. No one would ever make him run again.

"God rest your soul, Ilya Samovitch . . . and God forgive me!"

"Your father was a good man, Sara, may he rest in peace. He gave me this for you."

Shmuel Malka, Father's oldest friend, dropped a wrinkled note into my hand.

To My Darling Sara,

Thanks to God you are safe in Odenko. The Cossacks come shortly and I do not think I will be so lucky this time. We have talked about this day before, so now it is time. Each generation makes it better for the next, and as long as you are alive there is hope. Go to my cousin Mordechai in Drohobych. He will help you get to Budapest. Be bold, be brave, but do not be foolhardy. May God bless you always.

Your Loving Father.

"Oh, Papa . . ." I choked back a sob. "Peter Fedorovich should rot in hell!"

"Peter? After all he has done for us? If it weren't for him we . . ." Shmuel's raggedy sleeve smelled of damp earth and rotted beets when he touched my cheek.

"If it weren't for him my father would still be alive!" I shook off his hand. "With my own eyes, Shmuel Malka, I saw Peter shoot Papa last night. I was coming home from Odenko with my friend and saw them in the distance. I ran as fast as I could. I waved. I shouted. Still, he fired and galloped away. Papa was ill, but why should he die like this?"

"I don't know what you saw, Child, but it couldn't have been Peter. Why would he do such a thing—he loved your father and was a big brother to you. It must have been one of the young Cossacks. How could you see in the dark?"

He sat me down on a blackened chair—all that remained of our burned-out hut. Shmuel never married. He was like a gruff old uncle, ill at ease around children, but I knew he

4

loved me. "Dreska is no more, Sara. Count Peter warned us, but only 14 got away this time—including you and your friend. Fourteen out of 123 souls. A massacre!"

Shmuel wiped his rheumy eyes with his sleeve—his short, round body trembling with grief. "The czar is gone and still they hunt us down. Maybe the Bolsheviks will come, but who can wait? We leave for Podir in a few hours. Come with us Sara; it's safe there. Podir's too miserable for even a Cossack to waste his horse's dung upon it. And your friend Miriam is coming, too."

"She's not my friend; she's only 11. She acts like a child."

I took a deep breath. "Thank you, Shmuel, but we have relatives in Drohobych who can help me get to Budapest. Jews live like kings there. Here, the Cossacks still ride and peasants help them. Will the Bolsheviks be any better? I know they kill Cossacks and landowners but Papa said they also hate Jews; and if we could get to Hungary, life would be better there. That's where I'm going. I'll dig no more beets for the Fedorovich family—cursed be their name!"

"Sara, the count is not like his father. You curse Peter when you curse the Fedoroviches. That's a sin. It couldn't be Peter!"

How my heart ached to believe. I had always looked up to the dark-haired young nobleman who had done so much for Papa and me. In my mind he was as handsome as King David, as strong as Samson. The older girls of Dreska always acted friendlier to me whenever he visited. Count Peter was from a different world and as out of reach as my biblical heroes. He was gentile. He was the son of the landowner who abused us. Tears stung my eyes; for Papa, for me . . . and for Peter.

"Do not cry, little one. God forgives the sins we commit to survive from day to day in these terrible times. As long as there is life, there is hope."

"Not for Papa anymore, may he rest in peace. I still cannot believe it!" I dried my eyes. "If I hadn't gone to Odenko he might still be alive!"

"No, my child. What could you have done against Cossacks and drunken peasants?" Shmuel shook his head. "I beg you to come with us to Podir. Hungary is so far away."

"Papa talked about this day many times. Why don't you come with me, Shmuel? We can be Jews there and never have to worry again. There are no Cossacks in Hungary."

"I'm too old. Too tired." He sighed. "Besides, no matter where you go there are Cossacks. Maybe not by that name, but . . ." He blew into his handkerchief. "You were always stubborn, even as a baby. I will miss you, Sara." He sniffled. "How will you get over those mountains by yourself?"

"God will provide. Besides, Marya Petrovna and her husband are coming with me. I will miss you, too, Shmuel."

"Ivan Petrovna the woodchopper? They're not Jewish."

"No, but they are good people . . . like Count Peter. I'll be safe with them."

Muttering, he slipped out of his raggedy, long coat and draped it over my shoulders. "Take this. The cap, too." He withdrew a few coins from his pocket and dropped them into my hand. "I wish it were more, but it is all I have. Goodbye, my child."

We hugged. With another wrench at my heart, I tightened my grip around him. I was saying a final goodbye to Papa, to Shmuel, and to my life in Dreska. "God bless you, Shmuel Malka, for all you've done for me."

He cleared his throat. "May the Lord continue to watch over you . . . and our remnant of 14 wherever we go." The last of my protectors walked slowly into the dawn.

I had not the heart to correct him. Only 13 Jews had escaped the slaughter in our village. He did not know it was Marya who had gone with me to Odenko. She was 17 and a head taller, but I always acted older than my years. Her hair was golden blonde, mine was black, but we were like sisters, laughing and sharing secrets together. Before that terrible night, Marya and Peter were the only Christians I dared to trust. Now, she was the only one.

I did not know her husband, Ivan. People said he worked hard and never beat his wife. Marya had confided that they, too, were exhausted by the daily struggle to stay alive.

"Sara, we pray for the day when we can leave this wretched land. We all exist for the comfort of landowners. We do not hate Jews or Gypsies, not even cripples. We are all children of God, but Ivan and I are not like our neighbors. We are true Christians and we suffer like you." She made the sign of the cross.

"Except for the Cossacks," I said.

"True, but sometimes they beat us, too. They know we have Jewish friends, and Ivan will not join the neighbors when they ransack Jewish homes."

When Marya and I returned to find Dreska in flames, she decided to come with me on my journey westward. "This settles it! Ivan will not be surprised," she said, as we hurried past the smoldering ruins. "We've planned this for a long time. Ivan is an orphan, and my parents are too old for such a trip. When he sees what happened here he'll look in our secret place for the note I left. He'll know I've started for Stryi . . . that's our plan. He'll catch up to us in three or four days."

I turned for one last look. Our shtetl had always stood defiantly proud and apart from the gentile houses a short distance away. Two tiny villages side by side, yet worlds apart. Now, only gentile buildings were silhouetted against the bleak Russian sky. I took a deep breath and turned my back on the past.

Marya reached around her neck. "Take this, Sara; there aren't many Jews between here and Stryi." She looped a chain over my head. I looked down in horror at her gold crucifix. I lifted the still-warm cross quickly lest it burn my skin and sear my soul. I looked at her beseechingly. "I can't, Marya. It's . . . it's a sin for me to . . ."

"If Cossacks catch us, it will be a bigger sin to die when you don't have to. I'm sure your God will forgive you for wearing this if it keeps you alive another day."

Shmuel's words, but would he condone this? My mind was in turmoil. Marya seized my hand. "Don't be foolish. One more thing . . . I look Christian but you still need fixing." Rummaging in her sack, she took out a small kitchen knife. Holding my long black hair in one hand, she made quick, slashing strokes. "That's better, but you still look like a girl. Tuck it under your cap. That's better."

We kicked icy clumps from the side of the road, stomping and spitting on the frozen soil until we could trace black streaks across our faces. I pulled Shmuel's cap down to just above my eyes.

We examined each other carefully. Grimy, chapped hands with dirty fingernails hung loosely at our sides.

Marya wore Ivan's old trousers. My mud-caked skirt swept the snow with every step I took. With our heavy work shoes, we resembled all the tired, ageless, and faceless peasants working the same lumpy earth that would embrace them in death long before their time. With God's help, we would escape that fate.

Marya was still not satisfied. "We'll have to steal trousers for you, Sara. Dressed as boys, we'll be safer. Traveling only at night, we should be able to cover 20 versts before daybreak."

For two days we hid in lofts of deserted barns, never too far off the road. Luckily, we met no one. From our hiding places we waited for peasants to leave for the fields. Marya's daring was contagious. We stole men's shirts and trousers carelessly left hanging in open sheds. The frozen cloth crackled when we folded them into our sacks. I pitied the hapless wives who would surely earn a beating from their husbands. I hoped they weren't Jewish. Sometimes, we threw sticks at the geese sunning themselves at the front doors. If their flapping wings and loud hissing raised no alarm, we dashed inside to steal any scraps of food left around.

We took turns sleeping and keeping a sharp lookout for Ivan or any returning peasants. Marya slept soundly. No matter how often I changed my position on the hard floor, stalks of straw jabbed and poked from all angles. Our hut in Dreska was only slightly more comfortable than this loft; the thought unleashed a flood of memories. Papa always joked about purposely living in a hut so we'd really enjoy living in a mansion when we became wealthy. He was the peacemaker of Dreska. Before his latest illness, his tall, erect bearing inspired confidence in everyone. He always had a smile and a kind word, making light of the limp and the constant pain haunting him from old wounds. I covered my face with my hands and wept softly.

One part of life in Dreska had been good. I remembered little children laughing and playing outside the ramshackle wooden dwellings that leaned crazily against each other for support on Dreska's twisting streets. In stormy weather, mud sucked at our feet like clawing fingers, yet, somehow by Friday afternoon, every Jewish home was spotless and beautiful, ready to welcome Shabbos.

Papa said I was the woman of the house, so I lit the candles. He always sang the *Kiddush* softly and with such feeling that every Friday night brought the same bewildering ache—a longing for the mother I never knew. People said I resembled her—tall and slender with long, black hair. Neighbors also said she was pretty, but I felt they were just being kind because I had no mother.

I remembered the shy kindliness of Shmuel and loud neighbors who went out of their way to show affection. People eked out a living as best they could. While most toiled in the Fedorovich beet fields like my father and I did, there were laborers, water carriers, milkmen, scholars . . . and beggars. As poor as we were, there was always a small coin reserved for them. Giving charity was a mitzvah, and we could be as Jewish as we wanted inside our little ghetto. It was only when we ventured outside Dreska—or Cossacks came in—that we suffered for our faith.

I shivered, thinking how wonderful life really was then—in spite of the occasional calamities that befell us. My father enjoyed triggering my imagination, seizing every opportunity to point out the daily wonders other people took for granted. "Girls will have to know as much as boys to live in this 20th century, Sara. Wonderful things are in store. Forget yesterday—tomorrow will surely be better!" Papa was also the village optimist.

Not so Shmuel Malka. "I don't want you ever to forget how they oppress us!" Over and over he repeated, with the same dark intensity, the story of my first escape at the age of two. My parents ran from Cossacks on a dark and bloody night . . . Mother in one direction, Father in another. Shmuel scrambled in yet another direction with me tucked inside his overcoat. He flung himself deep in snowdrifts to hide from the raiders. He told me later how my father stood his ground swinging a scythe to ward off Cossacks and peasants. When it was over, Mama was missing. Neighbors said she escaped but froze to death in the forest. Shmuel knew otherwise and never let me forget it.

I had my own memories of once hiding under floorboards in a rickety prayer house. Another when I was four, cowering under the wide skirts of Gittel, the egg-lady, who stood like a rock outside her home while peasants torched her tumbledown hut.

Much later, Count Peter became one of my protectors . . . until the night he murdered my father! Over and over I relived that moment, unable to convince myself it was someone else. I took a deep breath to erase the past.

I slipped Marya's gold crucifix from around my neck and studied each detail in the pale moonlight. How could she have such faith in this statue? I know only God has such power. What bothers me is—will God really forgive me for wearing this?

2

Palestine. May 8, 1948, 1330 hours –

Kibbutz Yad Mordechai, in the soon-to-be State of Israel! Just writing these words takes my breath away. Only one more week until the British leave Palestine forever. Finally, we will have our own country.

I am Deborah Wiseman, Sara's youngest daughter. Another soldier and I are the first Haganah fighters sent to help this kibbutz defend itself against the Arab attack expected when David Ben Gurion announces statehood. Our orders are to hold this position at any cost and buy time for Haganah and Palmach fighters to reach Tel Aviv before the Arabs. We are proud to be entrusted with such an important mission.

This kibbutz was established in 1943, in memory of the Warsaw Ghetto Uprising led by Mordechai Anielewicz. It is both humbling and inspiring to be here. The kibbutzniks' high spirits are contagious.

2000 hours –

Too excited to sleep. I'll work on the manuscript that has occupied me for almost a year now—writing Mother's memoirs from her diary, aided by the conversations and stories

I've heard over these past 20 years. She was always candid, even when my questions bordered on the embarrassing. I hope Sara's voice comes through loud and clear, for I did my best to capture the essence of her independence and bravery. Her father also encouraged her to be respectful of authority even while questioning its values. She always said his curiosity was limitless—vexing even the rabbi with arguments about the customs shaping their lives. Mother said he told her he deliberately dropped the *h* from Sarah so his daughter would face the 20th century with an equally modern name.

She passed those same qualities on to her children, plus a keen imagination. "Deborah, you and your sister are native born; sabras need to be bold and brave, but do not be foolhardy," she would remind us. "Our freedom depends upon your strength and vision." Mother says we inherited our strong characters from her father. I wish I had known Grandpa Ilya.

Now comes our test. When the Arabs rejected the United Nations vote on partition for Palestine last November, we knew we faced a difficult future. It is awesome to know we are helping to shape destiny. Mother always said each generation has to make it better for the next; but here, in Palestine, people of every generation are involved. Hopes are high and we are confident. We will succeed because we must. I am surprised (and pleased) to find myself so calm, with an inner faith that we will prevail.

May 9, 1948, 0300 hours –

Late last night we were called suddenly at 2200 to unload a shipment of supplies. Having just now returned, I want to continue my thoughts about Mother. I always marveled at her amazing behavior as a 12-year-old facing adult situations. As a family, we often discussed the phenomenon of orphaned children—old before their time—forced either to overcome life-threatening dangers or perish. Father says our country has more than its share of such children. When this emergency is over I would like to go to a university— even if it's out of the country—to study how to alleviate the problems that plague some orphans in later life. Fortunately, Mother was strong enough to overcome hers.

May 9, 1948, 2000 hours –

This sudden hot spell does not bother me because our military operations are more exciting than those of last year when we brought illegal immigrants into Palestine. That phase was important for the country then and important for me, personally, because that's when I met Joel Aaronson. My unit was at the port when his ship—he was part of the crew—succeeded in running the British blockade, bringing in a load of immigrants and weapons. Joel is a British Jew (somewhat ironic!) and about my age. He made aliyah with his parents two years ago.

He thinks we're all arrogant and too sure of ourselves. I remind him that we can only depend upon ourselves for survival and that what he calls "arrogance" is nothing more than self-confident determination to do what we have to. If he thinks I'm bold, he's in for a surprise when he meets Mother . . . if our relationship gets that far.

Joel and I have known each other a comparatively short time and do not see one another that frequently. We do write a lot of letters. I find that people show their true selves easier on paper than in person, and from his letters I think he is the kind of man I could spend the rest of my life with. Of course, I wouldn't say this to him. He wants to have an "understanding," as he puts it, that we see only each other, but I'm not rushing into this kind of commitment yet. Before I was sent to Yad Mordechai, he said he was going to pull some strings and join me here. He does have a lot of contacts, but I doubt that will happen. It would be nice, though, I admit.

CHAPTER

3

RUSSIA. WINTER 1919.

Marya woke earlier than usual on the third day of our journey. "I had this wonderful dream," she said wistfully. "It was so real, Sara. Ivan was with us in Stryi, and a friend gave a party to celebrate our starting a new life away from Dreska. It was so real, I didn't want to wake up."

"I hope that's a good sign. Wouldn't it be wonderful to forget the past! Except, how can I forget that Papa is gone? Nothing seems real—Dreska destroyed, all those people dead, Shmuel leaving . . . and now we worry about Ivan."

"Don't look back, Sara. We're starting over. It has to be better than before. We've got to keep telling ourselves that." She stroked my hair. It was all I could do to keep from crying.

Marya was silent now, staring into space. Slowly, she broke the last of our stale bread in two and stuffed half into her sack. "It's no use. I can't rest while Ivan's out there. Our horse is old and slow, but they should have arrived by now." She hitched up her trousers. "You wait here. I'm going back to look for him. If we're not back by tomorrow morning, go on to Stryi without us. Are you afraid to be alone?"

"No, but we're together. I'm going with you."

"Don't be a fool. He's probably only a half-day behind us." She lowered the ladder to the barn floor below. "If

17

the horse lost a shoe, we'll catch up quickly. If it's a wheel, there's no telling how long it'll be. I don't want to jeopardize your chances."

I clung to her arm. "I can't let you go by yourself. Bandits on the road are as bad as Cossacks."

She shook off my hand. "No." Only the top of her honey-colored hair was visible as she lowered herself rung by rung. "Listen, Sara, we have to be practical. It's better that one gets away than three fail. With a little luck, we'll meet up with you in Stryi."

Hugging myself against the morning dampness, I watched at the opening in the wall until Marya disappeared behind the trees standing limb to limb across the road, branches drooping under the weight of ice and snow. Icicles sparkled in every direction as I squinted into the sun. It was warming up and I was feeling drowsy.

I thought I had slept only a short time, but when my eyes flew open I saw that the sunless, gray afternoon would soon be turning to dusk. I felt guilty for allowing Marya to go back alone. Chilled, I drew my coat tighter around me and descended the ladder.

Flickering lights in the nearby huts meant I'd meet no one on the way back.

If I hurried I might catch up to Marya and Ivan before dawn. Walking briskly, I ignored the frightening night sounds. The moon slipped in and out from behind black clouds as I hugged the tree line. Unseen branches grabbed my cap, showering snowy crystals down my neck and inside my oversized shirt. I broke into a half-run as the mournful cries of wolves seemed to be closing in. My mind told me they were far off but I shivered at the thought. Praying that Marya and Ivan would suddenly appear, I ran as fast as I could from the unseen terrors, my heavy shoes thundering on the frozen ground. I lost track of time. I was numb. I felt like I was floating in the air and looking down on this solitary, frightened girl scurrying back toward Dreska.

Suddenly, angry cries broke the stillness ahead. A sliver of light flickered off to one side. Drawing closer, I recognized Marya's voice coming from behind a thicket bordering the road. I dropped to my knees. Icy branches whipped and stabbed as I forced them apart for a better look.

Shifting moonlight and a small fire lit the clearing. A distraught Marya, hands pressed to her face, sat on the ground. Nearby, Ivan and a raggedy figure lay face down. A cart leaned on its broken axle, a pale white horse lying motionless between the traces.

A stocky, bearded figure strode into the firelight. A pistol in each hand made circles in the air as he cursed and raged. "Your man killed my partner over that miserable nag. A brave old Cossack he was, so now you will have to pay—stand up!"

Jamming one pistol into his waistband, he grabbed Marya's shirt and hauled her to her feet. She kicked at his shins, raking her fingernails across his face. With a torrent of oaths, the bandit dropped his other pistol.

From my hiding place, I parted the branches for a better look. His back was to me and I could not see where the weapon landed. Heart pounding, I thrust myself through the bushes. An overhanging branch knocked my cap off. I tumbled into the clearing.

"Get his pistol!" Marya screamed.

"Where?" I clawed the snow.

The robber whirled in a frenzy. "Sure, little girl, come help your friend. Now you'll both pay!" Turning back to Marya, he threw her to the ground. He grabbed for the pistol at his waist and I leaped on his back.

"Leave her alone!" Gripping his collar, I pulled with all my might. He toppled backward on top of me. Gasping for air, I grabbed his neck and dug my fingernails into the flesh. I reached around to claw at his face. He pried my fingers away. I grabbed his collar again. He grunted and kicked, but I held fast.

"Get the pistol, Marya. I'll hold him!" Out of the corner of my eye I saw her searching frantically in the snow.

"Oh, my God. I can't find it!"

With a mighty effort, the highwayman broke free. In a flash, he twisted around and came up with the pistol from his belt. "Don't you move," he shouted at Marya, "or I'll kill you right now." He glanced in my direction.

The gold crucifix had tumbled out of my shirt. "Give me that jewelry," he rasped.

"It's a crucifix," Marya pleaded. "She's only a little Christian girl. Let her be. You can see she's only a child."

The bandit leveled his pistol at her.

"Look," I screamed, "she's the Christian—blonde hair. I'm Jewish—*Shema Yisra'el Adonai . . .*"

"Stop the gibberish." He tore the crucifix from my neck. "Jew, Christian, who cares?" The back of his hand caught me high on the cheekbone.

I rubbed the bruise to ease the pain. Out of the corner of my eye, I saw Marya leap up and fly through the air. The bandit swiveled, firing as her body sent him tumbling to the ground. I heard him groaning somewhere off to my right. Marya lay face down on the ground. I screamed her name, but she did not answer. Scrambling furiously in the opposite direction, my fingers suddenly closed upon the lost pistol. Gripping it with both hands, I whirled to my right. The bandit was nowhere in sight.

Hearing a noise, I spun around. There he was, in a crouch, dagger poised. I never held a pistol before. Hands shaking, I raised it and tried to press the hammer back with my thumb. It didn't budge.

Pale moonlight glinted on his crooked teeth. He pointed the dagger at my waist. "Don't be a fool, little girl. Drop that pistol and I won't hurt you."

I froze. My cheek ached so badly that I could hardly see, and the gun seemed to be slipping out of my grasp. "Don't come any closer or I'll shoot."

"You're not even big enough to hold the gun steady. Come on," he cajoled, "give it to me and I'll let you go. I promise."

Keeping both hands on the grip, I slowly lowered the weapon.

Grinning, the bandit slipped his dagger into its scabbard.

"Stay where you are," I said, furtively inching both thumbs up to the hammer.

He advanced slowly, his toothy smile reminding me of the wolf my father had once cornered near our hut.

I raised the pistol, cocking it with both hands. The click sounded like a thunderclap.

He stopped. The dagger reappeared in his hand as if by magic. "Now," he grunted, "I'll have to teach you a lesson!" He lunged.

I closed my eyes and pulled the trigger. The dagger's hilt scraped my sore cheek.

"Rosalie, Rosalie, wake up before you freeze to death." Calloused fingers stroked my cheek. I blinked several times before the pinched face of an old woman came into focus. A fringed shawl was knotted beneath her chin. It was difficult to understand the words tumbling through the sunken mouth, but the concern in her watery eyes was unmistakable. A little old man hovered in the background.

"I'm not Rosalie. I'm Sara." Wincing, I touched my cheek and sat up.

"No games, Rosalie," she scolded. "How did you fall? You're face is black and blue."

"I . . . I'm not Rosalie." I looked at the old man. He shook his head sadly.

The woman squinted out of one eye and moved closer. "You're not Rosalie. Who are you? Where's my Rosalie?"

"Don't be upset, Grandma, I'll help you find her. My name is Sara."

The old man put his arm around the frail woman, helping her to her feet. "Rivka darling, Rosalie had to leave. She's fine. She said goodbye and not to worry." He kissed the careworn face.

The old woman looked sheepish. "I'm fine now, Mendel. I thought she was our Rosalie. How old are you, Sara?"

"Twelve."

"The same as our Rosalie."

"Rivka, look what I found." He pulled the bandit's lost pistol from his pocket.

"Throw it away this instant!"

"What if we meet bandits?"

"And if we did, would you know how to use it? You'll kill us yourself, God forbid."

She tossed the weapon aside. "Now, little one, what happened here? Who are those dead people?"

Rivka's eyes grew large as I recounted the terrible events of the previous night. She took me in her arms. "You poor child," she crooned, rocking me back and forth. Her gentle tone and soft embrace unleashed the sorrow lurking just beneath the surface since my early childhood. I choked back a sob for the mother I never knew. Reluctantly, I drew back from the warmth and safety of her arms. With an effort, I buried the memory once again.

"Sara, my darling, you shouldn't be traveling alone. Come with us to Miragon and we'll take care of you. We'll walk slowly until you regain your strength. Mendel, give her some bread and cheese from the sack. It's a little stale but you need . . ."

"I'm not hungry. Thank you, Grandma." God help them, I thought. If they could walk three versts in a day it would be a miracle. I felt guilty leaving them. "I'm old enough to take care of myself. Besides, I'm going in the opposite direction. First, though, I must dig a grave in the forest and bury my friends."

Mendel nodded. "I will help cover them with branches and rocks. It will be impossible, even with that axe in the cart, to dig graves. The two bandits we leave here for the wolves."

He didn't look strong enough to carry the sacks Rivka was guarding. I took his arm. "Mendel, you have a long journey ahead of you. I can manage by myself."

"No. I am helping."

I took the axe from the cart, averting my eyes from the bandit I had killed. I knelt next to Marya's body. Dear friend, I owe you my life. I'll never forget you.

Chopping furiously, I finally managed shallow graves while Mendel gathered broken branches and a few small rocks. I didn't know whether Jewish prayers were proper, but they were from my heart. When I fashioned a rude cross of two small branches and a strip of clothing, I heard a gasp from Rivka.

"Gentiles? They should all rot in hell!" Rivka trembled with anger.

"Rivka, Rivka, my darling," Mendel soothed, wrapping his arms around his wife. "Calm yourself. You promised not to think about all that. This is bad for your heart." He drew her gently to the ground, nestling her head on his shoulder.

I understood her grief; yet Marya and Ivan were not like that. "They were good people," I whispered. "My papa said we shouldn't hate all gentiles because then we become like our enemies, hating everyone who is different. That is a sin. God does not want us to be like that."

"Your father taught you well. We, also, thought like that—long ago," Mendel said softly. "But, where does God hide when tormentors oppress and kill us day after day?"

I nodded, for that always troubled me. Automatically, I repeated my father's explanation. "Papa said God sometimes hides, but not for long. He does not forget us, Mendel. And He doesn't mean for us to act like our enemies."

"I don't know what He means, but I will not blaspheme. Tell me, Sara, was the czar a Jew? Are Cossacks Jewish? I never heard of a Jewish nobleman, so if all our oppressors are gentiles, how can we not hate them?"

"But not all gentiles oppress us. Some are kind and loving like my friends were." I thought of Count Peter and the nagging doubts that never left me.

"Then you are most fortunate, little one. Our beloved Rosalie is dead. They have destroyed my Rivka with terrible memories that eat away her heart and mind. As for me," he whispered, "I try not to think." He kissed his beloved Rivka so tenderly that I thought my heart would break.

I pushed back the thoughts of my father. "May God watch over you both," I said hoarsely. "I have to think, though, that if I know three good gentiles then there must be more. Aren't there mean, despicable Jews, too?"

"Sadly, we have our share." Mendel's eyes blazed. "But do they burn your house and kill your children? And do they kidnap little Jewish boys to serve 25 years in the czar's army?"

Rivka uttered a little cry. She seemed to shrink within herself. Her eyes stared at me without recognition. Mendel helped her to her feet.

"You are right, Mendel," I answered weakly. "But if one hate begets another, it will never end. How can people go on living this way?"

"We cannot. Perhaps you can, Sara. You're old beyond your years, yet you're still a child. You call us Grandma and Grandpa, yet neither she nor I will live to see our 50th birthday. Why shouldn't we hate? We've been laboring and starving and running almost all of our lives." He sighed.

My heart felt like lead. "I understand, Mendel. Perhaps tomorrow will be a better day. I wish you both good luck."

"I hope so, little one." He hoisted both sacks over his shoulder. "Come Rivka, let's go look for Rosalie."

We turned from each other—they, in the direction of Miragon; I, to finish what I had started. First, I carefully searched the packed snow until I found Marya's crucifix. Next, I retrieved the pistol Rivka had thrown away and jammed it into my belt. Averting my eyes, I emptied the bandit's pockets of bullets.

Troubled by Mendel's words, I stood over the graves. How could I blame him and Rivka for hating everyone who wasn't Jewish? Yet, here was Marya in an early grave because she was trying to protect me. And where did Count Peter fit in? Was he the hero I looked up to or the murderer who killed my father? I longed for the days when my mind was free of such thoughts. Would they ever return?

I retraced my steps. Spying the same barn and realizing I shouldn't be walking in daylight, I ran as fast as I could, pausing only to make certain the building was still deserted. Exhausted, I climbed the rough ladder to the loft, loaded the pistol, and threw myself onto a pile of straw. Stretched out with the pistol at my side, I fell into a fitful sleep.

CHAPTER

4

I woke to the muffled sounds of distant workers on their way to the fields. Hiding until there was no one in sight, I set out to find any scraps of food left behind in the rude huts. Luckily, I came away with a small piece of hard cheese and three crusts of black bread.

For three days and nights I followed the same routine—dodging peasants and foraging in early morning; sleeping in the afternoon with the pistol by my side, and walking swiftly by night. I hoped I was going in the right direction.

At the end of the fourth night I found myself in the loft of a large barn that surely belonged to a nobleman or wealthy landowner. Tired from the night's exertion, I savored the last crumb of cheese, placed the loaded pistol near me, and proceeded to fall asleep.

I don't know how long I slept before a scratching sound sent my heart racing. I bolted upright. Only shadows and a few field mice were here when I lay down. A cold sweat chilled my forehead as a sense of foreboding swept over me. Searching for a handkerchief in my pocket, my fingers closed around the gold crucifix.

I studied the tiny figure. Statues and images were forbidden to Jews, but Marya drew much comfort from this one. Perhaps, as I got older, I would understand why.

A feeling of desperation came over me as I realized what lay ahead. Dear God, I prayed, help me get over those mountains and safely into Hungary where no one will care what religion I follow.

It was quiet, yet I felt a presence in the loft. I gripped the pistol and held my breath. The rustling sound grew louder. It had to be mice, I reasoned. I was not afraid of them. Tossing Shmuel's cap aside, I shook my curls free, wondering how long it would take for my hair to grow back.

A loud noise exploded above me. I threw myself to one side. Straw, arms, and legs showered down. I pointed the pistol. "Stay where you are!"

"Don't shoot!" A dark-skinned youngster scrambled to his feet, skinny arms waving high in the air. Eyes wide with fright, he stared at the weapon. "Please, Baba Yaga, do not hurt me. I am a good boy."

"Baba Yaga? I'm not that ugly old witch who rides around in a bathtub! That's a fairy tale. What are you doing here?" I grabbed him by the shoulder.

He shrank back. "You are trying to fool me again, Baba Yaga. I know it's you because only you could do such magic. First you are a man, then with my own eyes I see you turn into a girl!"

"I tell you, I am a girl dressed as a boy—never mind why. How long have you been sitting up there spying on me?"

"Only a few minutes, but I wasn't spying. I was up here waiting for my family when a man came in. I hid in the rafters. The man left and I started coming down. I lost my balance when you took off your cap and turned into a girl."

I unloaded the pistol and slipped the bullets into my pants pocket. Not wishing to scratch the crucifix, I transferred it to my shirt. His eyes sparkled in recognition.

"I'm Roman Catholic, too. My name is Stefan Miklos and I'm 10. What's your name?"

"Sara Samovitch. You look more like eight, and I'm not Catholic."

He came closer and peered into my face. "You're a little girl! How old are you?"

"I'm not little. I'm 12 going on 13. That's grown up."

He was not impressed. "You're not Catholic?"

"No."

"Sara? You must be Bilbodo!" he announced triumphantly.

"What's that?"

"Jewish. You are dark, but not like me." He drew himself up to his full height. "I am the only son of the Rom Baro. Gypsy chief."

"Stop bragging."

"Yes, you are definitely Bilbodo. That's why you are hiding. Don't worry; we'll protect you. Gypsies and Jews are much alike . . . everyone hates us." Frowning, he studied me from head to toe. "I don't know. First you change from boy to girl, then from Catholic to Jewish. Only Baba Yaga could do such things. Are you sure you . . . ?"

I kissed his cheek. "Baba Yaga has iron teeth. If I had them you would be bleeding."

"Ugh" He rubbed his cheek with his sleeve. "I hate being kissed. I believe you, Sara." He took a step back. "It will be dark before my father returns. Are you hungry? There's meat in my pack down below."

"I can't eat your meat."

29

"I have an apple, too. Can you eat that?" He turned toward the ladder.

"Don't you move." I pointed the pistol at his chest. "How do I know you won't turn me in?"

"I'm the son of the Rom Baro. And Jewish people are like us . . . we don't shoot people." Stefan squared his shoulders. "Besides," his dark eyes danced mischievously, "the bullets are in your pants pocket. Can I go now? I'm hungry." He walked away.

"Go," I said, feeling slightly foolish, yet undecided. Could I trust him? True, some Gypsies lived in ghettos, like Jews, but that didn't mean they liked us.

Stefan scampered back up the ladder, pack in hand. "Here. You first."

I pushed the meat aside. The apple was soft and mushy but I was starved. Between mouthfuls of meat, he sheepishly admitted that he was only eight but someday he would be the next Rom Baro. His father was the best horse trainer in the world and they would soon be heading back to Budapest.

My heart skipped a beat. "That's where I'm going."

"Why are you alone? Where is your family?"

"I have none."

"Who protects you?"

"I believe my God will watch over me, so I'm not afraid. Besides, I have this pistol."

"You're only a girl. You probably don't even know how to use it."

"I want you to know I just shot a bandit who thought like that."

"You did?" His eyes grew large.

I could see he didn't know what to make of this. I made a show of retying my shoelaces. "I did. How soon do you start for home, Stefan?"

"In a few months. My father has to train a few more horses, and then we have fairs in the North." His small mouth bulging with food, Stefan added thoughtfully, "Gypsies don't like the *gaje*—outsiders—so I do not think you will be allowed to travel with us."

"Tell your father I will work to pay for . . ."

Sounds of horses and creaking wagons came from below. With a seriousness belying his years, Stefan took my hand in his. "Come, I will talk to my father for you." Then, in a little boy's whisper, "Please not to mention Baba Yaga—the Rom Baro's son must never be afraid of anything."

From the doorway I watched the Gypsies make camp. Snorting and stomping, two well-fed horses were backing up a large covered wagon in front of the barn. Four wagons clustered nearby, their occupants deep in conversation. I couldn't understand Romany, but their colorful clothing reminded me of Gypsies I had seen as a little girl.

Stefan ran toward a tall, handsome man wearing a fur vest and slouch hat. He listened carefully, nodding and glancing in my direction. When the boy finished, the Rom Baro spoke sharply to a group of men standing idle and openly staring at me. Their women, dark eyes plainly hostile, scattered under the chief's stern gaze.

Stefan sauntered back. "After supper, my father will talk to you about coming with us. My father knows the owner of this estate, so we camp here tonight." He executed a half-bow and walked away.

I turned my attention back to the new arrivals. The women had disappeared; the men were now grooming their horses with loving care. No wonder the proud steeds moved and pranced with such grace. The sleek animals reminded me of how we used to fatten our geese—but our two-footed pets' comfort ended with our next holiday feast. That was a happy memory, but I missed Papa. He always said I should remember the past but not allow it to destroy the future. "We have been oppressed for so long that we accept the role of the hunted as our fate, but your generation, Sara, can change all that! Be bold. Learn everything you can and don't let them see you cry."

Feeling better, I retreated inside. Stefan came bouncing back, carefree and childish now that none of his people were around. "My father knows you have nothing to eat, Sara. Here's meat and bread for supper."

"Thank you. Did your mother make this?"

"My mother died two years ago," he said without emotion. "I'm looking for my jacket. Have you seen it?" He ran toward the ladder. "I must have left it up there." Stefan scrambled up the rungs, tramping noisily from one end of the loft to the other.

"I've got it!" came his muffled shout. The sound of running feet thundered overhead.

"Careful, it's slippery up there!" I gripped the ladder firmly.

Suddenly, there was a loud thump. "Hey!" Stefan's body came hurtling over the edge, his shoe catching the top rung. The ladder flew out of my hands.

Struggling to keep my balance, I reached up with both hands. "I'll catch you," I yelled, "take my . . ."

His head was a battering ram pounding my chest. My neck snapped back. Gasping for air, I clutched at his thin frame.

How could such a small boy cause so much pain?

CHAPTER

5

The pain in my chest woke me. I was covered with a blanket that smelled like fresh flowers. Tossing it aside, I was amazed to find a bright skirt circling my waist.

"Lay still, *gajo*." The comely Gypsy with black hair did not smile. "You're all right. Your chest is bruised, but nothing is broken. I rolled up your trousers under the skirt."

"Why am I dressed like this?"

"The Rom Baro's orders. You saved his son's life." Her dark eyes narrowed in a frank stare. "You've been sleeping three or four hours. I don't want to know anything about you, but during that time two constables came looking for strangers. They searched our wagons. They said four bodies were found not far from here. They recognized two old bandits, but the two in a grave were a mystery—a man, and a woman dressed as a man, both with yellow hair." She paused, giving me a knowing look.

I frowned but did not reply.

"The constables were puzzled because peasants reported seeing two young men—or possibly two women wearing men's clothes—skulking around and stealing things a few days earlier. One had yellow hair, the other black. The yellow-haired one is dead, so now they look for the dark-haired one." Her eyes challenged me.

"How's Stefan feeling?" I asked casually.

"Fine. While our people kept the constables occupied with foolish questions, the chief had me put a skirt on you and stain your face with herbs."

Instinctively, my hands went to my cheeks.

"Don't worry, *gajo*, it washes off. In a few days you can return to yourself. And you will be fine. Your chest will be tender for a few days."

I stood and put out my hand. "My name is Sara, and I thank you for everything. Let me give the skirt back to you now."

"Oh, no!" she exclaimed. "I mean, better not change just yet. Keep the clothes just in case. And the blanket, too." Ignoring my outstretched hand, she bowed slightly. "My name is Alepa." Turning on her heel, she walked away.

The tantalizing odors of cooking and frying drifted my way from campfires dotting the night. Everything smelled so good. How long had it been since I'd tasted hot food? Even though it wasn't kosher, as long as I didn't eat meat or chicken, I felt that God would understand. Fighting the temptation to devour everything, I sat in the doorway studying the Rom Baro's food. Impatiently, I pushed aside chunks of meat to look for the potatoes and vegetables. Suddenly, I realized that I had swallowed a piece of meat with one of the potatoes. Hunger conquered my good intentions—before I realized it, I finished the entire dish. Guilt-stricken, I looked around. No one had noticed my sin—only God. I sat there, feeling very much alone and expecting some kind of instant punishment. How I wished Marya were here with me.

Out of the darkness stepped Stefan and his father. "Excuse us for disturbing you, Sara Samovitch. It is good to see you up and well." The imposing Gypsy leader bowed. "I am Viktor Miklos and I thank you for saving my son. We are both indebted to you." He nudged Stefan.

"Yes, Sara Samovitch. Thank you for saving me. We brought cups and a pot of tea."

"Thank you." They sat near me on the ground while I served the tea. "I'm glad you weren't hurt, Stefan. And I thank you, Viktor Miklos, for hiding me. Now, we are even."

The Rom Baro chuckled. "You certainly are grown up for a little girl. We are now indebted to each other, Sara. Besides," his piercing eyes shone in the half-light, "the enemy of my enemy is my friend. Gypsies and Bilbodo both suffer under Russian boots." He sipped his tea. "Do you know where the name Bilbodo comes from? It is very interesting. Long ago, during the Inquisition, when Jews and Gypsies lived in separate ghettos side by side, a group of Gypsies elected a Jewish man, Yusef Bilbodo, to lead them." Viktor Miklos beamed.

"I never knew that," I said politely. I wondered whether Stefan mentioned my wanting to travel with them.

He studied the tea leaves floating in his cup. "My son says you have no family and you are going to Budapest. Traveling alone is dangerous. Aren't you afraid?"

I hesitated. "Yes. But then I think of my father, and I try to be brave."

"It is respectful to think that way about one's father." The Rom Baro nodded. "Stefan says you would like to join our caravan."

"I have no money, but I will work hard to pay my way."

"That would not be necessary; however . . ." He blew steam from his cup. "My son is a good boy and means well.

37

It is not easy to be Rom Baro for all the people; sometimes, your heart pulls you in a different direction. We—your people and mine—are much alike. Also, we are different. We do not wish to assimilate and lose our Gypsy ways. Frankly," his eyes held mine, "please excuse me for saying this, but it is honest. Experience teaches us not to trust the *gaje*—the outsiders. But, you may ride with us for a few days. Then we will see." He and Stefan rose to go.

"Thank you."

"Sara, constables are happy when trouble leaves their district, so we leave early in the morning. You will ride with Alepa and Stefan. It will be better if you continue to wear a skirt and dress like us." He chuckled. "You will be the first Jewish Gypsy!"

The red kerchief around Alepa's neck lit up her pretty features. Her trim figure moved gracefully and confidently under a long skirt as she grabbed the reins and sprang to the front seat of the wagon. She appeared to be about Marya's age. I wished she were as friendly.

Alepa pointed to the opposite end of the seat. "You sit there. Stefan is inside weaving baskets." She quickly turned her attention back to the horses.

Through the partly open flap I saw two men whittling away at small pieces of wood. A few children sat before a pile of twigs and branches. I climbed up and took my place on the seat, wondering who would sit between us. "Thanks for saving me from the constables, Alepa."

She nodded. With a brisk slap of the reins she eased our wagon into line directly behind the Rom Baro's.

Every wheel must have been thoroughly greased during the night for hardly a sound came from the five wagons in our caravan. Alepa maintained her cold silence the entire morning. From time to time, I stretched my arms and legs to steal a look in her direction. It was awkward being with someone who completely ignored me.

Careful to maintain the space between us, I tried looking over my shoulder at the wagons trailing ours, but the effort sent shooting pains across my chest. Swallowing hard, I kept my eyes fixed on the powerful hind legs of the horses pulling our wagon. Thinking Alepa was about to speak, I turned to her, but she had evidently changed her mind. That's the last time I'll do that, I vowed.

Around noon, one of the men came forward. He tapped each of us on the shoulder. "Lunch."

Alepa handed him the reins and stepped over the seat. Steadying myself, I followed through the open flap. The remaining man, still whittling, shooed the children away and pointed to the cleared area. I placed my sack of food next to a pile of twigs. Alepa still kept her distance. She ate her food while carrying on a lively conversation in Romany with the others. Ostracized, I stared into space, chewing resolutely on the tasteless, cold beans I had brought. The wagon lurched from side to side. Occasionally, I put a hand out to keep my balance. This driver was not as expert as Alepa—or else he didn't care.

Suddenly, a small clothespin flew through the air and landed at my feet. Looking up, I caught the amused glance of the Gypsy as his knife moved swiftly over a piece of raw wood. "Good morning, little one." He bowed slightly, his dark face breaking into a friendly grin. Hungry for any sign of friendship, I smiled back.

Behind me, Alepa spoke harshly. Probably rebuking him, I thought, but when I turned, she was scolding the children tossing twigs at each other. She left her seat abruptly. "Time to go up front again," she muttered.

By mid-afternoon I had had enough. Deliberately, I turned and stared at her. After an uncomfortable minute or two, she glanced at me. "Yes?"

I took a deep breath. "I'm sorry to be intruding into your life, Alepa. I didn't plan to, and I don't want anything from you. I'm not your age, but can't we be friendly?"

Still staring ahead, she spoke haltingly, "People are afraid of Gypsies and make us their enemy. For protection, we keep our distance and stick together. We do not associate with *gaje*, but . . ." She gave me a sidelong glance. "But you saved Stefan. Suddenly you are here and . . . and I am not sure how to act." She attempted a smile. "Being friendly with you is against everything we have been taught. It is hard for me to do that."

"I understand. I am Jewish and could repeat the same things to you. In our shtetl we . . ."

"'Stetull'—what's that?"

"You say it 'Sh' . . . like in 'shoe.' A shtetl is a little village. We are also forbidden to associate with non-Jews. I thought we were the only ones afraid of outsiders."

She seemed to be weighing my words.

"I don't think such customs are a good way to live. Do you, Alepa?"

She hesitated. "Sometimes I don't think so, but how can I go against tradition?"

"I have the same problem. We all wonder what our neighbors will think. My Papa said to do what's right and forget about the neighbors. But that's not easy. Can you do that?"

She shook her head.

40

"Neither can I."

We continued in silence for a few moments.

"You know, Alepa, I think you handle those horses better than some of the men."

Color crept into her cheeks. "The Rom Baro taught me." She eased up on the reins and on her private battle to remain aloof. "You are right, Sara. We'll be riding together, so I think it would do no harm if we became friendly—without changing our own ways."

"I'd like that." I extended my hand.

She hesitated. Then, as if testing the heat of a flame, she gingerly touched my fingertips. "We also avoid physical contact with non-Gypsies. For example, we buy and sell old clothing but are forbidden to wear anything *gaje* have worn. I say this because I saw the look in your eyes yesterday when I refused to take back my skirt and blanket."

"I had a friend named Marya. She was gentile but we were like sisters. We talked openly about our differences so we would not hurt each other. Do you think we can do that?"

"We can try. I never had a *gajo* friend before, Sara, and we never had outsiders stay with us. I wouldn't want to hurt you, so don't be surprised if I act like a stranger in front of others."

"I understand. I'm glad we can be friends, Alepa." I pondered a moment. "Let me show you something." I groped in my pocket, closing my fist around Marya's crucifix. It still seemed to generate a mysterious energy. My fingers flew open. The gold figure sparkled in the bright sunlight.

"But you are Bilbodo," she exclaimed. "Why do you—?"

41

"This belonged to Marya. She died to save me. Some- how, when I hold it, it's almost like she is here protecting me. You think I am doing wrong keeping it?"

Alepa paled. "I . . . I really don't know, but Christ died to save all of us," she whispered. She made the sign of the cross. "Did you know we are scorned for our part in His death?"

"No. Jews are blamed for that."

She shook her head. "The legend is that a Gypsy blacksmith was the only one willing to forge four nails, three of which the Romans used in the crucifixion. The fourth nail never cooled, so it continued to burn and sizzle as it chased the Gypsy blacksmith relentlessly. That fourth nail still wanders all over the world . . . and so do we."

"That story gives me the shivers!" I said, fingers still tingling as I carefully returned the crucifix to my pocket.

CHAPTER

6

Yad Mordechai, soon-to-be State of Israel. May 9, 1948, 1800 hours –

Today was another long day, most of it spent reinforcing the water tower on the hill. The settlers are friendly, grateful for our presence, and anxious to make us feel at home. It seems odd, somehow, that people about to go into battle must still concern themselves with the mundane chores of everyday life. The land has to be tended, cows milked, vegetables and fruit picked, horses and tractors carefully maintained, and eggs gathered from the henhouse. With weapons close at hand, people still have to mend fences and keep irrigation systems going—exactly what the early pioneers faced. I still marvel at Mother's facing those dangers at the age of 13.

We have two more days to shore up defenses. I can only imagine the preparation in Jerusalem. When the British leave on the 15th, it will be a race between us and the Arabs for key positions in that city . . . and many others. It is a race we must win, and win we will!

I am exhausted but happy. Mother's story is about three-quarters complete. We've heard the story of Marya's sacrifice so many times, yet writing about the bandits' attack almost moved me to tears. But for Marya, it is possible that none of us would exist. Mother lights a yahrzeit candle every year on the date she died.

When Mother's manuscript is complete, I'll add updates. I should easily finish everything by May 19th, my parents' 24th anniversary—God willing. We usually celebrate their anniversary in Haifa, but that is doubtful this year, even though our forces took the city last month and all the Arabs have fled. I don't know where Mother's Haganah unit is at this moment. Father is a medical and artillery officer in the Palmach, somewhere near Tel Aviv.

Theirs is such a wonderful marriage! Eelia (my older sister) and I often talked about the unconditional love and respect our parents have for each other. Is it possible such old-fashioned virtues still exist in this modern age? I love the story of how Father told her they were meant for each other. I hope Eelia and I find the same magic.

2230 hours –

The barrack is quiet and I am lying on my cot rereading Joel Aaronson's most recent letter. If we continue our friendship, it will take a lot of magic to make things easy between us. He keeps pressing me to stop seeing other men and date him exclusively. But the main issue between us is that he is Orthodox and I am not. "Listen, Deborah," he explains, "this is how I was brought up. As it is, my parents complain that I have strayed far since we came to Palestine." His parents are so Orthodox they don't consider me Jewish—which would be laughable if it weren't so utterly sad. Despite the fact that Joel does not subscribe to the rigidity of their beliefs, I know he is more uncomfortable with my Judaism than he admits.

Chapter 6

The religious issue between us is a serious obstacle. I cannot see myself subservient to Joel merely because he is a man, and when I go to pray, I do not want to be separated from the men in my family. Since I'm not inclined to make any kind of commitment to Joel at this time, there's no need to confront our differences head on. In the meantime, we sort of tiptoe around them.

I did learn he is one year older than I. We do enjoy each other's company, despite opposing views on many subjects. He keeps insisting that he wants to protect me, and I tell him I don't need protecting—I'm a big girl and a soldier. Mother and Father met Joel once, briefly. They think his concern for me is "touching," but they're my parents and I'm still their youngest daughter.

As long as we keep talking, however, Joel feels there is a possibility that we might make it work. I'm a fatalist. If it's meant to be, we'll find a way—although I doubt it.

CHAPTER

7

Russia. Early spring 1920.

At dusk, our caravan pulled up behind a dilapidated barn. Silhouetted against a darkening sky, a row of sorry-looking huts made a depressing sight.

"Nothing's changed," said Alepa. "Markova is so poor that even the Bolsheviks wouldn't come here. Tomorrow, the villagers will barter for clothespins and baskets and have their pots repaired. This place belongs to a nobleman who allows us to use his barn when he is away because we train his horses. When his estates were broken up, the peasants thought their troubles were over. Now they work for wages and scratch like chickens just to pay the tax collector." She turned to me. "I think the Gypsy way is better, Sara. We work for no one except ourselves."

I nodded. "If you can do that, it certainly is better. In Dreska, it would take a lifetime to earn enough to buy our little plot of ground, so the landowners still have their land. Maybe the revolution will change things, but who can wait that long? That's why I'm going to Hungary—there is so much opportunity."

"Aren't you afraid to travel alone?"

"Sometimes, but I try to be bold; and when I'm bold I feel brave. Do you think the Rom Baro will let me stay with the caravan?"

We dismounted from the wagon together. "He is a good man, Sara, but he must do what is best for the *kumpania*. Our community comes first, but I'm sure he will try to help you."

"I know." I watched her unhitch the horses. "Do you like living this way, traveling all the time?"

"I'm used to it. My father always says, 'Anywhere I fall is where I will make my bed.' I feel the same." She began brushing the horses' velvety sides.

"Isn't that a man's job?"

"Just like you said, I can handle horses as well as a man; besides, men and women don't have special jobs. We each do what's best for the *kumpania*." She paused. "Cheer up, Sara. The chief has a good heart. I'll see you tomorrow."

I headed for the barn. I probably would be eating alone again, but I didn't care now. I had made a new friend.

It was too early to go to sleep after my supper. I watched the women cleaning utensils while the men shooed youngsters into the covered wagons for the night. A few older children remained outside, talking among themselves. They never once looked in my direction.

The children reminded me of home. I could never lose myself for long in the childish games my friends played. I remembered all the dreams I had for a better life—fantasies about being blonde and gentile—not that I was ashamed of being Jewish, it was only that not being blonde and gentile in Russia prevented me from living freely and happily . . . and made me the target for Cossacks and drunken peasants.

Once I got to Hungary, though, I wouldn't have to apologize for being Jewish.

About to go inside, I became aware of the Rom Baro's voice rising above the others. He spoke in Romany, which I could not understand; but the soft cadences took me back to early childhood when, excited and frightened, I looked forward to the annual visit of those mysterious Gypsies who disappeared as suddenly as they appeared.

When Viktor Miklos switched to Russian, I was certain he did it for my benefit. "Tomorrow, we have only three hours to trade with the villagers before we resume our journey. It is important that each wagon has at least four armed men riding inside—two at the front flaps, two at the rear. It may be a tight squeeze and you may have to shift things around, but bandits and Cossacks are bolder in these parts, and we might even run into Bolsheviks as we approach Lvov. It is important that no one shows a weapon or fires one without my signal." He stepped out of the firelight and headed in my direction.

I heard the whispers as he approached. "Good evening, Sara." The Rom Baro's tone was friendly. "Alepa tells me you are getting along well together. That is good."

"I'm grateful to her, and to you for your protection."

He made a half-bow but said nothing.

I hesitated. "As long as you are continuing north to Lvov, do you think I could travel with you as far as Stryi?" I held my breath. How I missed the days when Count Peter would put his hand on my shoulder and assure me everything was going to be all right.

"What is there for you in Stryi? I have never seen a Jew there."

"I hear it's only a day's journey to Boryslav, and my father's cousin lives in nearby Drohobych. There, I can take a train over the mountains into Hungary." Please God, I prayed, let him say I can.

"Boryslav is not a good idea unless your cousin is a Cossack commander or nobleman. And because it is rich in oil, the Bolsheviks are sure to run there as quickly as they can. So, it is trouble either way. As for continuing with the caravan . . ." He cleared his throat. "The rest of our *kumpania* catches up to us in a few days. Then we will have a meeting and all the people will decide. We're still a long way from Stryi." He bowed and vanished into the night.

Immediately after breakfast I set out to enjoy the fair. It was early yet, and only a few villagers were present. The Gypsies joked and exchanged pleasantries with each other as they put finishing touches on their wares. There was a carnival mood in the air and my spirits lifted. Smiling in anticipation, I approached the first wagon. Conversation ceased immediately. No one looked me in the eye. Swallowing my disappointment, I walked away.

It occurred to me that I should have remained in the background until the crowds came. Alepa had cautioned me that my *gajo* presence offended many people; they tolerated me only because I saved the Rom Baro's son. Feeling guilty, I retreated, waiting until the eager citizens of Markova greeted their colorful, mysterious visitors.

Blending into the crowd, I was soon caught up in the exotic sights and sounds of a Gypsy fair. Rolled-up canvas sides exposed mounds of clothespins and rush mats. Sweet-smelling baskets and wreaths of dried twigs nestled comfortably amid fragrant pinecones. Little girls wearing long skirts darted in and out between the wagons. Attractive women with dark, flashing eyes hawked potions and charms promising undying love to sweethearts and pain-free limbs to the lame. Fortune-tellers whispered fantasies into willing ears. The citizens of Markova were plainly enjoying their brief respite from reality.

I trailed behind a group of villagers crowding the tinker's wagon. He was bald and sported a long mustache curled at the ends. "Shiny new pans, shiny new pans. Coppers or chickens—hold out your hands." His audience seemed mesmerized by the mustache that wiggled and waggled over every word of his singsong appeal. The tinker returned a dead chicken to a crestfallen housewife. "Can't take it, Missus. Our custom is to slaughter our own." His eyes swept the crowd, lingering when they met mine. I thought he looked angry.

The tinker beckoned to a wrinkled old crone carrying a live, one-eyed goose in a sack. "That one's fine." The fowl's thin neck bobbed up and down as its owner bartered its life away for three shiny new pots. As an afterthought, the tinker threw in a small jar. "No lover can withstand this potion, Grandma. Be careful!" The old woman giggled.

Laughing with the others as she melted into the crowd, I suddenly felt a tug at my sleeve. Suspecting a pickpocket, I whirled around. Stefan wore a serious expression on his face. "My father says to watch out for a tall man in a black cap. He's the town constable."

"Where?" Heart pounding, my eyes swept the compound. I turned, but Stefan had already disappeared. Edging my way back toward the safety of the barn, I noticed the crowd was thinning. No tall men were in sight. Only a few more steps and I'd be inside the cool safety of the barn. With a sigh of relief, I stepped across the threshold.

"Good morning, child." A pleasant voice greeted me from the darkness.

Black cap in hand, the tall man was most polite. "You are Sara Samovitch, correct? Don't be frightened. Our village has an old Jewish grandma who is ill and wishes to speak to another Jew before she dies. Will you please come for a few minutes? It's an act of mercy."

He had to be the constable, but how could I refuse a dying grandma? "I . . . I don't know. We are leaving soon and I cannot hold them up."

"It's only a question of minutes. I'll tell one of the Gypsies we'll be in the fourth hut down the road. Don't be afraid, girl." His fingertips rested lightly on my shoulder as we stepped into the sunlight.

I certainly wasn't leaving without telling someone. I held back, searching in vain for Alepa or Stefan. Gypsies scurried back and forth readying wagons. Suddenly, I recognized the bald-headed tinker. "Tell him," I said to the constable.

"Of course." He hurried ahead.

I watched as they conferred. The tinker glanced once in my direction before continuing on his way. The constable came back and took my arm. "He'll tell the Rom Baro. Come along . . . it's just a little ways off."

Somewhat reassured, I hurried down the road with him until we reached the fourth hut. He held the door open for me. "She may be sleeping, Sara, but it's all right to wake her."

"Grandma?" I approached the cot and bent over the tiny form under the blankets. "My name is . . . Why, it's just a bundle of rags!" I turned swiftly.

He pushed me onto the cot. "Sit down! You don't fool me like you did the others. I know the truth about you murdering those people."

I jumped up. "I did not! I killed a bandit who killed my friends. He was trying . . ."

Drawing a pistol, he shoved me back. "That's your story! You Bolsheviks start young . . . lying, stealing, and killing. No wonder you're in a hurry to reach Hungary. When the other constables return they'll put you in prison where you belong. Now sit, and be quiet." Edging backward, he kept his pistol pointed at my head. It looked like a cannon to me.

Frightened, I tried to stand again. My legs felt like rubber. "The Rom Baro will be here any minute, then you'll learn the truth. Let me go now and I'll say nothing about you kidnapping me."

"Kidnapping?" He snorted. "Sit, I say! If you take another step I'll shoot you for trying to escape." He slipped out the door. The key turned in the lock.

Heart beating wildly, I looked around. There was no window. A series of holes, high, near the roof, allowed the only ventilation.

Why had I ignored Stefan's warning? If I ever got out of this trouble I would never be so stupid again. Desperate and sick at heart, I fell back on the filthy cot. The tinker would have told the Rom Baro by this time, I told myself. They must surely be on their way now to rescue me.

An hour passed. Then two. I lost hope . . . I had been forgotten, the caravan long gone by this time. All my brave talk had been for naught. First, Count Peter's treachery—now the constable's. How could grownups treat children so cruelly? What hurt most of all was realizing I should have known better. Papa had warned me repeatedly about being foolhardy. A sob escaped me. This time, I let the tears fall.

Suddenly, the Rom Baro's voice outside sent my heart racing. "She'd better be unharmed!"

I brushed the tears away. A key turned in the lock and the Rom Baro burst in. "Are you all right, child?"

I buried my face in his jacket. "I told him the truth, Viktor Miklos, but he wouldn't believe me!"

"What did he say to get you here?"

"He said an old Jewish grandma was dying and she . . ."

The Rom Baro gripped the constable's arm.

The policeman paled and backed away. "Wait. One of your own Gypsies told me she murdered those people. It's true I made up the story of the old woman, but how else could I get her here? It was my duty."

"She's still shaking, you fool!" Viktor Miklos held me tight. "Sir, you are a monster and an idiot. Your superiors will hear about this—kidnapping a little girl. How could she possibly overcome and kill four people?" He pushed the constable aside.

As we walked out the door, the Rom Baro's comforting hand on my shoulder felt like the old days when Papa was alive and Shmuel Malka was always there, when Count Peter was my hero, and my world was secure. I blinked to keep back the tears.

"Thank God you're safe!" Alepa made room for me on the front seat as she picked up the reins. "It was lucky Stefan saw you walking down the road with the constable."

"Didn't the tinker tell the Rom Baro? He said he would."

"I don't know. I only know we were about to leave and you were not there. Then Stefan told his father." She clucked loudly to speed up the horses.

"Alepa, I can't stop thinking about what would have happened if I were traveling alone. No one would ever know I even existed."

"You mustn't think that way. You're here and safe with us, Sara. The Rom Baro is your good friend and so am I. In a week or so, the other half of our *kumpania* joins up with us, and we'll vote on your continuing with the caravan. You know that some find it difficult to accept an outsider in our midst; however, many feel friendly toward you in their thoughts but are afraid to show it."

"I hope they won't be afraid to vote for me at the meeting."

For several days our caravan made its way across the bleak countryside. I stayed close to our wagon when we stopped, talking to no one except Alepa and Stefan. Occasionally, the Rom Baro stopped by to see how I was faring. Stefan taught me how to start a campfire with wood shavings. "My father said I should keep an eye on you."

Being ignored had its benefits. I could study these interesting people without seeming rude, and I didn't have to worry about offending them any further . . . beyond my presence. Spending so much time with Alepa, it was natural for us to learn more about each other's worlds.

I was amazed by the similarities. From the beginning of time, she said, they were a people who had no graven images. They also believed in one God. Gypsies observed the ritual slaughter of animals for food; they were a peaceful people confined to ghettos alongside Jewish ghettos; parents changed the name of a seriously ill child to fool the Angel of Death; and they all had a fierce determination not to assimilate.

The more we learned about each other, the deeper our friendship grew. I told her about my father's determination that I should know as much as any boy. "If you had one wish, Alepa, what would it be?"

She didn't hesitate. "To be the wife of Viktor Miklos."

"Then I wish it for you with all my heart."

"And you, Sara. What would you wish for?"

"Above anything, I wish my parents were alive!" I sighed. "But that can't be, so I wish I lived in a free country. My father always said while there's life, there's hope. I believe that. I really do. I want to study at university, and I want a world where nobody cares if you're Jewish or Gypsy . . . a boy or a girl . . . or different in any way. And I don't want to have to do something just because my grandparents did it that way."

"It sounds too good to be true. Do you think that will ever happen?"

"I certainly do." I grinned. "And something more, Alepa. I really believe the day will come when women will have as much to say as men . . . although I would not like to hold my breath until that happens!" We both giggled.

At dusk the following day, we pitched camp in an open field, wagons drawn up in a semicircle. Alepa unhitched the horses and led them away. It took me a while, but I made a campfire like Stefan taught me. Grinning, he sauntered over after the flames caught. "You did a good job, Sara. My father said he will see you after the meeting tonight." He ran off to join the Rom Baro who was posting sentries around the camp.

Alepa returned with a loaf of black bread. "A neighbor sent this for you. She wishes you good luck in the vote. I told you there were others who like you."

"Thank her for me. It's a comfort to know I have some friends besides you and Viktor Miklos. What time do the others arrive?"

"They are overdue now. We may not vote for another four or five hours."

"In that case, you will have to tell me about it in the morning. I'm exhausted. I'm going to sleep right after supper."

We ate our stew in silence. After a short time, I put my dish down. "Something has been bothering me for days, Alepa. The tinker said he'd tell Viktor Miklos where I went, yet it was Stefan who told his father."

"Perhaps he forgot."

"I don't think he liked me to start with."

"You mean . . . ?" She gave me an odd look. "If he purposely withheld the information, his betrayal brings dishonor upon himself and every Gypsy—especially our chief. Such a disgrace makes the tinker *marime*—polluted! He would be banished from our community." She tossed the rest of her food into the fire. "I have lost my appetite. I will ask Viktor Miklos himself."

"Please, Alepa, don't say anything now. I don't want to cause more trouble. I need to stay with the caravan as long as possible."

Her face darkened. "I'll say nothing until after the vote."

"When would I have to leave if they decide against me?"

She shrugged. "Let's worry about that later."

8

Hearing Alepa outside at the campfire, I poked my head out, under the canvas. In the gray dawn the coffee smelled as bitter as my expectations. "Bad news, right?" My heart beat a little faster.

"Bad and good."

I bolted from the wagon. "The bad first."

She lowered her gaze. "I'm sorry, Sara. The newcomers didn't know you. They are against any strangers traveling with us."

"So, how can there be any good?"

Her eyes sparkled. "No one said when you had to leave. Maybe the Rom Baro will take you to Stryi after all."

"That would be wonderful!" I put my hand on her shoulder. "Thank you for everything, Alepa. You've been a true friend."

She gave me a quick hug and kissed my cheek. Her voice was husky. "I don't care who sees me. We're like sisters, Sara, and I'm proud of that."

The next sip of coffee didn't taste quite as bitter. "I feel the same, Alepa. And since I'll be leaving soon, I . . . I've been curious about something for a long time. Could I ask you something personal? It might be embarrassing, though."

She looked doubtful. "Embarrassing? I'm sure you wouldn't say something hurtful . . ."

"Oh, Alepa. Never! I want to be helpful. But it's up to you."

She took a deep breath. "Ask me."

"I was wondering if the Rom Baro knows how much you love him."

She laughed with relief, a slow blush filling her cheeks. "It's that obvious?"

"You should see how your eyes light up every time you talk about him. And the expression on your face, Alepa . . . it's beautiful!"

She shook her head. "No, it's not. I am so unhappy, Sara." Her expression darkened. "I'll have to be more careful. No one must know what I tell you now. I have secretly loved him even before his wife died of cholera two years ago."

"Doesn't he know? I can't believe it."

She sighed. "No one knows. My parents would be beside themselves that I even dared think such thoughts. The Rom Baro and I are in different worlds. It is our custom for the groom's family to give large sums of money to the bride's family before they marry, but any family would gladly accept a minimal *daro* for their daughter to marry this man. In fact, mine would forego the bride-price entirely because it would be such an honor to have him as a son-in-law . . .

"Sara, my parents are poor. I have already refused several offers that would have enriched them because I am waiting for a miracle. My parents are running out of patience because the older I get, the less money I'll bring."

"That's terrible. How old are you?"

"Sixteen." She was utterly dejected.

"Oh, Alepa. I feel so badly for you."

"Not a word to anyone, Sara. If my parents knew, they would marry me off quickly. Sometimes I think it is hopeless, when he treats me like a child. Most times, he treats me like a family friend."

"Why don't you tell him how you feel?"

"A girl can't do that, Sara. You're only 12. You don't understand."

"I'm almost 13. Why not?"

"She just can't. When you're older, you'll understand."

"Perhaps he's bashful and waiting for you to say something first," I ventured. "If I loved a man I would tell him, no matter what. Just think, Alepa, he might never find out how you feel and end up marrying someone else. That would be sad!"

She buried her face in her hands. "That's not our way."

"Then we have to find another way to let him know!"

She looked up with mournful eyes. "Could you go against your own traditions, Sara?"

"When your entire future is at stake? In that situation, yes!" I burst out. "At least, I think so . . . I have no family to upset. Couldn't one of your cousins or a friend tell him?"

Biting her lip in frustration, she shook her head.

"I have a thought. What if I gave him a note just before I left the caravan?"

She smiled sadly. "That's sweet, Sara, but I'm afraid not. I'll just keep praying for a miracle." She gathered up the coffee cups. "The others are preparing to leave. Come, let's get ready."

We strode across the clearing and climbed into the back of the wagon. As we sat facing each other at the open flap, Alepa handed me a rifle. "Ever used one of these?"

"Never. My people don't go hunting because shooting any animal for food is against our law. I'm afraid of such big guns."

"But you shot that bandit?"

"With his pistol. And it was the first time I ever held one. I guess I didn't have time to be frightened. It was him or me." I placed it gingerly across my knees.

"Now, it may be 'us or them.' Cossacks and Bolsheviks are roaming the countryside, and we're in the lead wagon. Two of our guards have been hurt, so I told Viktor we would take their places." She picked up the weapon. "Just hold it against your shoulder. Look down the barrel and aim along the sight . . . That's good . . . Then just squeeze the trigger. Brace yourself for the recoil. That's all there is to it."

"I wish I could practice once or twice."

"No time for that. You'll do well, Sara. Don't worry."

The morning passed without incident. At noon, Alepa told me to relieve the guard sitting with the driver. It felt good to stretch my legs. Picking my way carefully to the front, I stepped through the canvas opening.

The driver was Viktor Miklos. He smiled. "Good afternoon, Sara. Thank you for volunteering. We're changing our route slightly because Red Army units and a few straggling Cossack regiments are rumored to be roaming in this area. We'll probably come close to Drohobych after all. We'll know better tomorrow."

"I cannot thank you enough. I will be . . ."

The wagon lurched to a sudden halt. The Rom Baro struggled to keep the horses in place. "Trouble!"

A galloping horseman came to a halt alongside. His horse blew huge breaths, sides heaving. "Cossack patrol two versts ahead!"

"How many, Misha?"

"Twelve, fourteen. Resting by the side of the road."

"Did they see you?"

"I'm not sure. They may have."

Viktor shouted for the guard in our wagon. "Ride to the rear and turn the caravan around. Back to the forest we just passed and line up at the edge. Horses and children into the woods." He turned to Misha. "The other scouts?"

"Two remain to warn us if the Cossacks come this way."

"Rejoin them at once." Viktor turned to me. "We're now the last wagon. Bring Alepa up front."

Heart pounding, I shouted her name. Viktor coolly waited for the other wagons to reverse direction. Hooves churned the ground. Horses lunged, then stomped backward. Leather harnesses snapped sharply against the traces as wagons angled clumsily. Noise and turmoil reached a crescendo that magnified the terror.

Alepa sat between me and Viktor, who calmly braced himself to restrain our horses. Champing at the bit, the frenzied animals sensed danger. Tossing their heads angrily, they reared up on hind legs; their forelegs pawed the air to break Viktor's iron grip on the reins. He was immovable. How strong and brave he looked!

As I watched the string of wagons ahead careening from side to side on the frozen road, it seemed an eternity before the horses broke into a trot. Gripping the edge of my seat, I twisted around for another look. "No Cossacks yet!" I shouted. "How much farther?"

Alepa gripped my arm. "Any minute now. You'll see our scouts first, before the Cossacks."

I clutched the rifle. "I've run from them before, but I've never seen a Cossack up close. I hope I . . ."

Viktor glanced in my direction. "You'll do fine, Sara. Just remember how you shot that highwayman."

Thunder sounded behind us but the road was empty. In the meantime, we seemed to be galloping forever. The forest was nowhere in sight. My heart pounded as we rounded a bend in the road, and there it was. Pandemonium! Men running and shouting, horses whinnying, children dashing into the trees. Wagons ahead were jockeying into position as Viktor brought our horses to a stomping standstill. Above the milling noises, staccato hoof beats drummed at the rear. Why was the wagon in front having such problems? Our horses pawed the ground anxiously.

Cossack war cries echoed in the distance. "They've overrun our scouts," Viktor muttered. I held my breath. How much longer would he hold our wagon back? The Cossacks would be all over us before we got into position! Finally, it was our turn. Guiding the skittish animals skillfully into place, he tossed the reins to Alepa. "Into the forest. I'll get Stefan."

In a flash, she was down freeing the traces. "Yo!" Alepa screamed, gathering the reins and running between the spirited horses toward the woods.

I found Stefan and Viktor crouched behind the wagon. "They're not so good with the rifle," Victor said, "but a Cossack saber is deadly. Don't let them in close." Looking at me, Viktor stroked his son's curly head. "Stay close to Sara and Alepa. And keep your head down!" He ran toward the other wagons.

64

Stefan started after his father. I yanked him back. "Into the forest," I hissed. "Tell Alepa where I am."

Out of nowhere, a Gypsy came sliding alongside. "Now, you're not alone." It was the tinker, his bald head and fierce mustache no longer menacing. "No harm will come to you Sara Samovitch, I promise." This time he smiled. "I'll protect you, but keep your head down."

I felt guilty for misjudging him.

Viktor Miklos, standing off to one side, deliberately waited for the tinker to notice him. They exchanged looks. The Rom Baro slowly moved off.

Where were the Cossacks? It was one thing to be taken by surprise, but waiting for them to charge was unnerving. The tinker's hand was reassuring on my shoulder, but my insides were trembling. I crouched to make myself as small a target as possible.

"Sara, don't be afraid. I will not leave you under any circumstances. When they come down that road yell as loud as you can. It helps."

Minutes that seemed like hours passed without a sign of Cossacks. Viktor Miklos returned, looked at my protector, and pointed up the road. The tinker, rifle in hand, scrambled to his feet and ran toward the oncoming Cossacks.

Again that interminable wait. Finally, one of the scouts came running up. "They've gone back to their barracks, Chief. Looks like they were just trying to scare us."

Viktor Miklos grinned. "We live to fight another day. As long as we're here, we'll camp overnight in the forest." He helped me to my feet. "You did well, Sara Samovitch. I guess the Cossacks just wanted to have a little fun with us."

Alepa joined us. "False alarm. Thanks to God."

Finally, I found my voice. "I have to thank the tinker. That was very brave of him to stay with me. Where did he go?"

"Boris?" Alepa and Viktor exchanged glances. "I'll go find Stefan," he said, leaving abruptly.

I nodded. "He was a hero. He refused to leave me until Viktor ordered him to go."

She grimaced. "Boris was a traitor. He's not coming back."

"What are you talking about? He was ready to give up his life for me."

"He betrayed you to the constable—and purposely never told Viktor where you were."

"Why?"

Alepa shook her head sadly. "He hates all *gaje*."

"Oh, my God!"

"Only the Rom Baro and a few elders know of his treachery."

I put my hand on her arm. "I don't know what to say, Alepa. I should hate Boris, but he was ready to give up his life. He chose to stay with me and I can't forget that."

"He did not choose. The Rom Baro ordered him to protect you because he was a traitor. He bore false witness against you, Sara, an unthinkable crime for a Gypsy. He was banished from the tribe. Viktor Miklos gave him a choice: leave before the battle and be a public coward, or protect you with his life. Since there was no battle, he had no alternative but to leave and never come back. *Marime*! " She spat upon the ground.

CHAPTER

9

The new campsite, dark and foreboding, smelled of damp earth and rotted leaves. Though little sunlight penetrated the dense underbrush, the clustered tents and cheery campfires seemed more welcoming than before. Spared a Cossack attack, the Gypsies were jubilant. Word must have spread that I had carried a rifle as a guard, for suddenly people were smiling and nodding at me. I found Alepa mending the wagon's canvas. "I could help you sew those. I feel guilty doing nothing."

"This is the last one." She tied off the knot and stepped back to inspect her handiwork. "Not bad, if I say so myself."

"You are so talented." I helped her gather up the scraps. "You know, Alepa, I've been thinking about our last conversation. Let me give the Rom Baro a note about how you feel, just before I leave. That leaves you out of it, entirely."

"That would be very embarrassing for me, Sara."

"Better to be embarrassed than spend the rest of your life without the person you love."

"Some marriages are arranged at birth. Isn't it the same with you?"

"It used to be that way, but this is the 20th century. I think that if I loved someone, nothing would stand in my way."

"When you're 12, the world is different." Her dark eyes glistened. "I think he knows what's in my heart. The problem is that love is not enough for the chief of the Gypsies. Just like royalty within the *gaje*, marriage for him must be an alliance between important families. His bride must also bring wealth and power." Her voice caught. "My mother says it's time for me to be realistic. I'll be 17 in a few months."

"Alepa, I still can't understand why a person can't tell another person that she loves him and wants to marry him. It just isn't fair. And it doesn't make sense to me."

"Again, that's because you're 12." She sighed. "Life is not always fair, little sister. And grownups are not always logical. You'll see for yourself soon enough."

I did not sleep well that night. After breakfast, while wandering aimlessly around the camp I came upon the Rom Baro studying his maps.

"Alepa told me the truth about Boris . . ." I began.

The Rom Baro looked up, a troubled expression on his face. "I am ashamed and personally apologize to you for his betrayal. He is a disgrace to all Gypsies."

"Please don't apologize—the shame was his and his alone. Alepa said no one else knows, so I'll keep this to myself. I'm angry that he never told you I went with the constable, but you found me, thanks to God. Somehow, I can't forget that he was ready to give up his life protecting me from the Cossacks."

"You are a special person to be forgiving like that, Sara. Nevertheless, his betrayal and bearing false witness is a crime he had to pay for. It will take me a long time to forget his disgrace." Frowning, he put aside his papers. "You still look upset, Sara. Is there something I can do for you?"

68

"Yes, please, Viktor Miklos. I cannot forget what the constable said about going to jail. He said he would inform the other constables that I belonged in prison for killing the bandit. Can they lock me up for shooting a bandit who was trying to kill me? Who will believe me over a policeman?"

"Not to worry, child. Before we left, I filed an affidavit at the district office about the entire matter. I also sent an official copy to Maxim Zukhov, the nobleman who owns most of Markova. That put the fear of God in all of them. You have heard the last of that sorry affair. Banish it from your mind."

I breathed a sigh of relief. "I feel so much better now. Thank you."

"While you are here, Sara, I have just finalized our journey. This delay has caused another change in plans. Tomorrow, we come within 15 or 20 versts of Drohobych . . . but that's as close as we can take you—I am sorry. There's a trading post at the crossroad run by my friend Leonid. He is an honest man, and I trust him to take you to your relative in Drohobych. Do you have money for the train to Hungary?"

"No. I hope to hire myself out as a maid or a cook to fancy ladies."

"Commendable. Do you have such experience?"

"I cooked for my father and kept our house clean." I had to laugh at my own words. "Our one room hut was a far cry from a fancy mansion."

Viktor Miklos chuckled. "I think so. Anyway, that's an ambitious thought, Sara." He stroked his chin. "In the meantime, please allow me to advance you funds in case there are no fancy ladies. You can return it to my family in Budapest whenever you get there."

"I couldn't do that. You have done so much already. I'm sure my father's cousin will help me."

He gave me a long look. "One last suggestion, then. Being Jewish is an invisible problem, but everyone can see the Gypsy skirt and blouse you wear. We buy and sell old clothes, so ask Alepa to pick out the best *gaje* clothing for you."

"Speaking of Alepa," I said innocently, "she has been wonderful to me. She is so beautiful and brave. I want to be like her when I grow up."

"She is a good model." The Rom Baro toyed with his map. "Sara, you will be her age in a few years. You have no father so it is good we discuss this—not that I understand why and how women . . . and girls . . . think. Alepa is like my little sister. I worry about her. She refuses all offers of marriage. One of our young men has been in love with her for so long that I am afraid he will give up. Did she mention this to you . . . No? Maybe you could bring up the subject to her before you go. I've known her since she was a little girl. In fact, you remind me of her at that age." He patted me on the head. "I'm sure you will have more than your share of suitors, too, when you grow up. But one cannot continue saying no . . . they lose heart easily."

It promised to be a good day for traveling. Alepa, waiting in the wagon, handed me a slightly worn, but presentable, suitcase. The lock worked, though, so there was no need for string around the middle like the one I had in Dreska.

"You look good in those Russian clothes, Sara. I put extra dresses and petticoats inside; also a paper with a Budapest address. You're not surprised I can write?"

"No. Why should I be? You're a grown woman."

"Even so, Sara. Most of us can't read or write because we're never in one place long enough to go to school. But if I expect . . ." A faint blush appeared on her cheeks. "I want to be ready when that miracle happens. I am poor, but if I can read and write that will be something most brides cannot offer the Rom Baro. One of my uncles teaches me in secret. So, write to me at that address and my cousin will forward it no matter where we are. It may take a little time, but I promise to answer."

I took my seat alongside her, feeling guilty that wearing regular clothing again made me feel so good. "It's strange, Alepa, but in these clothes I feel I'm a different person than the one I was yesterday. I'm excited, but I'm sad at the thought of saying goodbye to you."

A wistful look clouded her face. "I, too, feel it. Dressed that way, you are suddenly the stranger we hid from the constables." Her sigh echoed inside my heart. She forced a smile. "We have another two hours before we say goodbye, Sara. Do you have money?"

"I'm sure I'll find work with a rich family."

"I hope there are some where you are going. Do your relatives live in Drohobych or Sambir?" She was having as much difficulty making small talk as I.

"Drohobych."

"I wish I had your confidence, Sara, and I wish I had money to give you. I have none."

"You've done enough. The Rom Baro offered to lend me money. I said no."

"Did you . . . did he say anything else?" Her eyes sparkled with anticipation.

"Well, he agreed with me what a wonderful person you are and . . ."

71

"What did he say? I hope you didn't tell him!"

"I didn't." Uncertain about what to divulge, I carefully rearranged the folds of my dress. "I wouldn't give up if I were you, Alepa. He . . . he considers you more than just a friend. He likes you very much." I was certain God would forgive me. Changing minor details was not really lying. "The grandmas in Dreska used to say that the smartest of men don't recognize their own feelings . . . it takes a woman to remind them. Which doesn't make sense to me, Alepa, because you'd think a smart man would be smart in everything, wouldn't he?"

"You would think so, wouldn't you?"

The caravan continued for another hour until we came to railroad tracks and a fork in the road. "The other wagons will wait here. I will take you into the post myself."

I jumped down as Viktor and Stefan approached. "Good luck, Sara. We rode on ahead so I could talk to Leonid personally. He is ailing but assured me he would take care of you." Viktor lowered his voice. "Listen carefully, child. Stay clear of his son Karoly. Do not tell them you are Jewish. You understand what I am saying?"

"Yes."

"One more thing, and I will hear no argument from you. I paid Leonid for his porter to take you into Drohobych. It is only a short distance."

"But . . ."

"No 'buts,' Sara. I know you will accomplish whatever you set out to do." He slipped a note into my hand. "My relative's address in Budapest. If you ever need help, he'll know where I am. Until our paths cross again, Sara, safe journey and thank you for saving my son's life."

72

"Thank you for everything, Viktor Miklos. I wish you a safe journey." We shook hands.

Stefan gave me a shy kiss. "Goodbye, Sara. I won't forget you." He scampered away.

Alepa drove slowly. "I wanted to say goodbye in private. I hope you don't have trouble finding work, Sara. You'll like Leonid—he's a kind man." She guided the wagon across the tracks and down the road. A dozen decrepit buildings crowded each other at the far end. Our horse pulled up in front of a weather-beaten stable.

I felt an overwhelming sadness. "God knows if we'll ever see each other again, Alepa; but we remain sisters wherever we are." I choked back a sob as we embraced.

"Oh, Sara!" Our tears mingled. "I cannot say goodbye."

I stepped down. Alepa slapped the reins smartly. The startled horse lunged forward.

Without a backward glance I walked resolutely ahead. No large houses with fancy ladies who might need a maid or cook. Only one small inn, a blacksmith shop, and a wide, rambling general store.

I squared my shoulders. Be bold. Be brave. Do not be foolhardy!

CHAPTER

10

WILD ANIMAL said the swinging sign in front of the inn. I had to laugh. Shmuel used to call me that in Yiddish—*Vilda Chaya*—when I was unreasonably angry or excited. A good omen, I hoped.

Straightening up, I pushed past the swinging doors. The dimly lit room smelled of boiled turnips and alcohol. The few peasants eating in a corner kept their faces buried in their bowls. A moon-faced bartender polished a stack of glasses behind the counter. He was stocky with a short neck and muscular, hairy arms—I expected to hear the sound of crunching glass each time he picked one up. He paused to wipe his brow with the same cloth. "Looking for your father?"

"I'm looking for Leonid." My voice sounded tinny in my ears. Papa always said a tavern was no place for a Jew.

"He's busy. What do you want?"

"Viktor Miklos spoke to him about me."

"The Gypsy?" He made a face and then pointed. "Next door." He breathed on a glass and carefully wiped the fog away.

It was a relief to be out of his presence, in broad daylight again. In the trading post a bearded old man squeezed his way through a maze of barrels and crates. I liked him immediately because he reminded me of Shmuel. "Leonid?"

"Yes?"

"Viktor Miklos said you . . ."

"Who?"

"Viktor Miklos, the Gypsy."

"What about the Gypsy? Who are you?" He closed an eye and leaned forward.

"My name is . . . I'm Marya Petrovna. He said you would take me to Drohobych."

"Oh. You're the girl Viktor told me about."

I nodded. "I have relatives in Drohobych."

"I know. What's their name?"

I hadn't thought of that. "Er . . . I really don't know. They're distant cousins. All I know is they came from Dreska—my village—a long time ago."

Leonid cocked his head to one side. That must have cleared his mind, because suddenly he was alert. "Of course. In a few days our porter goes there for supplies. He'll take you, but he can't wait there for you to find your relatives." He took my arm. "Go back inside and tell Karoly you'll share Sonia's room. I'll see you at supper." He patted me on the head and disappeared among his barrels.

Karoly did not like my message. "My father thinks we can take in every stray that comes along," he glowered. "You have money?"

"Viktor Miklos paid for the porter to take me to Drohobych."

"He doesn't go every day. Room and board is extra. You have more money? No? Then you work for it." He looked over his shoulder. "Sonia, get in here!"

A skinny girl, all arms and legs, appeared from nowhere. "Yes?"

"Take . . . what's your name?"

"Marya."

"You a Gypsy?"

"No."

"Makes no difference. Their money's just as good as anybody's. Take her upstairs, Sonia, and explain her job. Then get back to work. We haven't got all day to stand around socializing."

The girl fairly dragged me up the stairs and into a tiny room. She flounced on an unmade cot. "Just say yes to everything he says and stay out of his way. He says he likes everybody, but, really, he hates Gypsies and Jews. Put your bag under that cot. How old are you?"

"Twelve. You?"

"Twelve . . . or 13. I'm not sure. Maybe 11." She brushed her unkempt, corn-silk hair out of her eyes.

"Don't you know how old you are?"

"Not exactly, but what's the difference? Everyone tells me another age. My parents died when I was two or three. My aunt left me here about three years ago. Leonid's her uncle. A lot of overnight travelers stop here. Aristocrats and Cossacks, Jews and Russians, all running from the Bolsheviks and all dressed like peasants. It's hard to tell who's who. I help in the kitchen, serve meals, and clean rooms—anything else that needs doing when the porter needs help and Leonid is not around to see how Karoly works us. He's mean."

"Leonid seems a little strange, but nice. He lets his son mistreat you?"

"Sometimes I think he's out of his head. Karoly beats me when his father is not around, but it really doesn't hurt. How long are you staying, Marya?"

"A few days. Leonid said the porter will take me to Drohobych. What work do I have to do?"

"In the kitchen, with me, peeling vegetables, scrubbing pots and pans . . . and floors. When it's busy, we help the cook serve. Come on, I'll show you."

Sonia and I peeled potatoes and cut up vegetables and strange looking pieces of meat. I cut off the tops of more turnips than I had seen in my life. Karoly was everywhere, poking his nose into every detail. He brushed the sweating cook aside to taste the stew, told me to cut the vegetables in smaller pieces, and ordered me to bring in more firewood. Before we had a chance to rest, he reminded us that customers would be arriving shortly and we'd better eat quickly—but not too much.

Sonia and I joined the others at a long table. "Don't eat the meat," she said beneath her breath. "It's rotten."

"I don't like meat," I whispered.

Karoly sat next to his father, who seemed bewildered by the vacant chair on the other side of him. The porter, a tall, skinny man, sat between Sonia and me at the other end of the table. When the cook came in carrying two heaping platters, she first took her place at the vacant chair before placing the food on the table. As soon as she sat, a flurry of arms filled the air.

"Mind your manners!" bellowed Karoly. "You wait until my father and I take ours."

Hoping they would finish all the meat, I waited until they all filled their plates. Fortunately, there was nothing left to tempt me. I pushed the few remaining potatoes and vegetables onto my plate.

"When do you next go to Drohobych?" I asked the porter.

The scarecrow of a man kept his head down. "Whenever Karoly says," he muttered.

Karoly was busy shoveling food into his mouth, wiping stray crumbs away with the back of his hand.

"Doesn't he go tomorrow?" mumbled Leonid.

No one answered.

"Leonid said I could go with him." I looked to his father for support, but he seemed not to have heard me. "It's paid for."

"We'll see," Karoly said, patting the few stray hairs atop his head.

I glanced at Leonid again, but the faraway look in his eyes told me it was hopeless. A few customers straggled in as we finished. Karoly quickly herded us back into the kitchen before taking his place behind the bar. The porter and cook waited on tables while Sonia and I did the dishes.

The evening wore on and I was still elbow deep in greasy water when the weary porter tapped me on the shoulder. "Karoly says it's busy. Come help with serving. Now."

Drying my hands, I approached the burly bartender. He held out a heavily laden tray. "For those three men at the corner table."

"I never . . ."

"Use both hands!" Karoly carefully balanced the tray on my shoulder. "Don't dawdle—they've been waiting a long time."

With visions of me stumbling and food flying in all directions, I threaded my way gingerly through the crowded dining room. In front of their table, I froze. How would I get the tray off my shoulder without dropping everything? I looked imploringly at the men. "Help me with the tray, please," I whispered.

One of them took pity. Jumping up, he lifted the tray off my shoulder and placed it carefully on the table. "It is certainly heavy. Your first day here?" he asked in a low voice.

I nodded.

He began taking dishes off the tray. His companions did the same and soon my tray was emptied. They all smiled.

I breathed a sigh of relief. "Thank you, sirs," I said, hoping that Karoly hadn't witnessed my embarrassment.

But there he was, waiting for me in the kitchen, hands on hips. "If customers are going to do your job, why should I pay you?"

"I never carried a tray on my shoulder before. You made it too heavy."

"Carry it in front of you, stupid. Get back to the sink!"

His remarks didn't bother me this time because I was still basking in the unexpected kindness of the men I served. I'd been repeating Papa's words about there having to be other good people in this world, but this was the first time a complete stranger extended himself for no reason except to be nice. Another good sign, I thought.

CHAPTER

11

Unable to sleep, I dressed and tiptoed down the stairs. It was four in the morning but a light shone in the kitchen. The hollow-cheeked porter, startled by my entrance, wore a guilty look. "For a moment I thought you were Karoly." Eyeing me warily, he soaked up the last of his egg yolk with a crust of bread. "We only get eggs on Sunday, so I come down real early other days. I hide the shells in my pockets. I'm Sergei."

"My name is Marya."

"Stay clear of Karoly, Marya. He hates Gypsies and Jews and anyone who's different. He informs on aristocrats for money. Even when they're disguised, he has a nose for such things. You know that sign out front? People joke that *he's* the wild animal." He cocked his head to one side. "Listen, if you want eggs, boil them now. Don't fry . . . he'll smell it."

"I'm not hungry, thank you. Tell me, Sergei, when do you go to Drohobych?"

"In a week. You are going with me, no?"

"Yes. Is it nicer than Boryslav?"

"Much nicer. Why do you ask?"

"I need to find work in Drohobych. I have some relatives there, but I still have to take care of myself."

"Boryslav is an oil town full of adventurers. You'll like Drohobych." He had a faraway look in his eyes. "Since the others won't be down for a while, we can talk confidentially. Not to brag, but when I was a little older than you are now, I went to university in Petersburg and . . . well, another world exists outside this miserable trading post." He sat straighter in his chair.

"On the far side of Drohobych," he continued, "live rich Austrians, Poles, and Russians. Also, a few wealthy Jewish families, if you don't mind working for them. Some have maids. It's no paradise, though. Like everywhere, the rich love the place and the poor pray to escape. I don't think the revolution is going to help much."

I picked up his plate and washed the telltale yolks away. "I only intend to stay a short time. I'm going to Hungary."

"You say that as though it's an accomplishment—for all you know it might be as miserable as here. The rich on their estates don't care what happens to poor people. They encourage the peasants to have children but won't support schools. They're afraid that once a peasant can read and write, he'll send a letter of complaint to the authorities."

"I can read and write, but my friends couldn't. My father believed girls must be just as smart as boys."

"He was a wise man."

"He said it's wrong for a few to have everything while the rest starve."

"Was he a Bolshevik . . . a Socialist?" Sergei looked at me with suspicion.

"Oh, no," I laughed, "just a man who believed in justice. Anyway, I want to live in Hungary where everyone is free. I want to make something of myself—go to university like you did."

"Good for you, my girl." Sergei paced up and down. "Here the stupid peasants don't send children to school because they'll have no one to work the land. Plus, once boys can read and write they're drafted into the army. We're a land of peasants and priests. No wonder Bolsheviks riot."

"What's the answer?"

"The answer is," roared Karoly behind me, "get to work! The revolution's not here yet, and this is not a hotel for workers. Sergei, you making eggs again?"

The porter seemed to wilt before my eyes. "No." He pointed to the clean plate before slinking away.

I did not look up for fear Karoly would read my thoughts.

"Girl, as long as you're here you can start tonight's stew. I'm expecting more guests this afternoon. And the floors could use a good scrubbing." He paused. "And the answer to your question is to let well enough alone. If God meant all of us to be rich, we would be born to rich parents. Don't wait for the Reds to save you, either—godless people are doomed."

In the days that followed, I learned that business at the Wild Animal depended upon the time of day and flow of travelers. Some local villagers stopped by for a bowl of soup or a glass of vodka, but they were in the minority. Salesmen and peddlers rode in on horses or wagons, some came on foot. Located as we were on the crossroad, the inn attracted mostly distant visitors heading for Drohobych. Those stopping off before noon usually refreshed themselves with vodka, soup, or a sandwich. If they rode horses, Sergei watered and cooled them down before their riders resumed their journey. Later arrivals tended to stay overnight, so

Karoly usually knew by three o'clock how busy he would be that evening. A small number of these overnight guests—the merchants and businessmen who were dressed better than other patrons—were repeat customers like most of his local trade.

On the fifth day, Karoly told me that Sergei was confined to bed with a heavy cough. Accordingly, he would not be going to Drohobych this week. My stay, therefore, must be extended—unless I had other means to get to Drohobych. I didn't. And I didn't believe Karoly. All I could do was glare and grit my teeth. The gruff innkeeper was unexpectedly soft spoken. "I'm sorry. He's really sick. It's only a question of a few extra days, Marya. Cook is feeding him a lot of chicken soup—I need him back to work soon!"

I thought of appealing to Leonid but discarded the idea when Sergei did not appear for supper. He truly was ill and that meant extra work for everyone. Karoly did not scream as loudly as he normally did, but he drove us without pity.

We followed our normal daily routines, working furiously when Karoly was present, easing up when other duties called him away. Helping Sonia tidy up the guest rooms, I couldn't believe my eyes when I saw her stealing coins from a dresser while the occupant was eating downstairs. "He won't miss it, Marya, I only took a few."

"Stealing's a sin, Sonia."

"Oh, no. It's a sin only if the person is poorer than you."

"Who told you . . . ? Never mind. Does Karoly know you steal from guests?"

She shrugged. "He doesn't care. But if I see any sign that the guest might be an aristocrat, I have to tell him immediately."

"Why?"

"He reports them to a man in the next town. I think he gets money each time he turns someone in. Noblemen are bad people, you know."

Karoly hired a neighbor's son to do Sergei's work and made sure Sonia and I were not shirking our added responsibilities. After cleaning the rest of the house, it was into the kitchen for the most important task of all—peeling gigantic mounds of potatoes and vegetables for the never-ending pots of soup simmering on the stove.

"We must never run out of soup!" Karoly warned. "That's a sin as far as I'm concerned." He was at his meanest when guests showed up late in the day. Screaming and cursing, he stormed around the kitchen watering down the soup and yelling at us to cut the vegetables into smaller pieces.

In addition to my kitchen chores, I also served customers whenever the others fell behind, but I refused to carry a tray on my shoulder again. At the end of each day, sleep came as soon as my head touched the pillow.

Sergei returned to work several days later, skinnier than ever. It was just in time, for new guests had arrived in the afternoon. I was not surprised that evening when Sonia came for me with the familiar words: "Karoly needs you in the dining room. Bring potatoes and applesauce to the last table by the wall."

Drying my hands on a towel, I took pains to carry the loaded tray with both hands in front of me. Walking carefully, I kept my eyes on the slippery floor until I reached the table. It was crowded with dishes. When I shifted them around to make room, the conversation halted abruptly.

"Sara?"

A familiar voice sent shivers through me. I dared not raise my head.

"Sara, I know it's you."

I looked up into the eyes of Count Peter Fedorovich. "Sir, my name is Marya Petrovna. You've mistaken me for someone else." I scurried away.

Stumbling into the kitchen, I struggled to catch my breath. The handsome young man with curly, black hair was dressed in hunting clothes, but I recognized him instantly. My heart pounded. I should have confronted him then and there!

Karoly burst into the room. "Why did you run away from an important guest? Captain Ulanovich said he knew you and now you've upset him. He insists . . ."

I felt the blood rushing to my face. "Captain? He is Count Peter Fedorovich, a Russian aristocrat running from the Bolsheviks . . . turn him in!"

"Are you crazy? I saw his papers. How dare you lie about an officer?"

"Bring him here. I'll prove it!" At last, I would avenge Papa's murder. There was no longer a single doubt in my mind that it had been Peter that night.

"Do you take me for a fool? Who would accept the word of a kitchen girl against a brave army captain?" He gripped my wrist. "Now listen carefully. Captain Ulanovich is coming in here to speak to you privately. I'm going back into the dining room. Calm yourself! Throw water on your face if you have to, but do not upset our guest any further!" He slammed the door behind him.

CHAPTER

12

Yad Mordechai, soon-to-be State of Israel. May 10, 1948, 2200 hours –

Our work is progressing ahead of schedule only because everyone works practically around the clock. We are expecting additional fighters from Haganah or Palmach to arrive at any time.

My sister Eelia just celebrated her 23rd birthday recuperating in the hospital from a clash with Arabs. Her Haganah unit probes advanced areas for enemy buildup and she is not optimistic about this being a short war. How I pray she is wrong.

Eelia writes that she expects to be discharged from the hospital next week, and also that she met an "interesting" American bomber pilot there. He and a few of his friends came to help us fight the war. We are all so thankful for the volunteers who have come to our aid. She doesn't say anything more about him, but knowing her, I'm sure she finds him more than interesting. In any event, it's her news to tell, not mine.

In the mess hall today, I picked up an article about the first population census in 1922—taken two years after England received the League of Nations mandate over

Palestine and the arrival of Mother and Father in Palestine. There were 83,790 Jews (and 590,890 Muslims and 73,024 Christians). By 1939 there were approximately 475,000 Jews—mainly due to people escaping Hitler's rise to power. By 1945, however, only an additional 125,000 had succeeded in reaching Palestine because of the 1939 British White Paper that set up strict immigration quotas and banned further land sales to Jews.

Our love-hate relationship with the British is bizarre, and I daresay the Arabs feel the same about theirs. Father has been in Haganah since its inception in 1920. He seldom talked about it, but as a member of Palmach he was one of the British-trained, Jewish volunteers who parachuted behind enemy lines into Nazi-occupied Europe. Their mission was to organize local resistance and conduct rescue operations of Allied prisoners of war and escapees. Of the 32 parachutists who actually made the jump, 12 were captured. Seven of the 12 were executed.

I believe I mentioned earlier that Joel Aaronson is often sent on special assignments. His English accent must be a great asset on the "cloak and dagger" missions he undertakes for Palmach, especially against the British. I ask, but he refuses to discuss details.

My brother Aaron was also involved on special missions, but, for now, he is driving a truck in the convoys trying to break the Arab blockade of Jerusalem. Arab attacks began the day after we accepted the partition plan last November. Arabs control the roads, and their heavy fire on trucks and buses attempting to reach Jerusalem is bringing the city to a standstill. Food and medicine are in short supply. The Arabs have shut off the water lines. I am amazed at the ingenuity and tenacity of our people and know all the sacrifices will not be in vain.

It makes me sad to think we will soon be at war with the Arab nations. I know from personal experience over the years that while some neighboring Arabs hated and actively gave us trouble, just as many coexisted with us on varying levels of friendship—a sort of "live-and-let-live" relationship. I believe the Arabs that I myself know would have accepted the UN's partition boundaries . . . but they are obviously in the minority.

Although I am too tired right now to work on Mother's story, I did want to mention her recent comments about growing up wishing to be "blonde and gentile."

"No, Deborah, I *never* wanted to be anything but Jewish. My 12-year-old mind was trying to express my resentment and my longing to be just like everyone else. Being 'the other'—for whatever reason—makes one a target. I was then, and will always be, proud of being a Jew!"

13

RUSSIA. SPRING 1920.

The door swung open before I had time to collect my thoughts. The man I regarded as a brother—the man I hated now with a vengeance—strode into the room. He closed the door behind him, a puzzled expression on his face.

"Marya Petrovna, you say? Why . . . ?"

"For the same reason you are Captain Ulanovich!" I spat out the words.

He took a deep breath. "True. It's not safe to be who I really am. But why are you hiding from me, little sister?" He reached to put his arm around me.

"Sister?" I shrank from his touch. "You murdered Papa! I saw you!"

"You saw me murder . . . ? Oh, my God!" His broad shoulders sagged. "So it was you in the distance that terrible night. I didn't murder Ilya . . . I loved him . . . and you, too. He begged me to kill him before the Cossacks got there."

"I don't believe it! My father was a fighter. He never gave up . . . he . . ."

Peter held out his hand, his voice almost a whisper. "He was deathly ill, Sara. He said it made no difference if he died of his cough or by a Cossack's sword; but he wouldn't give them the satisfaction. You're a child, Sara. You can't understand this, but he was tired of running. He pleaded over and over with me to cheat the Cossacks of this last 'victory.'" Peter's eyes sought mine. "I shot him because I loved him, Sara. Can you possibly understand that?"

My insides trembled. How I wanted to believe him. "Didn't you hear me shouting . . . see me waving?"

"I saw a figure in the distance," he said hoarsely, "but heard nothing on account of the wind. Time was running out—the Cossacks were on their way, and I had to leave before they arrived. Your father was shouting . . . imploring me to shoot. How could I refuse? He was exhausted mentally and physically. Ilya was determined to die that night, one way or another. I loved him like a brother. It broke my heart."

He took my hands in his. His voice caught. "Sara. My dear sister Sara. I have had no peace ever since. What could I do? Please tell me you understand and forgive me."

Reliving the scene, I shuddered. Words from Papa's note came back to me: "*. . . I do not think I will be so lucky this time . . . we have talked about this day before, so now it is time . . .*"

My voice broke. "Forgive me for doubting you. Oh, Peter!" Flying into his arms, I felt the same, familiar love and security of before. My defenses crumbled. With every sob, all the pent up sorrow and fright seemed to wash away.

He gave me his handkerchief and waited for me to compose myself. "Why do you call yourself Marya?"

"Karoly hates Jews and . . . Oh, my God, Peter!" I thought my heart stopped beating. "I denounced you to him! He said he didn't believe me, but he gets money for every aristocrat he turns in."

He drew me to the far end of the kitchen. "Do not worry," he whispered, "I have good papers. I planned to go hunting tomorrow, but, to be on the safe side, I'll leave for home in the morning. We have a little time yet—tell me quickly, what are you doing here?"

I told him what had transpired since Dreska and my desire to get to Hungary.

"Stay in Drohobych, Sara, the Bolsheviks haven't gotten there yet. I hear that Hungary is not a good place for Jews these days." He pressed a handful of coins into my palm.

"I really don't need it, Peter. I only have a few more days to work. I was hoping to study and learn enough to enter the university in Budapest, but if Hungary is not safe, I'll just keep going until I find a place that is."

His eyes sparkled. "Good for you, Sara." He closed my fingers around the coins. "A loan from your big brother. Return it when you get to Budapest. I would take you there myself, but first I must go back for my father."

The old fury and hate boiled up inside me, but I could not hurt Peter. "How is he?" I asked, struggling to keep my voice even.

"Gravely ill. Thank you for asking. He is the old Russia and his world has collapsed. I do not think like he does, but he is my father and I love him. He hides now because peasants are denouncing people like us everywhere. If he is well enough to travel, I'll take him to our other home in Boryslav to rest. It's only a question of time before the Reds confiscate that estate, as well, but by that time we'll have left for Budapest."

"Karoly called you 'Captain'?"

"My papers say I am a cavalry officer going home on leave. I never mentioned your name—only that we both came from Dreska. I told Karoly my father ran the flourmill for the Fedoroviches, and you confused us with them. People like him are easily impressed by authority figures; besides, I gave him just enough of a tip to keep him hungering for more. He'll give me no trouble as long as I'm here. I know his kind." Peter kissed my cheek.

I collared Sonia at breakfast the next morning. "Captain Ulanovich is a friend of mine. Make sure nothing sticks to your fingers. You understand what I'm saying?"

"I don't know what you are talking about." She skipped away.

After the guests had eaten, Karoly sent for me. "Now, what is this business about Captain Ulanovich being a count? And how would you come to know such a noble person in the first place? I hope you apologized to him."

"I did. I made a mistake, like you said. His father, Ulanovich the miller, worked for the Fedoroviches in Dreska. I was a very little girl when the captain went into the army. I confused the families . . . everyone who didn't work the fields was an important person to me. I apologized profusely to the captain."

"And what about my apology? You lied to me."

"Yes, it was thoughtless of me. I apologize to you, too, Karoly."

"Good. I knew he was an important personage just by the way he carries himself. When he arrived he passed the kitchen and saw you working. He insisted that you serve him in the evening. I hope you told him how good we treat you."

"I told him everything."

"Good. The captain is leaving earlier than expected. Tell him again, and another apology wouldn't hurt, either.

He is out by the stables this very moment. Be sure to remind him to stop here whenever he comes this way."

Stepping out into the morning sun, I saw Peter adjusting his saddlebags. His sleek, red horse stood patiently as he tightened the cinch. "Rozalina!" I shouted.

The horse whinnied and turned its head.

"Rozalina, my old friend." I ran over and patted the velvety-soft muzzle. "She still remembers me!"

"Of course she does. It's less than six months since she saw you last." He withdrew an apple from his pocket. "You give it to her, Sara."

Rozalina's tongue tickled my hand. "I never forgot the first time you put me on her back, Peter. I was so frightened . . . but I loved it."

He looked down at me and smiled. "We had some happy times, didn't we? Do you remember the funny faces I carved on sticks you found in the forest?"

"And how the older girls who never bothered with me before were suddenly my best friends when you came to visit?"

Words and memories tumbled out in a stream. For a moment we were back in Dreska . . . back when life was reasonably safe, and each day followed the last in familiar monotony. "Will life ever be so good again, Peter?"

"Of course it will, little one—starting this very minute. Your work is finished here. I paid Karoly to hire someone tomorrow so the porter can take you to Drohobych. You'll see your uncle and be with family once more. And when you get to Budapest...." he withdrew a paper from his jacket. "This is a note for a good friend. Madame Olga owns an exclusive dress salon. I'm sure she'll have work for you. She will also know how to contact me should you need me."

How quickly he became my big brother again. "Oh, Peter, how can I thank you! Can you ever forgive me for doubting you?" I threw my arms around him. "God watch over you, forever. I do love you."

"And I love you, little sister. Remember, I will always be there for you."

We embraced. I hated to say goodbye. "I hope you find your father much improved." My heart was in my throat.

Count Peter Fedorovich galloped away and out of my life for the second time. I wondered when I would see him again.

CHAPTER

14

Emboldened by Peter's coins in my pocket, I confronted Karoly. "The captain said I should stop working immediately. What time does Sergei leave for Drohobych tomorrow?"

"I don't know what time he finishes his morning chores," he blustered.

"That's not what the captain told me," I said boldly. "He paid you handsomely, and I'm to let him know if anything goes wrong. He returns this way shortly."

"Oh, yes. I forgot." The innkeeper gave me a toothy smile. "Even if my neighbor's son is not available early tomorrow, I'll make sure Sergei takes you right after breakfast. The captain said there was no rush, but I said it would be my pleasure to get you there early."

I returned to my room and changed clothes. Sonia was just getting out of bed. "You're wearing a clean dress to peel potatoes?" she asked.

"I don't have to work any more. I leave tomorrow and have to wash my dirty clothes."

"Wish I was." She looked at me accusingly. "I'll have to work harder with you gone, you know. I hope you're satisfied."

I hung the wash on a line and waited impatiently on the front porch. I kept thinking about Peter and the coincidence of our meeting. Best of all, the sorrow of Papa's death had been cleansed of the hate poisoning my memory. Now I could mourn him properly. I felt the same numbing sadness building up inside again, disappointed that the truth made it no easier to bear. Papa was still dead, and I still missed him terribly.

I tossed in my bed that night. The joy of starting the final leg of my journey to Drohobych was tarnished by memories of Papa and having said farewell to Peter. Consoling myself with Papa's "while there's life, there's hope," I finally fell asleep.

Sergei was impatient. "Finish your breakfast, Marya. We leave in 15 minutes."

I looked for Sonia to say goodbye, but she had disappeared. She was an odd little girl with strange morals, but I liked her. Leonid was still asleep.

Karoly bowed as I got into the wagon. "Be sure to tell the captain how quickly I carried out his wishes. Tell him he honors me with his presence."

Sergei coaxed his dirty white horse down the road to Drohobych. The tired old nag stumbled over the deep ruts, every bounce of our rickety cart threatening to up end him. Raising each hoof with great effort, the animal snuffled and wheezed as though each step was his last.

"Is he strong enough to make this trip?" I asked.

Sergei exuded confidence. I hadn't noticed before that he had combed his hair and put on a clean shirt. With each step away from the inn he seemed to blossom further. Now, he was actually sitting erect beside me. The porter winked. "My horse is like me . . . you can't tell a book by its cover. Did I ever tell you about the time I went to university?"

"No. I'd love to hear about Petersburg—I mean Petrograd. I heard it's like a fairy tale. When were you there?"

"I was there years and years ago . . . when it was known as Petersburg. I was a country boy, overwhelmed and confused by the unfamiliar noises of a big city and its masses of people. People everywhere! The women were dazzling. Men looked heroic in dashing uniforms, and those in civilian clothes made me feel drab and alien, dressed as I was in country rags. What wonderfully awesome sights I saw in that fabulous city! I remember one occasion in 1912 when the Imperial War Department held an endurance competition for horseless carriages. It was the first time I ever saw an automobile! I even saw Czar Nicholas up close."

"I hope that devil is rotting in hell! Tell me about the horseless carriage, Sergei. I never saw one. What made it go?"

"It was long and made of heavy steel. Instead of a horse it has a motor—an engine that makes a lot of noise like pistol shots. That turns the rubber wheels. Who could ever imagine such a possibility?" His voice was dreamy. "Fancy balls took your breath away. A wealthy classmate befriended me. First, he threw away my country clothing and loaned me some of his fine suits. Then he taught me manners, and how to dance and say words young ladies wanted to hear. I fell in love with his sister, but the father threw me out. I was not of their class."

He paused. "There's a message in the rest of my story for youngsters like you, Marya. I met another girl. She saw my borrowed clothes and thought I was rich. I thought *she* was. We lied to each other and got married. Two years of fighting and poverty. I worked two jobs and she spent everything—and more—on clothes and perfumes. One day I came home to an empty flat and a note. She had run off with an engineer. That was the end of my carefree Petersburg days." His eyes glistened.

I felt embarrassed for him. I didn't know what to say.

After a moment, he roused himself. "Now I'm beholden to Karoly." He shook his head. "Don't ever let yourself be beholden to anyone."

"I know." I felt for the reassuring coins in my pocket. Empty! I picked up my suitcase and flung it open. Nothing. "Sonia!"

"What about Sonia?"

"My money is missing. No wonder she wasn't around to say goodbye."

"A strange child. Can't turn back now, Marya, we've gone too far. I'm sorry I don't even have a single copper to give you."

"I should have known better. No matter . . . I guess money is not meant to stick to me." I toyed with the chain around my neck.

"Why do you wear that?" he asked softly. His eyes held mine.

"What do you mean?"

"I've met many girls who looked like you but their names were never Petrovna. I see many things, but I say nothing because it is not my business. However, this I have learned: I would rather be a chicken among friends than a peacock surrounded by foxes." He gave me a knowing look.

He was right. I turned to face him. "My name is Sara Samovitch." I removed the crucifix. "This belonged to Marya Petrovna, my best friend. I'm not ashamed of being Jewish . . . I just wanted to survive."

100

"A laudable wish."

"Do you think God will forgive me?"

He hesitated. "You're still a child, but this is what I believe. Priests and rabbis might say otherwise, but I believe God understands and forgives. As long as our hearts are pure and we return to our faith. Now tell me so I know where to take you . . . what is the name of your relative?"

"Mordechai . . ."

"Stern?"

"You know him?"

"We buy supplies from him. A fine Jewish man. You are a lucky girl, Sara. He is wealthy and much respected by everyone. His wife died more than a year ago. Two boys, eight and ten, he raises by himself. Yes, I believe your troubles are at an end."

After a few hours, the deserted road finally gave way to warehouses and stables, then more substantial commercial buildings. We passed a telegraph office, a solicitor, and a crowded newspaper office. A bank proudly advertised its trustworthiness. People walking by looked prosperous, their clothes fancier than any I had seen before. What a splendid city, I thought. Surely, one of them needs a maid or a cook.

Our cart turned the corner and pulled up in front of a general store. Barrels and cartons lined the entrance. Sergei bounded up the wooden stairs with me trailing close behind. Several well-dressed women were examining merchandise stacked high on tables. Even from a distance, I caught the scent of their perfume. More exciting was the fact that they were conversing in Yiddish. It was almost like home, except that I had never seen such wealthy Jews before. Self-conscious about my secondhand dress, I moved quickly away.

"Hello, Mordechai," said Sergei to a tall man wearing a black cap and a clerk's black jacket.

"Just finishing with the ladies, Sergei. You and the little girl can rest on a chair or look around, in the meantime."

"Thank you, sir," I said, studying my uncle. Mordechai's ruddy, round cheeks made him look younger than Papa—despite his salt and pepper hair.

Strolling between the tables, I took in a display of more new clothes and supplies than I had ever seen in my life. The easy banter between the storekeeper and his fancy customers was a far cry from the drab shtetl life I had known.

A large picture book lying open on a table caught my eyes. It showed bejeweled women in fancy ball gowns. Why were they wearing long white gloves up to their elbows if they were indoors? I studied the men standing stiffly in starched shirts and funny little ties tied in a bow. I puzzled over their little jackets—tiny lapels on curved fronts that barely covered their chests . . . and didn't even reach their waists. The sides had been cut away, narrow backs hanging behind their knees like wide cloth tails. What strange fashions.

Sergei came over with the man in the black jacket. "Sara, this is Mordechai Stern."

The genial storekeeper took my hand. "It's nice to meet you, my child. What can I do for you?"

"I . . . think we are related. My father was Ilya Samovitch. I am Sara." I searched his eyes for some sign.

"Samovitch?" His brows came together. Slowly, a smile lit up his face. "From Dreska? Ilya's little girl? You must be around 11 or 12."

"Twelve, going on 13. Are you really my cousin? Or are you my uncle?"

"What's the difference? We're family. You can call me 'Uncle.'" He gave me a bear hug. "Wait . . . you said . . . you mean your father is dead? How did you get here?"

I related everything that had happened since that unforgettable night. Sergei listened open-mouthed.

"You poor child!" Mordechai could hardly contain himself. "My home is your home, Sara. I have always wanted a little girl, and my boys will love having a sister around. Tanta Hanna will be overjoyed." He picked up my suitcase. "Sergei, follow in your cart. After a quick lunch at home, you'll have enough time to get back before dark. Your horse could use the rest. He looks exhausted."

Mordechai led us out back where a fine looking horse and carriage waited. I stepped into the carriage first. As soon as Mordechai sat in the driver's seat, the horse took off at a brisk pace. Sergei's little horse plodded behind.

Bushes and trees along the road looked greener than any I had ever seen. I felt like I was beginning a new life.

15

Mordechai's living room had a large, round table with six chairs, a rug on the floor, a red overstuffed sofa with matching armchairs . . . and Tanta Hanna. Looking severe with her thin, white hair in a bun and wearing a black dress covered by a huge, white apron that hid most of her tiny frame, Tanta Hanna was busy straightening small white squares of lace on the backs and arms of furniture. No one in all of Dreska had as fine a home.

I inhaled sharply to take in all the smells of a Jewish home once again. How good it felt to be surrounded by my own people.

"Come, little girl, don't be shy." Tanta Hanna practically pushed me into an armchair. "After such a long trip you must have some hot tea and cake. Tell me your name again."

Mordechai gently put his arm around her. "Tanta Hanna, her name is Sara, my cousin Ilya Samovitch's little girl. You remember him, don't you?"

"What a question! I met him once when he was a little boy . . . so handsome he was. I think I went to his wedding. You come from Minsk?"

"Dreska."

"Of course, Dreska. So how is he?"

"My father died in a pogrom."

"May he rest in peace! Such a fine man. Those Cossacks should rot in hell!" She turned to Sergei. "And you, sir. Your name is . . . what is your name?"

"Sergei Malenkov." He bowed and kissed her hand. "A pleasure to meet you, madame."

"Of course. Such a gentleman I could never forget. You married the butcher's daughter Bessie, or was it Bertha? I forget so quickly. When did she die, poor thing?"

"I never . . . A long time ago, Tanta Hanna."

The sweet old lady rambled on. "You're still a handsome man, why don't you find a good woman and settle down? Remind me later, I have a lovely widow for you." She crossed to the sideboard. It was difficult to tell how old she was—her face was unlined and her movements were quick and sure as she moved a pair of brass candlesticks aside. It was her crooked fingers, stiff with age, that told her years. Teacups trembled in her hands as she opened the spigot on the highly polished samovar.

Afraid she might scald herself, I reached out. "Sit, little girl. One thing I can say—my hand is still as steady as a . . . as a . . . well, I never drop anything." She chuckled.

I stood by her side and passed each steaming cup from her hands. "Thank you, child. Call the boys in, Mordechai. I've got their favorite streusel cake."

Seconds later, two boisterous youngsters burst into the room. They could have been twins, with brown hair and the same round cheeks as their father. They hugged and grabbed her around the waist. Red-faced, a laughing Tanta Hanna held on for dear life as the trio bobbed to and fro in a noisy jig.

"Easy, boys!" Mordechai steadied her. "You'll knock her down! She's only . . ."

106

"Nonsense, Mordechai. They're just playing." She stretched to kiss the tops of their heads before pushing them toward us. "Michael, Aaron—this is your cousin Sara. And that is Sergei Menchikov."

"Malenkov."

"Of course, Malenkov."

The boys hung back, gravely shaking hands at their father's urging. "Michael's eight," said Uncle Mordechai. "Aaron is 10. Boys, finish your cake and milk in the kitchen, then go out and play till we call you."

Tanta Hanna turned to Sergei. "You must stay the night. Time enough in the morning to leave."

"Thank you, Tanta Hanna, but I must leave right after lunch. I'm sure you all have much to talk about."

"Before you go, let me tell you how I taught Mordechai to read. He was four, and I read him the same story every night until he could pick out the words by himself. I took him to show off for the schoolmaster, who turned each page while Mordecai read without a single mistake. I was so proud—until two pages stuck together and his words were not the words on the page they were looking at. He didn't know how to read at all—he had memorized every word!" She chuckled. "He's still trying to fool me, aren't you?"

Mordechai leaned over to kiss her cheek. "Never mind, Tanta Hanna, you're too smart for any of us. Tell them about the time Uncle Beryl stole the apple pies you had just taken out of the oven."

A smile crossed her lips. "Beryl the *Luftmensch* was a ..."

I leaned across. "Sergei, that's a man who makes a living from the air ... no steady job."

He chuckled. "Lots of them where I come from."

Tanta Hanna regaled us . . . from Beryl the *Luftmensch*, to Mendel the Lame, and then Herman the Beggar. An entire roster of relatives with colorful names describing their distinguishing characteristics: uncles who couldn't see or were hard of hearing, aunts with warts and goiters, skinny ones and fat ones, spinsters and patriarchs, dreamers and fools—and the daring ones who crossed the ocean to risk their souls in godless America.

She told each story with such love and tenderness that my heart ached. They were all strangers to me, yet every shtetl had neighbors like that. How I yearned to be part of such a wonderful life again. I grasped her hand. "Tanta Hanna, did you know my mother? Shmuel Malka saved me from the Cossacks when I was a baby." I held my breath.

The old lady cast a troubled glance at Sergei and Mordechai. She sighed. "I'm sorry, Little One. I only know this side of the family . . . and to tell the truth, sometimes I'm not sure if the things I remember really happened."

When it was time for Sergei to leave, we stood in the doorway and waved. On the way back into the kitchen Tanta Hanna stroked my hair. "It feels so good to have a pretty, little girl like you in the house."

Waking in a strange but beautiful room the next morning was one of the happiest moments of my life. Snuggling cozily under the goose-down comforter, I studied my surroundings. Never had I seen such luxury. The bed I slept in was at least twice the size of any I had ever seen. A tall mahogany dresser with six large drawers would surely hold all the clothes for three entire families in Dreska. To my surprise, the walls were covered with soft paper covered with tiny red roses. They looked real enough to pick off the wall. I felt I was living in a fairy tale. If only Papa were here to enjoy such luxury.

I leaped out of bed and opened the window wide. The sweet scent of an orchard filled the room. Bathed in sunlight, the view was crystal clear and pure. And so very quiet.

A graceful pitcher sat on the washstand. I poured icy water into a basin, splashing the last remnants of sleep from my eyes. Dressing quickly, I made the bed and straightened the room. What a wonderful way to start a day!

Tanta Hanna kept me company at the breakfast table. "It feels good to have you here, Sara, and you look so much better this morning. Your mother must have been a beautiful woman."

Lowering my head, I blushed. This was the first time someone said that as though he or she meant it.

Dishes rattled as she tidied up. "I don't want to rush you, but Mordechai usually leaves for work an hour before this . . . He waits for you in the living room."

16

"Good morning, Uncle Mordechai. I had such a wonderful sleep! It's been a long time since I slept in a real bed."

His eyes were as warm as his smile. "You know, Sara, I was so excited yesterday that I never asked what your plans are. You're 12—almost a young lady. We would love for you to stay with us. Would you like that?"

"It's so beautiful here, Uncle, I . . . I don't know what to say. Papa and I always talked about going to Hungary where everyone is free and no one hates you for being Jewish."

A long sigh escaped him. "Does such a place exist, Child? I doubt it. Bad things happen in Hungary, too."

"Also, I want to go to university."

He nodded. "I admire your ambitions, Sara. Don't you want to go to America—the golden land?"

"They say it's a godless country where people lose their souls, Uncle."

"So I've heard. But at least there is a choice . . . and couldn't you lose your soul here? However, it is your decision to make. How long would you like to stay with us before leaving?"

"Could I stay until I earn enough money to take me there?"

"As much as we want you to stay with us permanently, you could leave tomorrow if money is the only reason to stay. I will give it to you as a gift."

I ran over and kissed his cheek. "That's wonderful of you, but I couldn't accept that. I've got to earn my own way."

"But I'm your uncle—it would give me pleasure."

"Thank you. Maybe you could help me find a job as a cook . . . or a maid. That would be a big help."

"Just a moment. Let me think." He leaned back in his chair. "I have a better idea, Sara. My store has been neglected ever since my wife passed away. I've been putting it off, but now that you're here, I'd rather pay you than a stranger. Would you like to work for me and help put it back in order?"

"I couldn't take money from you, Uncle."

"God has been good to me, Sara, and now he has sent you. Would I take money from my own daughter . . . if I had one? No. So this is how it will be: You will receive a modest salary to help organize my store. You will live with us and give us the joy of having a daughter in the house. You will love it here, I promise."

Seeing the look on my face, he stood up. "Good. It is all arranged. Now, it's time for us to go to work."

The prospect of another ride in his beautiful carriage was exciting. Like the last time, no sooner had he settled into his seat then the horse took off at a brisk pace. Uncle Mordechai hadn't even touched the reins. "What a remarkable animal, Uncle. How long did it take to teach him that?"

"Actually, I never taught him. We're so comfortable with each other that it just happened. It works that way with people, too." He turned to me. "Don't be disheartened by the clutter in the store, and don't expect we'll change it overnight. Remember, our people wandered 40 years before they entered the Promised Land."

Once inside, the hodgepodge of tools, work clothes, and miscellaneous objects of all shapes and sizes made an intimidating sight. It would take forever to unravel such disarray.

Uncle Mordechai cleared his throat. "I warned you not to be discouraged. It took me almost two years to make it look this way, so I'm not expecting miracles. First, I'd like you to make a list of everything in the store, starting from the back. See that man waiting on a customer? That's Avram—we've been friends since we were boys. Call him to lift the heavy things. But before you do that, I want to introduce you to another friend."

I followed him to the cash register. A ferocious looking black dog blocked my path. He bared his teeth. "It's all right, Riga, Sara is family. Good boy." Uncle stroked his head gently. "Go ahead, Sara, pat him. He won't bite you."

Riga looked from Mordechai to me, then pressed his massive head under my hand. "I never saw a dog with purple eyes before, Uncle. He's beautiful."

"Riga's the best watchdog you could have. I never worry when he's around. At night, he guards the store. We haven't had a break-in since he has been here." He stroked Riga's fur. "Now I must get to work. Call Avram when you need help."

Avram was lean and ramrod straight, with receding hair and a strong chin. We spent the morning examining everything on tables and counters. He hardly spoke, parceling out the words like it hurt him to talk. Even he appeared overwhelmed by the detailed list I compiled. The disorder had become part of their daily routine. "It is good you are here, child. We were running out of space."

I worked alone in the afternoon. I enjoyed riding the ladder on rails encircling the store, but after an hour of climbing up and down and straining to inspect the topmost drawers and shelves, the novelty wore off. I ached all over and couldn't wait for the day to end.

During the ride home, Uncle asked me how I got along with Avram.

"Very well. He was a big help, but he hardly said a word. Is he always that quiet?"

"Always. He's had a difficult life. He's a Cantonist."

"I've heard that word before, Uncle, but I'm not sure of its meaning."

"In your village when a family had more than two sons, didn't they draft the other sons when they were six years old to serve in the czar's army?"

"Sometimes, but Dreska is . . . I mean was . . . a small village, and the army officers often looked for bribes. For 10 or 20 rubles, the boys could take a different family name and escape the draft."

"Here, too, but there were times when a bribe didn't work. Sometimes, boys were kidnapped from their families and sent to distant army posts. Those Jewish boys who served 25 years so far from home lost all contact with Jews. When they returned home they were hardly Jewish, yet they didn't want to be gentile. So they lived together, separate from the Jewish community but close by . . . on the outskirts. Those are the Cantonists."

"How sad."

"We were little children together. I feel guilty that I have so much and his life is so empty." He glanced in his direction. "I trust him with my life."

I spent the next two days making more lists. At the end of the week Uncle called me into his office. He pointed to the lists. "It is a mess, isn't it, Sara? Well, what would you like to learn about running a store?"

"How do you remember all of the things you have for sale and where they are? And how do you keep merchandise from spoiling—like some of the perfumes and face powders on the end counter?"

"Excellent question, Sara. We don't have too many things that spoil like those two, but that's one of the reasons we take inventory every so often—so that was good. Please tell me what is the condition of those perfumes and face powders? I see they've been here a very long time."

"Uncle," I started tentatively, "the seals are broken and there's loose powder over everything. When I sniffed the perfume bottles, I think I smelled alcohol. I don't want to insult you, but I can't imagine anyone buying them that way."

"I'm not insulted," he said with an approving smile. "Now, see if you can guess what I should do to get rid of them."

"Give them away to good customers?"

"A possibility, but if you charge nothing that's what customers will think they are worth. They were costly when I bought them, and there's still a good amount of powder left in each box. Attach a bottle of perfume to each box and tell Avram to make a sign showing the original price with a line through it. Then show a 'special' price of just a few pennies . . . that way the customer will feel he's getting a real bargain. Stack them next to the register so everyone sees them. Any other merchandise like that?"

"Two piles of work clothes." I looked up apologetically. "Some were so old that dirt worked its way into the crease lines. I don't think those creases will ever come out, Uncle."

"And customers must agree with you because they've lain there all this time. When Avram finishes in the back, ask him to dig out the bills so we know what we paid for them." He ran his fingers through his graying hair. "So, how did you enjoy the first week?"

"I did like it, Uncle, but I never realized being a storekeeper was such hard work."

17

For the next week, Avram and I continued working side by side, moving displays and counters. He was polite and shy, seldom looking directly at me when he spoke, but making sure I did not lift or push anything too heavy. No matter where he was in the store, I had the feeling he was always watching over me. That made me feel good.

Uncle Mordechai told us what he wished to accomplish, then left us alone to use our own imaginations in rearranging merchandise. If Uncle complimented us on a particular change, Avram's answer was always the same. "It was her idea." I soon learned that piling a stack of shirts one atop the other was not the best way to sell shirts. Gradually, I began looking at merchandise with different eyes.

One afternoon, I mentioned something to Uncle that had been puzzling me for some time. "We have all sorts of clothes for men yet nothing for women except a few old bonnets on a back shelf. Is it because women are concerned with style?"

He looked up from his ledgers. "Partly. Do you have an idea?"

"Well, I'm not talking about clothes for the well-dressed women I see here. I'm thinking about the wives of men who buy their clothes and tools here. Wouldn't reasonably priced bonnets and dresses interest them? I think it would bring in new business, Uncle, don't you?"

He took off the eyeglasses he used only for paperwork. "At the beginning, I only sold groceries and farm tools. Gradually, we added work clothes and other home necessities as people asked for them. I always planned to expand those ideas but never had time or the imagination to do anything about it. Now that you're here, perhaps it's time to . . ."

A knock sounded on the door and Avram poked his head into the room. "The aunt comes with the boys."

Uncle excused himself and left. I followed a few minutes later to find Michael and Aaron wandering in the aisles while their father chatted with a thin, plain-looking woman dressed in black. Her nasal voice carried all the way to the back. I started counting men's shirts.

After a short time, the woman came over to me. "You're the cousin—the niece? How old are you?"

"Twelve, going on 13. My name is Sara Samovitch."

Her narrow lips compressed. "I know. I am Frieda Goldschein, the boys' aunt. It's wonderful when families stay in touch. Did you write often to your uncle?"

"I never wrote him."

"Probably your mother did."

"She died when I was a baby."

"Oh." She searched in her purse for something she never found. "Was your father related to Mordechai?"

"I . . . I'm not sure."

"Then how do you know you're his niece?"

"My father told me we are related. He left me a note when he died."

"Humph. How fortunate for you that he did; otherwise . . . Well, I'm happy Mordechai finally got around to cleaning up this mess." She motioned to Aaron. "Wait for

118

me up front with your brother. I'll be in the office with your father. Don't run around—Grandma gets angry when we're late." She sniffed again, sweeping past me like a duchess dismissing her servant.

Avram came by with an armful of clothes. "Watch your step around the aunt," he muttered, his gaze riveted straight ahead. "What price should I put on these shirts?"

"I'll check with Uncle." I walked toward the office. From behind the closed door, snatches of Frieda's strident voice drifted toward me. I didn't intend to eavesdrop, but her words held me in place.

" . . . niece? . . . no word in years . . . not your obligation . . . be a fool!"

I turned around so quickly I almost knocked Avram down. He wore a grave expression on his face. "Forget what you heard, girl. She has nothing to say."

On the way home, Uncle wanted to know why I was so quiet. I told him it had been a long, tiring day.

The best part of my new life was at home, where Tanta Hanna fussed over me like I was really part of the family. That night, she and I were the only ones at the supper table. "Your borscht is especially delicious tonight." I dripped the sour cream into graceful pink swirls.

"That's because you're starved, Sara." She handed me a plate of boiled potatoes. "You were saying that Frieda Goldschein came to the store today. So?"

"I don't think she likes me, Tanta Hanna. Where are the others tonight?"

"Thursdays they eat at the Grandma's. Mrs. Goldschein and Frieda watch over them like mother hens. Mordechai was married to the younger daughter, Rose. A beautiful person. Just the opposite of her sister." She sighed. "May she rest in peace. Cholera . . . so young. The poor boys without a mother all this time."

The old familiar sadness hit without warning. "Tanta Hanna, I know how they feel—I never knew my mother." I cleared my throat, turning my head before she could see the beginning of a tear.

"Take more potatoes, Sara. They're good for you." Her hand lingered on my shoulder.

"No thanks."

Two potatoes tumbled onto my plate. "You're a growing girl. Now, what were we talking about?"

"Frieda Goldschein."

"Oh, yes. Frieda. She never married because no man was ever good enough. The way she fusses over the boys now I think she is anxious to make up for lost time. The man she marries is in for trouble . . . I hope it's not Mordechai." Her eyes twinkled. "I shouldn't say those things, should I . . . but it's just between us women, right, Sara? And there are so many other nice women to marry."

I cleared the table and followed her into the kitchen. Tanta Hanna looked up from the pot she was scrubbing. "I don't know what goes on in the store, child, but go slow. Some people have trouble accepting new ways. And new people."

Frieda Goldschein came to the store quite often after that. No matter where I was, I sensed her disapproval. If I failed to notice her arrival, Avram, my self-appointed guardian, would suddenly appear and mutter warnings in my general direction. Accustomed to his odd behavior, I was grateful for his concern.

When the old perfumes and powders quickly sold out at a penny apiece, I asked Uncle if he were ordering more. "I'd have to sell them for a hundred times that, which is why they remained on the shelf all this time. Running a store is a lot of guesswork, and I guessed wrong originally. A good merchant is careful about adding new merchandise, Sara."

"Now I understand why you hesitate about bringing in dresses."

"Actually, Sara, I'm still thinking about it. Frieda thinks it's a good idea, but risky. We're going to discuss it again this evening."

"Isn't this Tuesday?"

"Yes, but Mrs. Goldschein wants advice about some matters."

That evening, I was surprised to find the boys at the supper table. Aaron, at 10, was the serious one. "Papa says you have a good head for business, Sara. Did you work in a store before?"

Michael was not to be outdone. "Aunt Frieda says you turned the store upside down." He reached for another latke.

Aaron glared. "You know, Michael, if it's not a compliment you're not supposed to repeat it. And don't talk with food in your mouth."

I looked at Aaron. "It could be a compliment, depending on how she said it. Anyway, I'm taking it that way, so I thank you both."

Aaron was still curious. "Papa says you want to go to Hungary. Don't you like it here?"

"I do, very much, but people are more free there. Besides, I want to keep learning . . . go to university when I'm older."

"Girls don't go to university." Michael piped up. "Everybody knows that's a waste."

"It is not!" I tried to control my anger. "Girls are just as smart as boys."

Aaron couldn't hide his exasperation. "Why don't you be quiet, Michael? You don't know anything."

"Yes, I do. I'm eight. And I'm tired of being treated like a baby."

"Then you have to start thinking before you speak," Tanta Hanna soothed. "I agree with Sara. Girls should study and learn whatever boys do—no matter what the men say." She cast a loving glance at Aaron. "Tell Sara what you want to be when you grow up."

"A doctor."

Michael howled. "He's afraid of blood!"

Aaron ignored him. "I want to save people who have cholera. Like my mother had."

Michael's lips quivered. "Why did you say that? I miss Mama, Aaron." He looked like he was about to cry.

I swallowed hard to bury the bittersweet longings that had a way of surfacing without warning. I stared at the tablecloth.

"You know she's safe in heaven, Michael." Aaron put his arm around his little brother. "Let's go upstairs. I'll play a game with you."

Tanta Hanna waited until they climbed the stairs. "Those boys need a mother. I hope Mordechai makes up his mind soon."

"I hope it's not Frieda, Tanta Hanna. You know I would only say that to you."

We smiled like two conspirators.

I loved working in the store and meeting people. Two new developments took place the following week: Uncle decided to bring in dresses with matching bonnets, and Frieda Goldschein's visits became almost a daily routine.

Despite her obvious efforts to make me feel the outsider when Uncle was not around, I was happy. Avram, my self-appointed protector, managed to be close by whenever Frieda was present. If I could only hold out a few more weeks I would have enough saved for the rest of my journey, and I would no longer have to contend with Frieda's disapproval.

One afternoon, as I carefully unwrapped the shipment of bonnets and dresses from Petrograd, Frieda came to watch over my shoulder. "Be careful how you unwrap them. Pastels soil very quickly."

"They're beautiful, Frieda!"

"That's why Mordechai and I ordered them," she declared, pawing through the carton. "Where are the black and gray ones?"

It so happened that Uncle had asked me whether I liked black and gray, and I said no. Suppressing a smile, I stepped back. "This is all they shipped."

She stormed off.

Humming a happy tune, I walked to the back of the store where my uncle was getting ready to feed Riga. The black dog's behavior always mirrored his. When Uncle spoke softly, the dog relaxed; when a stranger appeared, Riga's ears stiffened until the relationship was established. Riga nipped playfully as Uncle stroked his head. "Good boy. Take care of the store tonight." He straightened up. "Did everything come in as ordered, Sara?"

"Yes, but Frieda was upset."

"You didn't say anything about you and I deciding against black and gray?"

"No."

"Good. No need to . . ."

"I understand." Our eyes met.

"She really means well, Sara. She does care about what happens in the store."

"I know."

He thought a moment. "And she is honestly interested in what happens to you."

CHAPTER

18

Mrs. Goldschein must have needed a lot of advice, for Uncle was now visiting two and three evenings a week, without his sons. An awkward restlessness that descended upon our household made up my mind.

"Uncle Mordechai," I said one morning on the way to the store, "I think I'd like to leave sometime in the next two weeks, or as soon as I finish whatever else has to be done."

"So soon?" I had caught him by surprise.

"It's time. The store is finished."

"Except for the dresses."

"They're in, did you forget?"

"I know that, but . . . Could you stay a little longer until we see how they sell and if we should reorder?"

"I thought Frieda was taking that over, Uncle."

He looked uncomfortable. "I never said that, Sara. You're part of my family and . . . What's that look on your face? Don't you feel that way, also?"

"Of course I do."

"Then what is it? You can trust Uncle Mordechai."

"Why doesn't Frieda like me?" I blurted out.

Taken by surprise again, he pursed his lips. "She does have a critical nature, I admit, but it doesn't mean she dislikes you. I think she doesn't know how to act around a girl your age. Give it another week or so and if you still wish to leave, so be it."

During the next few days Uncle Mordechai and I had an opportunity to talk about the wisdom of continuing with women's merchandise. By the end of the week Uncle finally decided he would gradually enlarge his selection, and I finally decided for sure that there was nothing further to hold me in Drohobych.

"I think . . . I think I'll start packing tomorrow, Uncle." How could I tell him how much I loved him and his little family—so much so that I felt guilty about leaving—and I certainly couldn't admit I had sometimes daydreamed about staying with them forever. No, all I could do was look at him with my eyes slowly filling with tears.

He read my thoughts. Clearing his throat, he stroked my hair tenderly. "We will miss you, Sara, but you are going to love Budapest."

The following morning, I awoke feeling achy and out of sorts. It was an effort to get out of bed. I crept back under the goose-down comforter, realizing the cold I had been fighting all week had finally caught up with me.

Tanta Hanna touched her lips to my forehead. "Just as I thought. You've got a fever, child, and you're staying in bed. Does your throat hurt?" She handed me a cup of hot tea with honey. "I'm sitting here until you drink it all. While I'm waiting, tell me something. I hear Frieda spends a lot of time in the store. How does she treat you?"

I pushed the tea away. "Please, Tanta Hanna, I'm tired. Can we talk tomorrow?"

"I thought so."

I slept in fits. When I awoke there was no warmth to the sunbeam shining on my covers. Michael's high-pitched voice came in waves through the open window. They must be having bread and jam at the old table just below. I wondered whether all brothers fought as much as they did.

Now, I heard Aaron's voice clearly: " . . . how I'd like it if she came to live with us. Did she ask you, too?"

I threw the comforter around me and crept to the window.

"No. They didn't ask me. I hate when they treat me like a baby."

"Well, you are, Michael."

"You said you wouldn't call me that."

"Anyway, Grandma says we're all family and nothing will really change. I told you, Michael, I'll take care of you no matter what happens."

"I can take care of myself." A long silence. "Will Aunt Frieda still be our aunt? Why can't she just stay where she is with Grandma and we can see them every Thursday night?"

"It doesn't work that way. Anyhow, it's not definite."

"Maybe if we stopped fighting, Papa wouldn't be aggravated. Then, Aunt Frieda could stay home with Grandma. What do you think, Aaron?"

"Our fighting has nothing to do with it, Michael. Grownups don't think like we do."

Crawling back into bed, I couldn't help feeling sorry for them . . . and for my uncle.

Uncle Mordechai's face lit up. "You look so much better, Sara. You know you've been sleeping for almost three days?"

"I'm still a little groggy. But I do feel better. How are things at the store?"

"Avram sends his regards. Riga looks for you every day. Are you well enough for a little conversation?"

I nodded.

He cleared his throat. "I know you're anxious to leave, but the doctor says influenza takes time to get over."

I blinked, struggling to stay awake.

Uncle cleared his throat. "I will be getting married soon, Sara, but we both want you to stay . . . permanently."

"Frieda . . . ?" I couldn't help it—I was asleep before he could answer.

Tanta Hanna pressed her lips to my forehead. "You still have a bit of fever. Are you nauseous?"

"A little." I leaned on one elbow. "What time is it?"

Uncle Mordechai and Tanta Hanna leaned forward, their faces seeming to tilt to one side. In an instant I was asleep again. Each time I woke, another disembodied face floated into view . . . Tanta Hanna, Uncle, Aaron. I wasn't sure whether Frieda was reality or a dream. Sometimes they were all together; other times, only one. Their lips moved but I never heard a word—not even when their faces seemed only inches from mine. I tried to speak but words never came out. I had never slept so much . . . never felt so tired.

One afternoon, the wallpaper roses suddenly came into focus. I blinked, and Tanta Hanna was leaning over me, the delicious smell of frying chicken fat clinging to her apron. "Thanks to God, Sara. Now, a little chicken soup with your favorite *knaidlach* stuffed with *gribenes* and you'll be yourself again. It's been a week."

After I had eaten, she threw a robe and blanket around my shoulders. "At least you have a good appetite." She led me to a chair by the window and pounded the pillows until they were plump. "Have to air this bed out . . . and you, too, Sara. You're coming downstairs for supper. It's Shabbos, and we have company coming."

"Frieda?"

"Sheila Morganstern."

"Do I know her?"

"No. She is my secret weapon against . . . against you know who. Mordechai has known Sheila since childhood. She never married—stayed home to care for her sick mother, who died last year. Lately, Mordechai would run into Sheila at *simchas*, but nothing came of it. So, what do you think I did, Sara?" She giggled like a schoolgirl. "I invited Sheila one afternoon, months back—before you came—to show me a new embroidery stitch. Could I help if I'm a slow learner?" Tanta Hanna gave me a broad wink. "I kept her until Mordechai came home from work. Naturally she stayed for supper. They've been keeping company for some time now, and I finally convinced Mordechai it was time to invite her for a Shabbos meal. You know—someday you'll learn—that sometimes men need a push to get them started." Tanta Hanna became serious again. "Mrs. Goldschein will be disappointed but, after all, Mordechai and Sheila were friendly in their teen years, so why shouldn't they be friendly—and maybe more now? You will like her, Sara. She makes you feel like you've known her all your life."

"That's so romantic!" I began to feel lots better.

"What were we talking about? Oh, yes—Sheila Morganstern. Remember this, too, for when you're older, Sara. There are times when love, also, needs a little help.

And some men—like your uncle—need to be reminded they're in love."

We laughed. She tucked the blanket around me. "Listen, Sara, the doctor says you need to recuperate for at least six or eight weeks. Influenza takes a lot out of a person. I know you're disappointed, but first you must get well. Now, I've got to prepare supper. Call me if you feel cold."

It was strange. I was anxious to leave for Hungary, yet the prospect of being part of this remarkable family for a little longer eased the discouraging news. In some ways, I looked forward to it. In Uncle's house I could go back to feeling like a child in a Jewish home again . . . and not have to push myself to think like a grownup in order to stay alive.

I was drawn to Sheila Morganstern immediately. Her glossy black curls framed a sweet face with rosy cheeks. She had a warm smile, and I saw what Tanta Hanna meant about her having a special warmth that invited you to be her friend.

Tanta Hanna made sure the boys were scrubbed clean and neat when they went off to the prayer house with their father, but when they walked up the front path, after stopping on the way home to pick up Sheila Morganstern, Michael's shirt was twisted and hanging loose. Before he took two steps inside, Tanta Hanna was tucking in his shirt. "Michael, that's no way to greet the Sabbath. Go bring me the candles."

This was something I looked forward to every Friday afternoon, and it was a custom I knew I would observe when I was older. Tanta Hanna's freshly laundered apron and lace shawl matched the snow-white tablecloth. Reciting the *brachas*, Tanta Hanna moved her hands in gentle circles over the candles' flames and then covered her eyes. Each Friday since my arrival I'd felt the same lump in my throat, as I imagined my own mother doing this when I was an infant—though I had no such memory. Papa, of course, I remembered—and when Uncle Mordechai chanted *Kiddush* over the wine—with Sheila Morganstern looking at him with such love in her eyes—it was all I could do to keep from breaking into tears. As always during *Kiddush*, Tanta Hanna's worn hand would reach for mine and squeeze until my weak smile acknowledged hers. Then, I followed her into the kitchen to help serve the gefilte fish.

Waiting for the boiling hot chicken soup to cool, Uncle related the latest neighborhood news, heard in the store while I was out.

"Mordechai says you have a talent for business, Sara," Sheila added. "I think that is remarkable for one so young."

I blushed. "Thank you, Miss Morganstern."

"You must call me Sheila."

All during the meal, from the looks passing between them, it was obvious she was the woman Uncle planned to marry. I wondered how Frieda was taking this sudden turn of events. It was a happy thought.

"Such a big smile, Sara. Did I miss a joke?" Uncle looked puzzled.

"I'm sorry, Uncle. Something funny just popped into my head." I took a sip of tea to keep from laughing aloud.

"Good. Since you cannot travel yet, Sara, why don't you come back to work? That is, if you're feeling well enough. Nothing strenuous, to be sure."

"I would like that, Uncle. A few more days and I'll be ready." I helped myself to another *rugelach* from the dessert platter. "I'm going to miss your baking when I get to Hungary, Tanta Hanna."

The three of them exchanged looks. Uncle Mordechai placed his teacup carefully on his saucer. "We'll talk about that when it's time, Sara."

We were silent during the carriage ride on my first day back to work. The only words Uncle spoke were to his horse. That intelligent animal, sensing his master's mood, neighed softly and kept a steady pace until we reached the store. My mind was occupied with plans to leave Drohobych as soon as possible. If he was getting married soon, I would only be in the way.

Avram greeted me with a big smile. "It's good you are back, Sara. I put the new dresses in the first empty space I found. Where do you think we should put them?"

I sat on a chair studying the overflowing racks. Suddenly I felt Uncle's hand on my shoulder. "Sara, let's have a cup of tea in the office. I have something to say to you."

He waited until we each took a sip. "Sara, so much is happening that I don't know where to begin. It is all good, though. I don't know why I'm so nervous." He put his cup down. "Actually, I do know—Sheila and I are going to be married shortly, and . . ."

"*Mazel tov*, Uncle!" I threw my arms around him. "I'm so happy for you. I like her, a lot."

He took my hand in his. "Now don't say anything until I'm finished. I love you like a daughter. You know that, don't you?"

I knew what was coming, and wanted to save him the embarrassment. "And I love you, too. That's why it's hard for me to leave. I'm better now and really should be on my way to Hungary. I don't want to stay another six or eight weeks."

"No, wait . . . wait!" He sprang to his feet. "That's not what I mean. You're not well enough to travel alone yet. Sheila and I want you to stay and be our daughter!" He took a deep breath. "We want to adopt you."

"Adopt? I'm going to Hungary, Uncle. Why would you . . . ?"

"It takes a long time to recuperate fully from influenza. For however long it takes, Sheila and I want you to stay with us. It would make our happiness complete if you agreed."

"But why do you have to adopt me? I . . . I already have a father."

His face reddened. "Of course—may he rest in peace. I don't want to take his place; I just want to protect you. As my daughter, you would be taken care of if something should happen. Life is strange, Sara; you might even change your mind about leaving."

"I don't know what to say, Uncle."

"Say nothing. Just think about it. You're almost a young lady, and that's where Sheila comes in. She has nieces and knows how girls think. The thought of you on your own, with no family, troubles us. We've talked it over thoroughly and promise not to interfere with any of your personal wishes. Don't give me your answer now—think it over."

CHAPTER

19

---

*Yad Mordechai, soon-to-be State of Israel.
May 11, 1948, 1800 hours –*

Joel Aaronson left just a second ago, and I still find it hard
to believe he is assigned here! As soon as I heard that
British accent outside the barracks door, I knew it was him.
Joel's announcement that another 15 men will be arriving
tomorrow was met with cheers by my bunkmates. At this
moment, he and the others are planning how to best utilize
the manpower—and womanpower, I reminded him—to
halt the Arab advance. We must buy time for our forces to
seize Jerusalem and Tel Aviv before the Arabs.

Joel arrived about two hours ago with four other
Palmachniks in a truck full of supplies. After everything
was unloaded, he and I went for a walk around the kibbutz,
for privacy is nigh impossible under present conditions. He
wouldn't tell me how he managed to get himself assigned
here. All he said was he misses me and wants to be close to
me when the action starts. (Isn't that a strong, reassuring
declaration!) I really shouldn't have been surprised by his
visit, for he is a most resourceful fellow.

Like my father, I am a strong believer in fate; there is no
such thing as coincidence. For example, I'm at the point in

Mother's diary where she talks about her *Uncle* Mordechai, and here I am in *Yad* Mordechai. Mordechai and Sheila just got engaged, and Mother—Sara—was torn between remaining safely with them and leaving for Hungary. Here is Joel trying to convince me we should become engaged, and I am torn between my love (strong feelings?) for him and the knowledge that his very Orthodox parents do not think I am Jewish enough.

Joel points out that they accepted his departure from their long-held ultra-Orthodoxy, but I don't know how long it took him to accomplish that. Besides, a son is one matter—a mere future daughter-in-law, another. I will not wait under a cloud until they choose to accept me, yet I cannot disregard his parents or their influence upon him.

Writing about all this helps me think logically, although logic may not help with the problems we face. It has to do with my feelings. *If* we are ever to marry . . . (first time I ever even thought of marriage!) . . . do I have the strength, or desire, to wait out his parents? I wish to be respectful, but they make it most difficult for me.

My bold opinions about equality for women clash with Joel's, but that's way down on the list of problems. As he puts it, "I'm pretty open-minded, Deborah, and inside I feel I have slowly but surely moved far from my parents' ways. I don't know how much more I can bend without becoming a traitor to my own parents and to my religion."

And for my part, I don't know whether I want to become that *frum*—I just can't be as observant as he is. I never thought my Jewishness would cause me trouble with another Jewish person.

We managed to discuss all those points by the time he had to leave and rejoin the others. When he kissed me, all our problems melted away, even though my head told me I was fooling myself. As I write this, lying here on my cot, I know that love is not enough to solve the problem . . . but love has to be there in the first place before we can go forward. We will both have to have lots of faith and courage. I hope we are capable of doing that. I'm not even thinking about *my* family's reactions to this matter. I believe they can be just as stubborn . . . that's not the right word . . . just as determined as Joel's parents.

My sister, Eelia, would probably advise me not to waste my time on him; my parents and brother would counsel patience and "follow your heart"—which is why I won't discuss it with anyone before I make up my own mind. Off the top of my head, I'm enough of a romantic to feel *anything* is possible when love is present.

Now, I'm going back to Mother's manuscript. Then, sleep on my dilemma.

P.S. Someday, I'll draw up a coat of arms for our family: Be bold. Be brave. Do not be foolhardy!

CHAPTER

20

DROHOBYCH, POLAND. LATE SPRING 1920.

Tanta Hanna dried her hands on her apron. "No, it's not being disloyal to your papa. What's to think about, child? It's for your own good, and it is fortunate he marries Sheila. Frieda would never adopt you."

"Does she know he's marrying Sheila?"

"Oh, yes. I think she's relieved. I don't believe she ever wanted to marry Mordechai in the first place—there is a schoolteacher she used to see from time to time. The mother's heartsick. She thought Frieda could do better ... and marrying Mordechai would have kept the store and her grandsons' inheritance in the family." Tanta Hanna shook her head. "Sometimes life gets very complicated."

Michael and Aaron came into the kitchen for a bread-and-jam snack. I followed them outside. "Would you tell me the truth, no matter what I asked?"

Aaron hesitated. "It depends."

"On what?"

"Well, Papa says we shouldn't hurt people un-necessarily."

"That's very considerate, Aaron. But if I told you that I had a problem and needed your absolutely honest and truthful answers—and nothing you said would hurt me ... ?"

"In that case, I would tell you."

"Your father wants to adopt me." There was no change in their expressions. "Would you want me to be your sister?"

Michael wiped jam from his chin. "Will you boss me around?"

"Never."

"It's all right with me. Can I go now? My friend is waiting."

There was a smile on Aaron's face. "I think it would be fun having you as a sister. We told Papa that the other day."

"Thank you, Aaron." I paused. "Are you upset about Sheila Morganstern?"

His smile disappeared. He shrugged. "She seems nice. But we have Tanta Hanna to take care of us. We really don't need a stepmother. Grandma and Aunt Frieda live close by." He eyed his piece of bread. "Want a bite?"

"Not hungry, thanks. Maybe your father's lonesome."

"He has us and Tanta Hanna. And every Thursday we go to Grandma's."

"I don't think that's enough for grownups, but you're too young to understand that."

"Why do you say that? You're not that much older than me!"

"Girls are more grown up, but let's not argue. Would you rather have Aunt Frieda come live with you?"

He made a face and we both laughed at the idea. "Aaron, I think Sheila Morganstern is a very nice person and she truly loves your father. He likes her a lot, I can tell. You don't have to think of her as your mother. Think of her as another aunt."

He sighed. "I guess you're right, Sara, but I'm worried about Michael. He's only a child and doesn't understand. I think he's worried that Papa won't pay as much attention to us once he gets married."

"I don't think your Papa will do that. And," I whispered, "I really think she's nicer than your Aunt Frieda."

"I hope so."

Early the next morning, I found Tanta Hanna sitting forlornly at the kitchen table. "What's wrong, don't you feel well?"

"Just a little tired, child. My rheumatism."

"Get back into bed. I'll give Uncle breakfast."

She sighed. "I'm getting old, Sara. And I'm forgetting more things than usual."

"That's not true, Tanta Hanna. You're the youngest old person I ever met. Come on, I'll help you."

She didn't budge.

"Don't you want to go back to bed?"

Her voice wavered. "If I tell you something, do you promise not to tell anyone?"

"You can trust me, Tanta Hanna."

Her shoulders sagged. "What will happen to me when Sheila moves in? No kitchen is big enough for two women. Where will I go?"

All of a sudden, Tanta Hanna looked her age. Frightened, I held her close, alarmed by the trembling of her frail body. I put my cheek next to hers. "Don't worry, Tanta Hanna. They're going to need you more than before. They'll need you to run the house and handle the boys. Who else could do all the things you do? Cook, bake, the boys . . . everything!"

Helping her back to bed, I kissed her soft cheeks and smoothed her hair. A tear formed in the corner of one eye. She brushed it away, but I pretended not to notice she was crying. I bit my lip to calm myself and hurried back to the kitchen.

Uncle's face mirrored my concern when I told him. "I feel terrible, Sara. Of course nothing changes. You did right to tell me. Sheila wants to work in the store with me, and I'm going in right now to tell Tanta Hanna."

I waited in the carriage. It was taking Uncle too long. I pictured him trying to console her and Tanta Hanna refusing to talk. The horse turned and stared, as though reminding me he would not move until Uncle arrived.

When the front door finally opened, a completely recovered Tanta Hanna stood there, waving vigorously. She cupped her hands around her mouth. "I forgot to tell you, Sara, we're all invited to the Goldscheins' for supper tonight."

I was nervous about meeting the matriarch of the family in person. Mrs. Goldschein was short and plump, with a piercing stare. She looked old, like all grandmas, but there was none of Tanta Hanna's gentleness.

"So you are Sara Samovitch." With probing eyes, she slowly inspected me from head to toe. I felt like I was itching all over.

"I am happy to meet you, Mrs. Goldschein."

She muttered something, brushed past me, and pulled her grandchildren close. Michael and Aaron disappeared into her embrace. Out of the corner of my eye I saw Michael wipe his cheek where she had kissed him.

Mrs. Goldschein obviously knew Sheila, but when the younger woman attempted a polite kiss, Mrs. Goldschein pulled back. "I can do without the kissing."

Sheila turned red. Uncle whispered, "Mother!" He put his arm protectively around his fiancée's waist and glared at his former mother-in-law.

Mrs. Goldschein arched her eyebrows. "I don't kiss people over eight. Germs."

Frieda escorted us into the dining room, surprising me by putting her arm around my shoulder and telling me how happy she was to see me again. I noticed Uncle Mordechai nodding in approval as I took my seat with the others around the table. Frieda ladled out the soup. "I hear you're planning to go to Hungary, Sara. When do you leave?"

"I . . ."

Uncle's foot tapped mine under the table. "Actually, Frieda, Sheila and I insist that she stay with us until she is completely recovered from influenza."

Mrs. Goldschein spoke up. "And I hear you want to go to university some day. I think that's a waste. Women belong at home raising a family. What do you need an education for?"

I looked at Uncle. He nodded encouragement. Trying to keep my voice respectful, I kept my eyes fixed on the brooch pinned to Mrs. Goldschein's dress. "My Papa said girls should know as much as boys. I just want to learn everything I can."

Sheila spoke softly. "I believe husbands and wives have more in common when they each have a good education. Don't you agree, Frieda?"

"Um . . . I never thought about it before. But what if the husband has no education and his wife is smarter than he is?" She offered the meat platter to her mother.

Mrs. Goldschein shook her head. "A smart woman doesn't let her husband feel she's smarter—even if she is. She should stay home and let her husband be the wage earner."

Frieda, still holding the platter, stared at her mother. Mrs. Goldschein bristled. "I worked in the store only because your father had no interest in business—or for that matter, in working!"

Frieda put the platter down. "I wasn't referring to us, Mother. I was thinking about husbands who might resent their wives working."

Uncle picked up the platter. "For my part, I welcome Sheila working with me because that's her wish. This store can use a woman's touch. If it weren't for Sara, the store would still be in a mess. She did wonders!"

Mrs. Goldschein had regained her composure. "A family business belongs in the family. No outsiders." Her gaze lingered on me.

I felt very much the outsider here, just as I was in the Gypsy camp. Would I ever belong anywhere? I contemplated the slice of brisket on my plate, feeling I'd choke if I took another mouthful.

"Exactly," said Uncle, beaming. "Sara's family, and after our wedding Monday, Sheila is, too. No outsiders here, Mother!"

"Frieda said you're planning a raffle," Mrs. Goldschein continued. "It's a good way to get rid of those old bonnets. Did you sell many tickets?"

"It's a free drawing, Mother, not a raffle," her daughter corrected. "Every woman who comes to the store gets a ticket. We'll have two winners for bonnets, and Sheila's donating a pillow she embroidered, as a third prize. Isn't that wonderful?"

"Better make sure good customers win. Don't waste prizes on strangers."

"We can't choose the winners," Uncle explained, "and we can't give old bonnets in the drawing. We all agreed that the bonnets should be new. Frieda's friend, the schoolteacher, will draw the winning tickets. He's a fine young man. I like him, Mother."

"Herman Bookman, who came to the house last week?" Mrs. Goldschein asked.

Frieda blushed.

"Humph. I thought the rabbi would draw the tickets. I'm not impressed with Mr. Bookman." Mrs. Goldschein turned up her nose.

Uncle spoke up. "Excuse me for interrupting, but did the rabbi say anything about the cemetery? Hoodlums knocked over a few gravestones last week, and I was wondering whether they discovered who did it."

"The rabbi said nothing to me," said Mrs. Goldschein. "He should report it to the authorities."

"According to the rabbi," observed Sheila, "it's nothing more than a schoolboy prank. What do you think, Mordechai?"

"I don't think it's children this time . . . too many disturbing things happening lately. Jews are now forbidden to work for the railroad. A customer told me his brother was just dismissed after 20 years." Uncle Mordechai looked around the table. "Frieda, you'd better tell Herman the latest bit of news: Jews will soon be barred from teaching and all other government jobs."

"I told you a schoolteacher is nothing," muttered Mrs. Goldschein.

Frieda paled. "Thank you, Mordechai. We heard the same thing. I told Herman to start looking immediately for something else. This new Polish government is not too friendly toward us. How are we Jews supposed to earn a living?"

"Uncle Mordechai, maybe the whole family should move with me to Hungary?"

I never saw Uncle so angry.

"Never, Sara! I fought for this country in the last war. So did my father, my grandfather, and my great-grandfather in other wars. No one's driving me out of my own country. We'll earn a living, somehow. We'll survive because this, too, will pass."

"Enough of such talk," said Tanta Hanna raising her water glass. "Here's to Sheila and Mordechai's marriage next week. Now that's something to look forward to!"

CHAPTER

21

I thought getting married was a happy occasion, but almost every woman was in tears when Sheila and Uncle Mordechai stood under the chuppah. He stomped on the glass. *"Mazel tov!"* they all shouted. Everyone, with the exception of Mrs. Goldschein, kissed everyone else.

Dressed in Sabbath finery, the women milled around the tables loaded with Tanta Hanna's delicacies. The men, not quite at ease in their best clothes, crowded the side table where schnapps and slivovitz sent them slapping each other on the back between coughing fits and gales of laughter. They made the most of turning an ordinary workday into a festive occasion.

I strolled from group to group, standing respectfully at the fringe, to hear the latest gossip. In the kitchen, the butcher's heavy hand on the scales was the main topic. In the living room, the consensus was not to bother the authorities about a few mischief-makers toppling gravestones in a cemetery, and a few serious people in the corner debated the wisdom of leaving Drohobych.

I felt a tap on my shoulder. With a broad smile on his face, Avram stood holding a glass of schnapps in each hand. *"Mazel tov!* Little One. This is such a happy occasion that I feel like talking, especially since you are leaving us soon. Come sit with me a bit."

He downed one of the drinks before drawing up two chairs. "A few things you should know. When I returned from the army after 25 years, the gentiles said I was Jewish, the Jews said I wasn't because—even though it was against my will—the army baptized me. Well, that's true. I don't observe the rituals, Sara, but in my heart I am as Jewish as anyone here. Anyway, when I came back only your uncle would give me a job. He's a good man." He kissed me on the forehead. "Never forget who you are, Sara."

"I won't, Avram."

"I say that because in the army all those years I did forget. I met no other Jews. It was every man for himself and I became a person without feeling. I remember one time when we were drinking in a tavern, an old Jew wandered in for directions. I paid him no mind for I was only interested in my drink. My comrades were pulling the old man's beard and playing catch with his hat—but what had that to do with me? Nothing. I bought another drink and watched the peasants join the fun. They spun the old Jew around and around. My comrades slapped each other on the back and had a good laugh.

"Suddenly, the old Jew fell. One of the men in my squad pulled me off the bench. 'Hey, Jew, go help your papa.' Now, this is the strange thing, Sara—I had been in this new troop for more than a year and never once had I uttered the word or indicated that I even knew what a Jew was; and here was this drunken, ignorant ox reminding me and announcing to the world who I really was." His voice thickened.

Avram inhaled sharply. "I helped the old man to his feet, dusted off his coat, and saw him safely outside. Then I returned to thrash the loudmouth, after which the entire tavern joined in giving me the worst beating I ever got. But they also gave me back my soul."

He swirled his drink 'round and 'round. "It's important to know why people dislike us, Sara. Anti-Semitism has a good side—it never lets us forget who we really are. Those who dislike us just because we're Jewish—a pox on them, I say. On the other hand, Mrs. Goldschein and Frieda dislike you and Sheila—or anyone—who might take away from Michael and Aaron's inheritance." He tossed down the last of his drink.

"I never looked at it that way before, Avram. I think I understand Frieda and her mother better, now . . . and I'm beginning to feel guilty."

"Don't feel guilty. Good reasons do not excuse bad manners. As for your uncle, let him adopt you, girl. Yes, Mordechai's a good man. I said that before, didn't I?" He stared at the empty glass. "We're in for a bad time here. Much talk in the taverns about the 'new Poland only for Poles.' If I were young, I'd go to Hungary . . . better still, I'd go to Palestine. If I'm going to die fighting for my life, why shouldn't it be for my own country? I'm going to give you a pamphlet to read about Zionism. Right now, I need another schnapps." He patted me on the head and walked away.

Aaron came over with two pieces of pudding on a plate. "One's for you, Sara. Avram's the best 'uncle' you could have. I like him."

"Me, too." I took a bite of the pudding. "He thinks we're in for trouble. What does your father say?"

"You heard him the other night. This is his country, so why should he leave?" Aaron licked his fingers. "Tanta Hanna makes the best pudding in the world. I like you,

Sara. You don't act silly like the other girls. I can't wait until you're our sister."

"It's nice of you to say that, Aaron. If I wasn't an orphan, maybe I'd be just as silly." I took a deep breath. "Can you keep a secret?"

He nodded.

"I think it's best that I go to Hungary. I don't think your grandmother likes me, and I don't like her. I know it's not respectful . . . is it a sin for me to say that, Aaron? She's really mean to me. I know she doesn't want me here."

He thought a moment. "As long as you don't show it, Sara, it's not disrespectful. I'm not sure whether just thinking about something can be a sin. But she's that way with everyone." He sighed. "Grandma worries a lot about Michael and me . . . especially Michael. Outside of Aunt Frieda, we're the only relatives she has. Papa says we have to look away because she acts out of love."

"But love shouldn't hurt others, should it? I don't think I can stay where I'm not wanted. Please don't say anything to your father or anyone."

"Well, let me think this out. If I tell him, he wouldn't be able to change Grandma, so why upset him? What if . . . "

"It makes no difference. Even if your grandma liked me, there is no university here. So, I really must go to Hungary."

"Is university that important to you, Sara?"

Our eyes met. "I do not see myself growing older and not knowing more about the world and other people, Aaron. There is so much to learn. Why should only boys and men have an opportunity to better themselves?"

150

"I never thought about it that way, before." He made a face. " I don't blame you, Sara. When will you leave?"

"I don't know, I just made up my mind. Soon, probably. I have to find the best way to tell your father."

The following week began innocently enough. The free drawing was a huge success. The constable's wife, who normally never came into the store, won a bonnet; a woman who came in for the first time to buy a spool of thread and some needles won the second bonnet. The local midwife won Sheila's embroidery.

"It's terrible," lamented Mrs. Goldschein. "Not one regular customer!"

On Wednesday, when Simcha, the kosher butcher, opened the door of his shop a live pig ran out squealing into the street. "I'm ruined!" cried Simcha, throwing out everything in his shop.

"A desecration!" said the rabbi.

Our little community was in an uproar. And I didn't know what to do. If I left now, I would be deserting in the face of danger.

Supper that night was a grim affair. "Uncle Mordechai," I said, "Avram feels we're in for bad times. Do you think maybe . . . maybe all of us should consider leaving Drohobych?"

He looked around the table, choosing his words carefully. "No one drives me from my own country! I admit the pig in Simcha's shop was not a boyish prank, but the troublemakers here are using the Bolsheviks running wild in Russia as an excuse to blame Jews for everything. I'm sure the good people of Drohobych are as upset as we are.

It just calls for us to be more cautious and to sit tight. It's nothing we haven't lived through before."

Thursday, the district constable came into the store asking for Uncle Mordechai. After speaking in private for a few minutes, Uncle called Sheila, Avram, and me into the office. "I want you to tell my family what you just told me."

The constable, sitting stiffly in his high-collared uniform, chose his words carefully. "Since we are now Poland again, certain hooligans are getting bolder. Like my friend, Mordechai, I am a patriot and I believe in 'live and let live.'" He paused. "It seems that a few hotheads in my Polish fraternal society do not feel kindly toward your people.

"While I cannot act officially *before* a crime is committed, I came to warn you to be on guard. Hooligans may try to burn your store tomorrow night."

Sheila gasped. I could feel my heart pounding wildly. Remembering how Count Peter's warnings preceded a pogrom, I reached for Sheila's hand. Uncle's expression did not change as the constable continued. "I assume you can arrange a suitable reception, Mordechai? . . . Good. I see we understand each other."

"We do, thank you." Uncle shook his hand. "My regards to your wife."

When the constable left, Uncle looked at Avram. "You were right. You and I will sleep in the store tomorrow night."

"I'll bring a few comrades."

"I am staying with you," said Sheila.

"Me, too," I added quickly. "I know how to handle a pistol."

Uncle exploded. "No, you both will stay home! This is man's work."

CHAPTER

22

Sheila nudged me as a few aging strangers strolled casually toward the back of the store and disappeared into the warehouse. At first glance, they seemed no different from the other balding and potbellied older men of our community, but even from a distance they carried themselves with quiet authority.

"Avram's Cantonist friends," she whispered. "Can you imagine being kidnapped when you're five or six and serving 25 years in the army?"

All I could do was stare and shake my head. I thought of the little boys in Dreska who suddenly disappeared when I was growing up, but I always thought some were away visiting relatives.

Avram and Uncle accompanied the last man into the warehouse. While Sheila checked bills in the office, I waited on the lone customer in the store. As I wrapped her purchases, a burly young man at the entrance watched my every move. When my customer left, he took a few tentative steps across the threshold. After a quick glance around the store, he strode toward me.

Riga, who had been lying quietly at my feet, stood erect. Ears pointing, he growled and bared his teeth.

The youth stopped in his tracks.

"Can I help you?" Riga's body tensed against my leg.

"No. I mean, yes, little girl. I'm looking for a job. Does your father need a clerk or deliveryman?" He looked at Riga. "Does he bite?"

"Yes." Hearing Avram's footsteps coming down the aisle, I took a step forward. "We have enough help."

Backing away, the youth mumbled something and left in a hurry.

Avram studied the retreating figure. "Something tells me we'll see that one again tonight. He's probably reconnoitering. Come, Sara. Time for you and Sheila to leave. Your uncle and I are well prepared for those hooligans."

I kissed Uncle good night. Sheila held him tight. "Be careful, Mordechai."

"Don't you worry, it will be nothing. When you come to work in the morning, I'll take the carriage back and freshen up."

Sheila and I could hardly wait to get to the store the next morning. The constable was just helping four disheveled looking young men drag themselves into a wagon. I recognized the burly youth from yesterday. Hands tied behind their backs, bruised and bloody, the four sat dejectedly as the constable drove off.

Uncle and his friends watched in silence. Some of their clothes would need mending, and a few bloody scratches would need attention, but they were smiling.

"Thanks to God, you are all safe!" Sheila hugged Uncle.

"Good riddance," he said. "We were lucky to have just a few scorch marks on the outside."

"You men are too old to be fighting with such youngsters," scolded Sheila.

"We gave better than we got!" Avram said with authority. "Fight them head-on from the beginning, we say. No turning the other cheek. Right, gentlemen?"

His friends were vocal in their agreement. Uncle wore a grim look.

Sheila fussed over her husband. "You look tired, Mordechai. Are you all right? Please go home and rest."

"All I need is a shave." He kissed my cheek and climbed into his carriage. Riga bounded past and leaped up on the seat beside him. "No, Riga." Uncle pushed him away. "Stay with Sheila and Sara."

Avram pulled the dog out of the carriage. "Don't come back today, Mordechai. I'll take the ladies home at the end of the day."

As the afternoon wore on, Sheila's anxiety increased. "I don't like the way he looked, Sara. I'm telling Avram to close early."

"We did have quite a struggle with those hooligans last night," Avram admitted on the way home. "I'm sure Mordechai will be fine after a day's rest, Sheila. Your husband is quite a man, you know."

"I know. Everyone says he is unusual." Sheila seemed uneasy. "He didn't look well at all. I'm going to make him stay home tomorrow."

I reached for her hand. "Uncle will be fine, Sheila. Isn't it amazing how his horse and Riga respond to him?"

"Animals are quick to sense a man's character," said Avram. "Did you know he and the constable were comrades in the 1905 revolutionary movement?"

Sheila kept folding and unfolding her handkerchief. "I'm worried about my husband, Avram. He's so stubborn.

I wish I had his faith and patience. I think those hoodlums are just the beginning. What do you think?"

"I'm afraid we're in for some bad times, Mrs. Stern."

I reached for her hand. "Please don't worry. I'm sure Uncle will be all right. And if there is one good person like the constable, then there must be others who will stand up for what's right."

"From your mouth to God's ears," whispered Sheila.

Rounding a bend in the road, I craned my head for a better view of our house. "I see a few other carriages in the driveway, Sheila. We must have company."

Tanta Hanna and Frieda were standing motionless in the doorway as our carriage drew near. Sheila gripped my arm. I felt a sudden chill.

"What's wrong?" I shouted, leaping to the ground.

Sheila hurried ahead. Frieda hugged her with unusual fervor. "Oh, Sheila. I'm so sorry!"

Tanta Hanna threw her arms around me. "Sara," she gasped. "Mordechai is gone."

"Gone? Where?"

Frieda led us inside the crowded living room. "Such a tragedy. I still can't believe it. I brought Tanta Hanna to see Mother while the boys were at school. When we got back, the carriage was standing in front of the house and Mordechai was lying on the front seat. I don't know how long they were standing there."

"Where are the boys?" Sheila asked.

"With Mother."

The elderly doctor drew us aside. "My condolences, Mrs. Stern. You, too, Sara. Mordechai was dead for some time before I got here. A massive heart attack. I'm certain he felt nothing."

156

Sheila's knees buckled. Someone held smelling salts under her nose. My mind went numb, and suddenly the acrid ammonia smell stung my nostrils. I pushed the bottle away. "I'm all right."

Still in a daze, I went over to Tanta Hanna. Looking forlorn and smaller than ever, she seemed oblivious to the comforting neighbors. "Come." I took her hand. "Lie down for a while, Tanta Hanna."

"No, I can't," she moaned. "He was like a son to me."

"I cannot believe he's gone," Sheila repeated over and over as a neighbor helped her to a seat on the sofa next to Tanta Hanna.

"What will become of us, Sheila? Where will I go now?"

Sheila roused herself with an effort and put an arm around the frail shoulders. She moistened her lips but her voice, breaking, was barely a whisper. "Nothing will change, Tanta Hanna. Nothing." Then she seemed to notice me for the first time. "And nothing will change for you, Sara. I promise."

23

The funeral was stark and quick. Almost like Papa's. There hadn't been time to sit shivah or mourn then, and I hadn't been able to cry. Now, the enormity of Papa's death, coupled with Uncle's, descended upon me like a sudden storm. I don't recall ever crying for so long a period of time. Tanta Hanna, looking lost, consoled Michael and Aaron. Sheila, walking around in a daze, did her best to console me, but she was having difficulty dealing with her own sorrow. Frieda, with Herman the schoolteacher at her side, quietly managed everything despite her mother's constant advice.

I stayed close to Tanta Hanna and the boys during the week of shivah. We alternated between bouts of sorrow and laughter with the crowds of people coming to offer consolation and fond memories. At first, I couldn't understand how visitors could laugh when we were hurting so badly. Sheila explained that it was their way of paying homage and dealing with the death of someone they cared for. "Life still must go on, Sara, no matter how badly we feel."

Sheila, Frieda, and Mrs. Goldschein spent much of the time in the upstairs bedroom, emerging tight-lipped and serious after each session. I felt sorry for Mrs. Goldschein, who seemed to have lost all her aggression.

"Why do they look at us so funny when they come out?" Michael asked. "What's going to happen to us, Aaron?"

"Nothing's going to happen, Michael. Stop worrying. They're probably talking about the store. We'll still live here with Sheila and Tanta Hanna . . . just like before. I told you, I'll always take care of you. We'll always be together, Michael."

Near tears, Michael turned to me. "Are you still going away, Sara?"

I put my arm around him. "I . . . I think so, Michael. I really must . . . unless there is some way I can help in the store until things settle down. But Aaron is right. You know that Frieda, your grandma, Tanta Hanna, and Sheila all love you very much. They'll take care of you like they always have. Nothing will change for you."

"I don't know. I heard them talking the other day. I don't want to move to Grandma's, and I don't want Aunt Frieda and Herman living here when they get married." He rubbed his eyes. "I miss Papa, Aaron." It was sad to see the utter desolation on his baby face.

"Michael, did I ever tell you about the time the Cossacks chased us?"

"No," he whined, still rubbing his eyes.

"I had this big rifle and . . ."

"A real one?"

"Oh, yes. And it was very heavy."

"Girls can't shoot guns!"

"I did."

"At real Cossacks? You're making that up!" He looked at his brother.

Aaron nodded.

"Honest? How did that happen?"

160

"You know that a Gypsy caravan brought me to Drohobych. Well, on the way a Cossack patrol chased us into a forest, but I didn't have to use it then. It was before that that I fired a pistol at a bandit who was attacking my friend and me."

"Was it fun?"

"No."

"Did you kill him?"

"Kill . . . ?" I shook off the memory of the murderous highwaymen. I took a deep breath. "No, Michael. Lucky for me the bandit ran away."

"Were you scared?"

"Very scared. But it happened so quickly. It's scarier talking about it now than when it actually happened. I try not to think about it."

"If I had a gun, I wouldn't be scared of anything." He sauntered away.

Toward the end of the week, Sheila asked me to come to her bedroom. She took my hand in hers. "You know I love you, Sara. I was looking forward to being . . ."

I saw the pain in her eyes. "I know."

"Mordechai is gone, but I still want to adopt you . . . if that is agreeable with you. I'd be a good . . . I'd take good care of you, Sara." She held out her arms.

Inhaling her perfume and feeling the warmth of her embrace, I was tempted. I drew back. "Thank you, Sheila, but even if Uncle were alive, it's time for me to leave."

"You're certain of that?" Her eyes searched mine.

"I think so. Yes. Yes, I am."

"You don't sound convinced."

"I want to go, yet I feel I'm deserting everyone just when you're all facing trouble. Like I'm a coward running away. I don't . . ."

"Absolutely not! We could all leave if we wished, Sara, but it's our decision to remain. You do whatever your heart tells you. When would you go?"

"If you don't need me in the store, in a week or so. If you need me, I'll stay as long as you wish."

"That's sweet, but unnecessary. Between Avram, Frieda, and Herman we'll be fine." She smiled. "We can start getting you ready tomorrow. Now go join the others. I'll be down shortly."

Aaron was waiting at the foot of the stairs. "Is everything all right? You look as serious as the grownups."

"I just told Sheila I'm going to Hungary if they don't need me in the store."

He looked around. Satisfied we could not be overheard, he whispered, "Good for you! Listen, Sara, I saved seven gold coins. I don't need them. I'm giving them to you for your trip."

I kissed him on the cheek. "That's sweet, Aaron, but I really don't need money. Your father has been paying me each week and I have enough."

"Did Sheila tell you what they were talking about?"

"No."

I didn't discover that until the following week. "Sara, you're almost a young lady, so I wanted to discuss this privately with you. Mrs. Goldschein, Frieda, and I have been talking all week to find the best solution for the boys. I wanted to stay and raise them because I truly love them. Besides, I felt . . . it makes no difference what I felt, because—well, you know how protective Mrs. Goldschein is of Michael and Aaron. She and Frieda convinced me there would be less upheaval in their lives if I were not . . . not in the picture. So, I'm going away."

"Leaving Drohobych? How will that help the boys?"

"Frieda and Herman will get married and live here with them and Tanta Hanna. That way, there is no change in their surroundings. Also, and more important," Sheila cleared her throat, "Mrs. Goldschein was worried that I . . . that the boys would suffer financially if I stayed. I assured her I didn't want that to happen."

"That doesn't sound fair to me. After all, you're Uncle's wife."

She sighed. "We were only married a short time, Sara. She owns the store, not Mordechai. He must have had an intuition, for he left me some money. Also, an envelope in his handwriting for you—money for expenses at university in Budapest." She brightened. "And everyone is happy. Right?"

"I'm not sure. I hope so. Where will you go, Sheila?"

Her eyes held mine. "That depends upon you. How would you like company on the trip to Budapest?"

My heart leaped with excitement. "You mean that?"

"I do. Once we get there . . . well, who knows? It's the beginning of a new life for each of us, Sara."

24

It was heart-wrenching stepping into the carriage without Uncle. Sheila sat in his seat and picked up the reins. The horse didn't move. She gently shook the reins. He turned to look at her, but still did not move. "Go!" She shook the reins harder this time. The horse took a few halting steps before settling into a steady gait.

Entering the store for the first time without Uncle was a sad moment. The instant Sheila slid the key into the lock we heard Riga scratching inside. He bounded through the barely open door, knocking me down. Herman held on to Frieda and Sheila as Riga sniffed their clothes, then lowered his head in disappointment. His beautiful, purple eyes had lost their gleam. Back on my feet, I felt like crying as Riga slowly retreated to a corner, curling up near a black jacket.

"That's Uncle's!" I reached to pick it up. He growled, baring his teeth.

"All right, Riga. I'll leave you alone."

"He's waiting for his master," soothed Avram. "Wouldn't let me touch the jacket either. The store was closed all week like Mrs. Stern said, but I came every morning to feed him. He misses Mordechai."

"I know. Even the horse seemed to have lost his spirit."

Sheila cleared her throat. "We all miss him. Avram, please throw open the doors and let some fresh air in."

Avram waited on most of the customers that morning while Frieda took Herman on a tour of the store. Sheila sat quietly on a chair in the back, looking lost. My heart went out to her. She had spent so many years taking care of her mother before marrying Uncle Mordechai. Now, after only weeks of a happy marriage, she was a widow. I wondered why some people are visited with misfortune while others are not. Was this all decided by God during Rosh Hashanah . . . "Who shall live? Who shall die?"

Entering Uncle's office, I could feel his presence in the cold room. His scent lingered, reminding me of all the things I never got to tell him. He died too soon . . . like Papa . . . or was it that I waited too long? How I wished I told them how much I loved them. How much I loved Uncle for taking me in and making me feel part of his family. Through the open door, I could see Riga stretched out, head resting between his paws. From time to time he nuzzled Uncle's jacket. I left the office and gently took him by the collar. "Come, Riga, let's go outside a bit. We both could use some fresh air." Reluctantly, he left his vigil.

Sitting on the back step, with the brush Uncle always used I patiently groomed the black fur until it sparkled. His beautiful, purple eyes gazed plaintively at me. He looked as depressed as I felt. I missed Uncle Mordechai, and the thought of saying goodbye to Tanta Hanna and the boys was keeping me awake at night. While the prospect of traveling with Sheila was exciting, this was the closest to home I'd been since Dreska. It seemed like another lifetime.

"Sara?" Avram called from inside.

I gave Riga a hug. "Stay here, boy. I'll be right back."

Avram handed me a wrinkled envelope. "I forgot to tell you, Sara. Sergei, the man who brought you here from the inn, delivered this last week. Said it came some time ago but he couldn't get here sooner. He apologized and sent his regards."

After first checking to make sure Riga was still on the back step, I studied the envelope. Alepa's name in the corner sent my heart racing. Her letter was dated two weeks before I had written her.

> *Dear Little Sister Sara,*
>
> *I hope you are well and that your work is not too hard wherever you are. Is it with a rich family? The Bolsheviks say they love everybody, but they treat us no better than before. Sometimes, even a little worse. Conditions are not good wherever we go. Is it the same with you? Our caravan detours for a special council meeting. People say Viktor's intended bride's family is going to America where even Gypsies are rich. Her departure may be the miracle I was hoping for. You should go to Budapest as fast as you can before our relatives leave for America, too. If you write quickly to the address I gave you they should get the letter in time. Stefan and Viktor send good wishes. I send love to my dearest Sister and Friend.*
>
> *Alepa*

I immediately wrote a short note to her relatives and a longer one to her. We're leaving just in time, I thought. If Alepa's relatives leave Budapest before we arrive, at least Sheila and I will have each other.

After posting the letter, I went up front to help Avram and Sheila. It wasn't until closing time that I discovered Riga was not in the store. I was frantic. "It's my fault," I wailed. "I left him sitting outside at noon and forgot to bring him in!"

Sheila forced a wan smile. "Don't worry, Sara, he'll be all right. Tomorrow morning he'll be waiting at the door."

But Riga was not waiting the next day. Nor the day after. No matter how much the others tried to console me, I could not stop blaming myself. I had been careless and because of me, Uncle's beloved Riga was missing.

The next morning after breakfast, Michael came running back into the house. "Aunt Sheila, Riga's sitting by the mailbox! I tried to bring him in but he won't budge."

Sheila handed me a plate of meat and potatoes. "He likes you, Sara, perhaps you can coax him in."

A bedraggled looking Riga eyed me apprehensively. His eyes were dull, his coat matted and dirty.

"Come, Riga. Have some breakfast."

I let him have one bite before leading him back to the house. He wolfed down the food while I picked burrs from his fur. Licking the dish clean, Riga walked uncertainly from room to room sniffing the air. He halted at Uncle's favorite armchair before stopping in front of the staircase.

"Riga's coming up, Tanta Hanna," I shouted.

I could hear her comforting the dog before he padded slowly downstairs again to sit dejectedly by the front door.

"Good boy, Riga. Come ride with Sheila and me in Uncle's carriage." I gripped his collar firmly, but once outside he bolted. Off he went at a brisk trot until he was far ahead of us. He stopped and turned to stare. He howled at the sky. I shivered, remembering the wild wolves that night I searched for Marya and her husband.

A crestfallen Avram greeted us at the store. "He's still not back, Mrs. Stern."

Sheila bit her lip. "We just fed him at the house and he ran ahead. I thought he'd be here waiting for us."

Avram shook his head sadly. "If that's the case, I don't think Riga's ever coming back."

"Why do you say that, Avram?"

"He's a one-man dog, Mrs. Stern. He stayed near Mordechai's jacket all that time, just in case. Then, when he couldn't find him at home, he knew for certain. I think Riga just went off into the forest to die of a broken heart."

"Stand still, Sara, so I can fix this hem." Tanta Hanna handed me a piece of thread. "Chew on this so I don't stick you with the needle."

"How will that help?"

"It does. My mother told me that and it always worked for me."

"Why is the hem so heavy, Tanta Hanna?"

"I'm sewing gold coins in it. My gift, so don't say another word. Bandits are everywhere. This is something to fall back on in an emergency. Please stop fidgeting, Sara."

"Avram's waiting to take us to the station."

"So he'll wait a little longer." She sniffled. "I'm going to miss you, child."

I had said all my other goodbyes, but leaving Tanta Hanna was something I dreaded. That wonderful cinnamon-raisin smell would always remind me of her. Combination mother, grandmother, and confidante, she had been my champion right from the start. Helping her to her feet, I hugged the slender frame for the last time. With a pang, I suddenly realized how fragile she was.

"Thank you for everything, Tanta Hanna. I'll never forget you. I'll write as soon as I'm settled." I kissed her, then ran blindly out the door.

Avram helped us into the wagon and climbed on board. Before he could even settle into the driver's seat, the horse took off.

"That's remarkable!" Sheila exclaimed. "This is the first time he's done that since Mordechai . . . He must like you, Avram."

To my surprise, he was blushing. I took another look at Avram, realizing I had never really looked at him as an individual—only as a kindly father figure who went out of his way to watch over me. He was nice-looking, in a rugged way.

Avram smiled. "I don't know about that, Mrs. Stern, but I try to treat animals like I treat people. They have feelings, too. So, life goes on even for horses." He paused. "Be careful of strangers, dear ladies, especially Hungarians—they have a bad reputation." He reached into his pocket. "Here's that travel permit I promised you, Mrs. Stern."

"How on earth did you get it so quickly, Avram? It would have taken me forever." She glanced at the official-looking paper before handing it to me.

AUTHORIZATION TO LEAVE THE BORDERS OF RUSSIA

The Jewess Sheila Stern and daughter Sara, having expressed a desire to depart for Hungary, are declared to have left the borders of Russia forever.

Signed,
K. Papreszewski, Commissioner of Travel

Avram chuckled. "I have my sources. You'll notice it is right up to date; it's even got the latest Polish stamp for good measure. Doesn't mention the Russian Empire at all. And they really mean it when they say you've left 'forever.' They don't want you back!"

Sheila looked wistful. "They're getting their wish. First, Mordechai. Now, Sara and me." She sighed. "No, we're definitely not returning, ever."

"I don't ever want to come back!" That was all I could bear to say.

Avram frowned. "I worry about you two. A beautiful widow and pretty daughter are easy prey. What will you do if Sara's Gypsy friends have left Budapest?"

Sheila roused herself. "Like always, Avram, we will do whatever we have to."

"Well, if they are gone, you should consider going to America . . . or Palestine." He took a pamphlet from his pocket. "Sara, here's the article I promised you. Theodore Herzl talks about Zionism and a Jewish state. Very exciting."

"Thank you, Avram." I stuffed it inside my bulging handbag.

He stared at the bag. "Now, give me that old pistol you're carrying, Sara. You're not that grown up yet. Besides, Budapest is much more civilized than Drohobych." He took my pistol away. "However . . ." He handed Sheila a small, square package. "For protection, Mrs. Stern. This is a lady's pistol that once belonged to nobility—very accurate. And less noticeable."

Sheila held the package gingerly. "Thank you, Avram. Perhaps one day Sara will show me how to use it. In the meantime, I guess it's safer with me."

The train was already at the station when we arrived. Clouds of steam obscured the engine as its boilers took on water from the lopsided tank bordering the tracks. Avram hoisted our suitcases to the train platform. He removed his cap. "May God watch over both of you," he said huskily.

"Thank you for helping us and being such a friend, " said Sheila sadly.

Avram cleared his throat and waved awkwardly before turning away.

Sighing, I studied the retreating figure. Another protector was exiting my life. "He's such a nice man, Sheila. I wonder why he never married."

CHAPTER

25

After a two days' journey, our train pulled into the station. Never before had I seen such crowds of people, all carrying bundles or suitcases and scurrying like ants. And the noise inside the terminal! "Where are they all going in such a hurry, Sheila?"

"They must be late for an important occasion. I wonder why that sign only says 'Buda'?"

I hailed a porter. "Sir, could you please tell us how to get to Budapest?"

He chuckled. "You are there. This is Buda, on the west bank of the Danube. Right across the river on the east bank is Pest. Buda-Pest, understand? Can I take your bags?"

Sheila and I exchanged embarrassed looks. "No thank you, sir."

He was already in search of another prospect. Glancing at the paper in my hand, I called out, "Excuse me, sir. Which way to Magyar Street?"

Without stopping, he pointed. "Ten, twelve squares that way. Now, I've got to find paying customers." The porter shoved his cart boldly through the crowd.

We stood on the sidewalk dodging an endless stream of pedestrians rushing to and fro. Carriages driving at a pace to threaten one's life made crossing the wide boulevard a frightening experience. And the street noises were almost as loud as inside the huge terminal. "I never saw so many buildings in one place."

Shaking her head, Sheila held onto my arm until we had safely reached the other sidewalk. "Let's rest a moment and enjoy the view."

The sun felt good on our backs as we sat on a bench and studied the snowcapped mountains of Pest in the distance. "I can't believe I'm finally here. Isn't it exciting?"

"It's beautiful, but let's not wait too long, Sara. We may have a great distance to go, and these suitcases get heavier by the minute."

Alternately asking directions and resting, it took only an hour to find Magyar Street. We paused in front of the elegant Hotel Astoria, where an imperious doorman hailed carriages for stylish guests.

"I've heard of this hotel, Sara. It must be grand staying here. Isn't it odd—the wealthy people don't seem to be in as much of a hurry. Have we much further to go?"

"I think it's only a square away." I had committed the street number to memory, and in the distance I could make out ROMANY CAFÉ emblazoned on a blue canopy.

Double-checking the number on the door, I rang the bell. While we waited, we studied the half-brick, half-wood building. It was old but in excellent condition. Colorful flowers bloomed in gaily painted window boxes. Just the kind of house I imagined Hungarians lived in. I rang the bell a second time.

Sheila pointed to a small sign we hadn't noticed before: Open 6 p.m. "Oh, my. That's two hours from now."

Somewhere above us a window slid open, and a man's voice bellowed something about reading signs. The window slammed shut. Minutes later, the door opened. A stout, middle-aged man with bushy white hair confronted us. "That was enough noise to wake the dead. I was sound asleep. What do you want?"

"Alepa said . . ."

"My cousin? Why didn't you say so in the first place? I am Sandor. Come in!" A broad smile transformed his features. "Sara Samovitch, you must be. I received your letter and I am honored." He bowed.

"Our travel permit says my name is Sara Stern and this is my mother, Sheila Stern."

"I understand perfectly." Even, white teeth flashed in a knowing smile. He bowed again. "Welcome to my home. Please follow me." Sandor led us past tables set with fine linen and sparkling silverware into a spotless kitchen.

"Sit, ladies. Questions later. Tea or coffee?" Without waiting for a reply, he drew three glasses of hot tea from a bubbling samovar and filled a platter with cookies.

Placing a lump of sugar between his front teeth, he sipped loudly. "Ah. Now I am awake. Tell me everything I should know."

"In truth, Sheila was married to my Uncle, Mordechai Stern, who recently passed away. May he rest in peace." Every time I thought about Uncle I thought about Papa—I couldn't help it. Out of the corner of my eye I noticed Sheila's face turning grim.

"I am sorry for your misfortune," said Sandor in a soft voice.

Regaining my composure, I told him all that had happened since I last saw Alepa. "We were worried you might have left for America."

"Not for some time yet. I'm sorry I barked at you. Last night lasted until daybreak this morning, but the money

175

flowed along with the wine, so I didn't care." He shrugged. "Who knows how long it will last? Now, what can Sandor do to make you happy?"

"We need an inexpensive place to live," said Sheila. "And jobs."

He pursed his lips. "A tall order in these unsettling times. The city is full of refugee White Russians, with and without money—mostly without. Also, thousands of Jews like you. Not that Jews are bad—we Gypsies are in the same boat. This government no longer looks kindly on either of us. Yet, some of us manage to remain 'darlings' of the rich, while others are cursed and ostracized."

Sheila leaned forward. "Are you one of the 'darlings' or one of the 'cursed'?"

He passed his fingers through thick, white hair. "There is a saying that all a Hungarian needs to get drunk is a glass of water and a Gypsy fiddler. I am proud to say my family is a dynasty of gifted musicians . . . one generation after another. We make the fiddle laugh; we make it cry. So it is only fair to say, at this moment, we . . . I am one of the 'darlings'. But it is precarious. How long our Romanian masters will tolerate us is another matter. But we think positive, no? What kind of work are you good at?"

The sweet pastries revived me. "I worked in a general store. I can take care of inventory. I can cook and wait on tables. Also, I can shoot a pistol."

"That's good—except the pistol. We have enough trouble as it is."

Sheila added, "I managed a household. I embroider and sew."

He nodded. "Excellent. My friend, Madame Olga, has a fancy dress salon. A very elegant trade. She waits on the nobility herself; but she might need another seamstress, Mrs. Stern, especially one who embroiders. My restaurant doesn't need another cook or waitress, Sara, so let's see if Madame Olga can find something for you."

Her name had a familiar ring, but I could not recall where I'd heard it before. "Sheila and I would be forever indebted to you, Sandor."

He cleared his throat. "It is nothing. In the meantime, you can sleep on cots in the storeroom for a night or two until we find a decent rooming house for ladies. The only problem is that you can't use the storeroom until after our performance this evening."

"That's more than we expected. And we thank you again." Sheila smiled. "In the meantime, where do you wish us to wait?"

"First, you must eat. We serve dinner at six, and the show follows. The help is starting to arrive now, so I must talk to the chef. After you freshen up in the ladies' room, sit at that corner table. I know you will enjoy the evening. I'll see you after the performance."

In the ladies' washroom, I took a dark dress from my suitcase. The skirt was wrinkled, but if I remained seated the entire evening no one would notice. Sheila changed into the black dress she wore at her wedding. After viewing herself in the mirror, she turned to me. "You know, Sara, we will not be eating kosher food for a while, so I suggest we just stay away from meat and chicken while we're here."

"I wonder how people travel far from home and still keep kosher—and what do soldiers do, Sheila? Maybe they'll serve fish tonight also."

We took seats at the corner table, hiding the suitcases behind our chairs. "I have to tell you something amazing,

Sheila. Do you remember, I told you some time ago that Count Peter gave me a note for a friend in Budapest? Well, I looked at it again—his friend is also Madame Olga. I'm saving his in case Sandor is unsuccessful."

An attractive woman with long, flowing hair approached with three bowls of soup. Purple skirt swirling around her slender form, she slid onto the chair opposite us. Large, gold, hoop earrings dangled gracefully as she leaned forward. "Welcome, ladies. I know you are Sara and Sheila. I am Carmen, the hostess. If this Hungarian apple soup is not the best you have ever tasted, this meal will cost you nothing." She laughed heartily. "A joke—I know you are Sandor's guests. You see I eat this soup myself, so it can't be too bad. Oh, oh. I just thought of something." She bolted from the chair.

Returning shortly, Carmen stood behind Sheila and slipped a long strand of pearls around her neck. "Many of our customers will be wearing long dresses and jewels." She clapped her hands in delight. "Excellent! They're just the right length."

"They're breathtaking. I can't . . ."

"Shush." She took a short, pearl necklace from her pocket and hung it around my neck. "Just the right touch for a young lady. Now, let's eat."

"Who do these belong to? We can't wear them!"

"Of course, you can. They're fakes . . . like some of our finest customers and most of their jewelry. Only another pearl would know yours are not real." Studying Sheila carefully from across the table, she nodded in satisfaction. "Severe, but elegant. You could use a bit of makeup, but that can wait for another time. Some of these gigolos are sure to spot you hiding in the corner. If you need rescuing, send the waiter to me."

As we ate, Carmen informed us that Sandor was the owner, and mostly everyone working there was Hungarian, Gypsy, or Polish. The customers were primarily White Russians—titled and pretenders. "They all put on a big show, hoping to marry money. Most are penniless—we can tell by the tips, when we get them. But this is a fun place to work, and we eat like royalty."

"Carmen," I said, "I never tasted apple soup before. It's delicious. I . . ." Looking past her shoulder, I froze at the sight of a uniformed figure in the doorway. "Cossacks!" I knocked over the water glass.

Sheila dried my dress with a napkin. Carmen murmured sympathetically, "I'm sorry, Sara. Gregory's the doorman. Claims he was a general in the czar's army, but everyone knows he's a starving actor. This is the longest job he's ever had."

"He looks real enough to me." My heart still beat furiously. "I'm sorry. I feel foolish, Carmen, but those Cossacks murdered and pillaged us for so long that . . ."

"I should apologize to you, Sara. You're not the first . . . mostly it is a Jewish customer who reacts that way. We only have a few, but Sandor has told Gregory several times to change his uniform. Some of the terrible stories I've heard make my hair stand on end . . . and that's not easy when you look at my hair." Carmen sighed. "Not really funny, am I? But even a bad joke is sometimes necessary in these times. Listen, I have to go now. If you were not Jewish, I'd recommend the pork goulash in sour cream and kummel liquor. Instead, order our chicken paprikash, made with just enough melted chicken fat that you'd swear your grandmother came down from heaven to cook it herself. Cabbage strudel for dessert, and you think you are in heaven. I must get back to work. Enjoy the meal."

A young waiter took our order and touched his fingertips to his lips. "A pleasure to serve connoisseurs of fine dining. Mesdames, tomorrow you must order Gypsy Chicken Schnitzel—mouthwatering! In the meantime, Sandor sends this bottle of wine with his compliments."

Extracting the cork with a loud pop, he deliberately placed it on the tablecloth in front of Sheila. She and I exchanged looks.

He bowed, and in a voice so low only we could hear, his words were precise. "Smell the cork. If moldy or vinegary, shake head. If good, nod."

Mystified, I watched Sheila follow his instructions. She nodded.

He bent low again. Pouring a little into her glass, his lips barely moved. "Swirl glass and sniff. Small sip. If not vinegary, nod."

I watched as Sheila completed the odd ritual. The waiter smiled, speaking normally as he filled our glasses. "Thank you, mesdames. Enjoy your meal. My name is Josef."

"Thank you, Josef." Sheila waited for him to leave before raising her glass. *"L'chaim!"*

"L'chaim!" I took a small sip and put the glass down carefully. Feeling as though the entire dining room was watching, I glanced about. To my disappointment, no one paid us the least bit of attention. "I'm curious about something, Sheila. Why didn't the waiter check the wine himself before bringing it out? Isn't that silly?"

Sheila smiled. "It's one of those polite customs rich people observe. Just look around at all those fancy ladies and gentlemen. Don't they look grand?"

The dining room was almost full. Handsome men in evening dress hung on every word of their bejeweled ladies. From the gaiety in the smoke-filled room, it was obvious the elegant diners had not a care in the world. How I envied them!

Sheila looked pensive. "How Mordechai would have enjoyed this experience, Sara."

"Papa, too. What a difference from how we lived in Dreska. Are you all right?"

Nodding, she dabbed at her eyes with her handkerchief. "I wonder if I did the right thing leaving Michael and Aaron. I feel guilty about abandoning them, Sara."

"You didn't abandon them, and I'm sure they don't feel you did. Your leaving was in their best interests. I know I would feel that way if I were them."

She sighed. "I hope you're right."

We continued in silence. The cabbage strudel was delicious enough to lift one's spirits. The waiter refilled our glasses. Soon, both Sheila and I felt more at ease. This was my first experience in a restaurant, and it was dazzling. A waiter catering to my every wish, an unending flow of exotic dishes on fine china . . . everything fit for a countess. I wished the evening would go on forever. Could there be a better way to live and enjoy life?

How wonderful to be wealthy and carefree . . . and never have to worry about Cossack war cries or drunken peasants! How pitiful and sad my life had been. Swallowing hard, I breathed deeply to shake the sudden despair.

My dark thoughts must have been contagious for, suddenly, the bleak look reappeared on Sheila's face. We reached for the wine glasses that some invisible hand kept refilling.

The room had grown unaccountably hot, and I was unaccountably thirsty. Draining the last drops of my third drink—or was it my fourth?—I turned the glass upside down. I had had enough.

Across the table, Sheila's face was like a mask. "Sara, I think we've had too much to drink. I wish we had a room to go to. The show hasn't even started yet. Or has it?"

It was becoming difficult to keep faces in focus. I struggled to stand up. "I think we need some fresh air."

"Yes." Sheila steadied herself with one hand on the table and took my elbow. We tried unsuccessfully to stand upright. A white cuff and black sleeve suddenly appeared between us. A man's voice, low and reassuring, sounded in our ears. *"Ich bin a Yid.* Hold on to my arm and follow me."

26

Yad Mordechai, soon-to-be State of Israel. May 12, 1948, 2400 hours –

This has been the longest day of all, so far. Fifteen additional Palmach fighters finally got here around 1300 hours, and in short order everything was solidified. Yad Mordechai's total population is now about 150. Each person knows exactly what is to be done and that is comforting. Ben Gurion's expected announcement about statehood should be coming soon. Our resolve is high', as is our spirit.

We have a stretched-out perimeter, but our leader is a bold, young, seasoned Palmach veteran who inspires confidence. He knew some details of Haganah's capture of Haifa a few weeks ago. When the British announced on April 21 they were leaving key positions in Haifa, Haganah immediately shelled the city and stormed those positions. Though Arabs controlled the port and the trade, tens of thousands suddenly fled the city on foot, by car, and by boat. Tens of thousands of Arabs also mysteriously left Jaffa.

No one knows what caused them to leave homes and material possessions in such panic. One rumor is that they left on orders from Arab leaders, fully expecting to return in a few weeks after their armies make good on their promise to "throw all the Jews into the sea." Well, we are more determined than ever not to move one inch from this spot! The capture of those two cities is a great accomplishment. Arab threats to annihilate us only stiffen our resolve. With everything now in order, all we can do is wait.

Joel and I have been able to sit and talk candidly. He insists that we will lose our identity and disappear as a people unless we fully observe our religion. "But here I am, just as alive as you," I tell him. I felt he was rushing me to make a commitment. He was blunt: "This is wartime. We don't have the luxury of playing drawn-out games, Deborah. I love you and I think you care about me." He'd wrestled with his own convictions and was positive he could live with my brand of Judaism if I could live with his Orthodoxy. Joel was confident his parents would accept anything we agreed upon. "In any event, I'll be marrying you, Deborah, not them."

He is honorable and determined, and I do care for him. I promised him an answer by the end of the week. Grandpa Ilya's advice to be bold and brave is pushing me to go along with Joel. Will we be able to live happily with our religious differences? I'll have to sleep on it.

Mother's manuscript fascinates me. I am just beginning to appreciate what immigrants went through coming out of a shtetl wearing shtetl clothing and thinking shtetl thoughts—always the "other" as they made their way on foot, by wagon, train, and ship, to a strange, new world. Police and border guards pushed and pulled them (at best) according to rules they did not fully comprehend, in a language foreign to their ears. Making themselves understood was almost impossible; earning a living, chaotic. Mother told me how many of them were frightened by the mere sight of a uniformed fireman or postman in their new, friendly country. Every day brought another adventure with shifting players and surroundings, until their very existence resembled a ride on a merry-go-round.

Somehow, I do not picture my parents like that. Perhaps it's because they were so young and hadn't spent half a lifetime in a shtetl. Their early years in Palestine were backbreaking and dangerous—malarial swamps, a stubborn land of rocks and boulders, and highly coordinated Arab attacks in 1920 and 1921. The attacks of 1929 and during the 1930s I remember well, but nonetheless, I was fortunate growing up on a kibbutz surrounded by a loving family and supportive friends. The peaceful years in between were wonderful, and when this initial trouble is over, Joel and I will do everything we can to make peace with the Arabs. I believe most of them want that as much as we do.

CHAPTER

27

BUDAPEST, HUNGARY. SUMMER 1920.

"Why do I smell onions?"

"You've been sleeping on sacks of them, Sara." The gallant waiter of last night stepped out of the shadows. "This storeroom was the only place available before the show started last night. I'm afraid those old linens don't make much of a mattress. How do you feel?"

"Achy and thirsty. Where's Sheila?" I tossed aside the pink tablecloth someone had thrown over me.

"You call your mother by her first name?" Josef gave me an odd look. "I left her having coffee in the kitchen. It's five-thirty in the morning."

My fingers flew to my neck.

"Carmen took your pearls last night. Come, let's join your mother."

Sheila looked wide awake. "Sara, you'll feel better after a hot coffee. I've already thanked Josef for his wine lesson and for escorting us from the dining room before we passed out."

"I'm so ashamed. Was I sick or loud, Josef? The last thing I remember was feeling very dizzy. Did we fall? Tell me everything."

He grinned. "Nothing like that at all. You and your mother were very quiet, considering the amount of wine you consumed."

He handed me a steaming cup of coffee. "It happens to the best. I feel responsible because I kept refilling your wine glasses, just as I do with all customers. You both were enjoying the evening so much. When I realized you were drinking the wine like water, I decided to stay close. You each took my arm like perfect ladies. Be assured, it was a normal exit with nothing amiss."

He looked at his watch. "I have classes at university in a few hours. You ladies can use the cots in the other storeroom now. There's a bolt on the door, and the cooks won't be going in there until at least mid-afternoon. Get some rest. Will you be having dinner here tonight?"

"Possibly," answered Sheila. "I'm curious about something. Did I hear you correctly last night? Did you say *'Ich bin a Yid'* as we left the table? Why would you tell us you are a Jew? Are you?"

Frowning, he lowered his voice. "I was walking away when you toasted each other, but I did hear you say *'l'chaim.'* I said it because I needed your immediate trust."

I had an uneasy premonition. "Why did you whisper?"

"You're strangers here. These are difficult days. The Romanians came in to clean up our government but they take away our liberty. They hate Jews with a passion!"

"Are you Jewish?"

He hesitated. "What if I said 'no,' that I'm studying German at university? Would it make a difference?"

Sheila and I looked at each other. "I think so," I said slowly. "I can't imagine a gentile saying he is a Jew in Yiddish. So, if you say you aren't . . ."

Sheila spoke up. "Like you said before, Josef, these are difficult days—but you really don't have to answer that question if you don't care to. Your religion and politics really do not matter to us."

"It's complicated." He ran his hand over the stubble on his chin. "I need to shave before classes." He headed for the door. "Why don't you ladies get some more sleep?"

It was past noon when we woke for the second time that day. This time my head was clear when we returned to the kitchen. Carmen greeted us. "Heard you moving around, so I waited. The coffee's fresh and the rolls only a trifle stale. You're both looking much better than the last time I saw you." She laughed.

I was hungry, and the hard roll, dunked in coffee, tasted sweeter than cake. "I feel like a new person, thanks to you and Josef." I hesitated. "Carmen, does everyone here know we're Jewish?"

Her expression changed. "Uncle Sandor and I would never discuss your religion with anyone. We know what it means to be Bilbodo."

"Does anyone else know Sheila is not my mother?"

"No."

"Good," said Sheila. "Now Josef knows. What kind of man is he, Carmen?"

She pursed her lips. "Sandor assigned him your table because he trusts him. Josef always treats me with respect, but then I am Sandor's niece. He has a reputation as a lady's man. Some of the older aristocrats . . . women . . . find him especially attractive. Please pass the butter, Sheila."

"Is he Jewish?" I asked.

Carmen concentrated on putting the exact amount of butter on her plate. "I honestly don't know. I know he's Hungarian . . . some say he's part Gypsy, part Cossack. Why don't you ask him yourself? Remember, though, a lady's man usually says what you want to hear."

"You make him sound like a . . . like a liar, Carmen. He seemed friendly and respectful to us, didn't he, Mother?"

"Somewhat. He didn't answer when we asked if he were Jewish. You're young, Sara. As you get older, you'll learn that people aren't always what they seem. Anyway, we're forewarned. Changing the subject, Carmen, is Madame Olga's far from here? Sandor said . . ."

"I almost forgot!" Carmen reached into a pocket. "He gave me a note of introduction in case you were up before him. Her salon is only six or seven squares away. If you'll wait till I get dressed, I'll take you there."

"Thank you, but if you'll give us directions I believe we could find it ourselves."

The wide boulevards sparkled in the sunlight. Young, well-dressed students carrying books overflowed the sidewalk. The girls appeared to be only a few years older than I, but I felt like a farmgirl in my clothes. Arm-in-arm, laughing and joking, they passed us by as though we were invisible. All had the same carefree attitude. How I wished I were headed for university with them, instead of Madame Olga's to beg for a job. I hurried to catch up to Sheila as she rounded the corner. For a moment, I lost her in the blinding sun.

"Sara!" Josef's face suddenly emerged from the sunlight. "Where are you going in such a hurry? The Romany is in the opposite direction."

"Madame Olga's." Sheila shifted her embroidery bag to her other hand. "Excuse us, Josef, but we don't want to be late for a job interview."

"May I walk with you?"

"You just came from that direction."

"Yes, but I'm done with classes, Mrs. Stern, and I can take you directly there. It would be my pleasure."

I gave him a sideward glance. He looked 18 or 19. Something about him reminded me of Count Peter, but Josef was much more intense. If only we could trust him. "I hope you didn't fall asleep in class."

"I'm used to working late hours. May I say that both of you ladies look beautiful."

"Thank you. I see why they call you a lady's man."

"Who told you that, Mrs. Stern? Don't believe it. I am a struggling student trying to get by in a difficult world. The salon's just around the next corner. I can wait and go back to the Romany with you."

"That's not necessary. I don't know how long . . ."

He consulted his watch. "I can wait exactly 43 minutes. The help uses that side entrance and that's where I'll be. If you're not out by then, I'll see you at the café tonight. Good luck."

Madame Olga looked exactly like the picture in my mind of a true aristocrat. Chin held high, with a ramrod posture, she studied the embroidery Sheila brought. "Fine workmanship, Mrs. Stern. Sandor is not only a good friend, but an extraordinary *artiste* with a heart too big for his own good—always going out of his way to help people— but that's what makes him best *prima*—first fiddler—of all the Gypsy orchestras in Hungary. Come, let us enjoy a demitasse while we decide what to do with you." The tiny cups she gave us probably held two teaspoons of the thick, black liquid. Madame Olga sipped daintily.

I held my cup exactly as she did. The demitasse tasted like burnt, bitter coffee.

Madame Olga arched her slender neck. "The story you tell is most interesting, but working in a general store, I'm sorry to say, is another world from my salon. The cream of society comes to Madame Olga's for exquisite design and style. Our workmanship is incredible, but my clients are merciless in their expectations. They are ogres. I keep them away from my workers because the client is never wrong. Never!"

Sheila nodded. "Of course, Madame, but ogres do not frighten us. My daughter is young in years, but she has faced Cossacks. We are not afraid of anything, and we're willing to start any . . ."

"Cossacks, you say?" She held up her hand. "Be quiet a moment and let me think." Depositing her cup and saucer on an ornate desk, she strode to the window. After a moment, she turned to face us again. "I have decided. Mrs. Stern, we can use your talents in our design department. Sara, can you sew—a little, perhaps?"

"A little, Madame. I also kept inventory in the general store."

"Better," she murmured. "Report tomorrow morning at eight. If you need a place to sleep, you may use our storeroom. It needs tidying, but it is clean. Now, I must go. An important client waits." Madame Olga swept out of the room.

During the walk back, Josef was full of advice. "I suggest it will be easier if we pick up your clothes now and bring them back to the salon. You probably won't be able to rearrange the storeroom this afternoon, so you'll have to stay at the Romany one more night."

"We don't need help with out clothes. Sheila and I are perfectly capable."

"Of course you are, but you and your mother are Sandor's guests. I insist." He turned to Sheila. "Mrs. Stern, last night you asked me . . ."

"Forget what we asked you last night. We were only making conversation."

"Didn't you say it was a matter of trust?"

"It makes no difference now."

"Meaning it might at a later time?"

Sheila shrugged. "Meaning nothing. We are more concerned with earning a living and finding proper lodgings. As I said before, your religion and politics are of no concern to us—we had many gentile friends in Drohobych."

CHAPTER

28

Sandor frowned. "I see Josef waiting near your suitcases. Are you going somewhere with him? I normally do not interfere with *gaje*, but I feel responsible. Carmen said you had questions. Josef is a charming young man. Some women find him irresistible. Personally . . ." He coughed discreetly. "Sometimes I wonder if he thinks about anything other than having a good time."

"Do you trust him?"

"I do, Sara. Why do you ask?"

Sheila answered quickly. "We asked him if he was Jewish and he evaded the question. There is something secretive about him."

"But Sheila," I added, "in all fairness, he wanted to discuss it later, and you told him it wasn't important."

Sandor looked thoughtful. "He never talks about himself. From my observations, he's a good waiter with a talent for ingratiating himself. I think he is honest, but if you feel he is not truthful, then follow your intuition."

"Sara and I appreciate your advice. From now on, we'll be more careful about what we tell him. At the moment, he has offered to carry our luggage back to Madame Olga's, that's all. And we have you to thank for her hiring us. We start tomorrow."

Impulsively, I hugged the kindly Gypsy. "She even said we could sleep in her storeroom. Thank you for everything, Sandor."

His eyes twinkled. "It is my pleasure. If it's not comfortable there, come back here at once. And don't forget, we are serving Gypsy schnitzel for supper tonight. It will melt in your mouth."

Josef picked up our suitcases as we approached. "This is everything? You ladies certainly travel light."

"We don't own much," I replied, as we walked down the street. "Tell me, Josef, what are you studying at university besides German?"

"German? I never said . . ." He chuckled. "You have a good memory and the makings of a bad detective, Sara. I study archeology, architecture, and economics."

"Economics? In case you starve at the other two?"

He grinned. "You might say that. Tell me, if you were a student, what would you be studying?"

"Girls were not allowed to study in my shtetl . . . my village . . . but Papa . . ."

"I know what shtetl means, Sara. But surely, you don't want to live like your parents. That may have been good enough for them and their parents. This is the 20th century! I believe in equal opportunity for men and women. Wouldn't you like to attend university?"

Sheila interrupted. "She's only 12, Josef. A little too young, don't you think?"

"Mrs. Stern, there are students not much older in some of my classes. Sara strikes me as a very bright girl. I'd be happy to help her study for entrance exams, if she's interested."

I blushed. "I'd love that. Papa did teach me to read and write, and much of what the older boys . . ."

"That's very kind, Josef," Sheila said as we arrived at the side door of the salon. "Once we're settled, perhaps we'll take advantage of your offer. Thanks for carrying our clothes. We'll bring them inside and be out in a moment."

"I have to go inside myself, Mrs. Stern."

The young woman behind the counter barely looked at me. "Put those in the storeroom, girl. Hello, Josef," she beamed. "You're early. Madame Adrienne's gown will not be ready for two hours. But let me check for you."

"Thank you, Sonia." He hummed a little tune. "You'll like it here, Sara. What will you be doing?"

"I'm not exactly sure. Mother will be working in the design department."

Sonia returned quickly. As far as she was concerned, Sheila and I still did not exist.

"Because it's you, Josef," she smiled coyly, "they'll have it ready in 30 minutes."

"I'll be back." He held the door for us. "Unless you're in a rush, there's a great pastry shop around the corner. My treat."

"I'd love that! We're in no rush, are we, Mother."

Sheila hesitated. "Maybe you two can go. On second thought, we're not watching the clock, Josef. We'd love a pastry. Please let us pay—you've done so much for us already."

"I wouldn't think of it." He escorted us out the door and down the street.

Overhead bells tinkled merrily when I opened the pastry shop door into a world of chocolate smells and confectionary delights. My eyes grew wide as I took in the curved glass showcases overflowing with mouthwatering delicacies. I moistened my lips, remembering Tanta Hanna's kitchen on baking day. But this was a shop entirely devoted to pastries—I never imagined such a thing existed!

Settling in a wire-backed chair, I rested my elbows on the green marble tabletop and feasted my eyes. Mounds and mounds of cookies. Square shapes and circles, triangles and narrow strips. Enough dried fruit and powdered sugar to last a lifetime. Wouldn't it be wonderful to have enough money to buy anything I wanted!

Josef brought a tray with three tall mugs brimming with whipped cream. Flecks of chocolate nestled in the foamy whiteness. I took a sip. "Nutmeg and cinnamon, Mother. Did you ever taste anything like this before?"

Sheila grinned, handing me a napkin. "Never. Do I have a whipped cream mustache like you?"

"No," answered Josef. "Sara, would you like one of those strudels?"

"Oh, yes! And could I also have one of those long pastries with cream bursting out the ends? I'll share them with Mother."

He looked at me sideways. "I think when you grow up it will be cheaper to clothe you than feed you."

"Tell me how much Madame Adrienne's gown costs, then I'll tell you if you are right."

"You'll have to ask her, Sara. I just pick it up and deliver it." He headed toward the counter.

"It's really not our business," Sheila whispered.

Josef returned with the pastries. The thin dough dissolved in my mouth like a snowflake. "This is a real treat. I love this country! It's such a far cry from Dreska and Cossacks."

"Not so far as you think!" His mood changed instantly. A darkness seemed to settle in his eyes.

198

"Did I say something wrong?" I put the pastry down.

"No, Sara. Enjoy it all while you can—I don't want to spoil your fun."

"What is it, then? What are you trying to tell us?"

He leaned forward so only we could hear. "The regent, Admiral Horthy, is murdering thousands of innocent people, especially Jews, and the rest of the world closes its eyes! He is destroying Hungary. We have to . . ." His voice trailed off in frustration.

"We can do nothing, Josef. We're ordinary people."

"We can do plenty, Sara! First . . . well, this is not the place for such a discussion. We'll talk another time. I think we should go." He scraped his chair back.

Sheila and I exchanged looks as we filed out. This time, the bells above the door did not sound as joyful. Proceeding in silence until we reached the salon door, Josef put his hand on the doorknob, but did not open it. "Mrs. Stern, did you tell Madame Olga you are Jewish?"

"No. Why?"

"Just curious. Don't." He held the door open.

The package was waiting for him at the counter. He tucked it under one arm, and we started back at a brisk pace. "I'm sorry to rush you, but we took longer than expected."

"I'm glad you're in a better mood now, Josef," Sheila remarked. "Please don't bother walking back with us. The lady is waiting for her gown and we know the way."

He sounded relieved. "Then I'll turn here. Be careful, ladies."

We resumed our walk in silence. My mind was busy trying to make sense of Josef's words. "What did he mean, 'we can do plenty' about Horthy? Do you think he's a Bolshevik, Sheila? I don't think he's Jewish."

"He's either *not* Jewish, or not sure he can trust us. I don't know whether he is a Bolshevik, but he doesn't paint a pretty picture of conditions here. I keep wondering why he is so friendly to us." She looked troubled. "Sara, I think we should leave Hungary as soon as we can. We'll be better off in America."

Carmen joined us for supper. "How did it go with Josef, Sheila—a charmer, isn't he?"

"He is. Tell me, who is Madame Adrienne?"

"You found out so quick?" Carmen's eyes sparkled. "A rich, old widow. Past 40. At least, that's what they all say."

"Does he have a second job—delivering gowns for Madame Olga?" I asked.

Carmen smiled. "Students do earn extra money making deliveries, but I think he would deliver Madame Adrienne's for nothing." She rubbed her thumb and forefinger together. "The lady has plenty of money . . . and she does look good for her age, I admit. Loves young men, but then again— who doesn't? Josef is one of her escorts to balls, nightclubs, and other society places. Sandor loves when they come here because she always brings a big group. On those nights Josef is a customer, not a waiter. And all of us here are proud of him for being able to mix with such high society."

"Interesting," Sheila observed.

"It gets better. Her friends are White Russian émigrés who act like they own the world. Most are penniless, but their noses are up in the air and they order us around like the servants they used to have. They resent Josef but can't say a word because Madame Adrienne pays their way. She doesn't give a fig that Josef's only a waiter."

"That's to her credit," I said. "Is she beautiful?"

"Yes, for a 40-year-old. I hear she pays him to be her escort. Are you disappointed to learn that about him? By the way, where is he now?"

I thought it was petty of Carmen to say that. "He's delivering a gown. As for the way he chooses to live, who's to criticize? We do whatever we must to survive."

Carmen thought a moment. "True, but your mother knows that a gigolo is not exactly a thing to be proud of." She made a face. "He must know those aristocrats hate him. Why doesn't he stick to his own kind? There are so many girls younger and prettier than the widow. That is so unfair."

Sheila shook her head. "Who said life is fair?"

I turned to Carmen. "What's more sad is what you said about the White Russians still lording it over people . . . like they did when the czar was in power. You've no idea what it was like. He was a monster! The Bolsheviks did us a favor getting rid of him—if I were older, I might have been one of them!"

Carmen crossed herself. "God forbid! Don't even joke about it, Sara. If one of our White Russian customers heard you, he'd report you to Admiral Horthy's secret police."

CHAPTER

29

After sweeping floors and running up and down stairs all day, I collapsed on a pile of remnants in the long, narrow room Madame Olga said we could sleep in. Sheila was still in the design department, which gave me an opportunity to straighten out the musty, windowless room. Where were the beds? It took me a few minutes to realize that a towering pile of remnants hid two rickety cots. Resigned, I patiently removed and folded each piece of material until the last remnant uncovered three baby mice and a number of crawling things that had nested on the sagging mattresses.

"That's awful," said Sheila, over my shoulder. "And how could we sleep in a room without a window? I just finished work. Let's look for the student hotel Josef mentioned was nearby. Otherwise, we'll go back to the Romany."

We let ourselves out the side door. It was dusk. Not a light showed from any of the stores except the pastry shop. "We'll ask the baker for directions." I tried the door but it was locked. The shade on the door was up, but a dim light came from the rear of the store. I thought I heard voices as we knocked.

"I'm baking, what do you want?" asked a gruff voice over the tinkling bells. The jowly proprietor peered around the partly open door. "Who sent you, girl?"

"Nobody sent us. We saw the light. We're sorry to disturb you, Mr. Baker. Can you tell us where the . . ."

He pushed tiny, flour-smudged glasses up to his forehead. "You were here the other day with that young man. Come in." He pulled the shade down all the way before opening the door just wide enough for us to slip inside. Shutting the door quickly, he blocked our path. "Did he tell you to come here?"

"You mean Josef?" Sheila tried to look past him.

I craned my neck to see who else was in the store. It was too dark.

He shifted his weight to block my view. "I don't know names. He bought you hot chocolates and pastries." The baker moved his eyeglasses down to the end of his nose. He pulled the towel from around his neck, smudging more flour onto his spectacles. "Now, I can't see a thing," he muttered. "That was you, right? What are you doing here?"

"Yes, it was us." I wondered why that was so important. The flour all over his face made him look like a clown, but why was he acting so mysteriously?

"Look, " Sheila exclaimed, "we just got jobs at Madame Olga's. All we want is directions to a hotel for students somewhere around here. Can you help us, please?"

He made a face. "The Magyar is a few squares away to your left. Please leave now. I'm busy." He opened the door a crack. "Don't come back here again at this hour!"

"Thank you," we said, squeezing through. The light in the back of the store went out.

"What do you make of that cloak-and-dagger scene, Sara?"

"What could be going on in the back?"

Sheila shrugged. "Who knows? We have our own problems to worry about. I hope the hotel has clean rooms."

In a few moments we were facing the night clerk at the Magyar Hotel. Nodding in sympathy, he said he'd give us a student rate because a student recommended us. Payable in advance, of course. Possession, however, would not be until the next night since the room's current tenant was still asleep, unaware he was being dispossessed for owing three month's rent. "I am the owner of this establishment, but I have a soft heart. I don't dispossess anyone until a cash customer takes his place."

He pointed to a pair of couches in the lobby. "You can sleep there tonight. Better still, go to supper, and perhaps the young man in your room will decide to come down. Then I can dispossess him." Satisfied with himself, he straightened his tie. "Where are you ladies from?"

"Russia."

"Poland," added Sheila. "I am curious, sir. We are new to Hungary. We have heard so many stories about your regent. What kind of man is he?"

The clerk gave her a searching look. "Admiral Horthy is our regent. Mind you, I am not political, so I only repeat what I hear." He paused until a group of young people passed out of earshot. "No need to tell everybody our business. As I was saying, some folks—like those students there—think Horthy is as bad as the Habsburgs. They say he interferes with university life. I don't know. One thing for sure, he is chasing all the . . ." he peered into our faces . . ." all the . . . troublemakers . . . out of government. We can't let the Bolsheviks strangle Hungary like they did Russia. Some people say he destroys freedom. Others say he

205

saves Hungary from anarchy. Mind you, I only repeat what people say. I am not political."

"Of course," said Sheila.

I held my tongue. Whatever the Bolsheviks are, they are the enemy of my enemy. They killed our killers and that was good enough for me.

"Well, it's suppertime," the man continued. "If you want an inexpensive meal, just follow those students waiting near the elevator. When their friend comes down, they'll lead you to a tasty . . ." The jangling telephone interrupted. "A moment, please, ladies."

He whispered a few words into the receiver before hanging up. "A wonderful invention, the telephone. Did you know Ferenc Puskas, who established the first telephone exchange here in 1881, came from right here in Pest? He and his brother Tivadar. A wonderful invention, but now people talk on it all the time—mostly nonsense, if you ask me. What news is so important it can't wait to be told in person?" He shook his head. "You can wait over there, on the sofa."

We took seats on a creaking couch and kept our eyes on the group of students. After ten minutes of scanning every passenger leaving the ancient elevator cage, Sheila gave up. "Let's go, Sara. Their friend must be asleep. We'll find a place on our own." Sheila crossed the lobby with long strides.

"Sheila, wait!" I caught up to her at the revolving door to the street. "I think I saw Josef at the newsstand."

"I know, but don't wave, Sheila. I'm not in the mood for more of his dark predictions." The door swished behind her. I slipped into the next section of the revolving door.

I heard rapping on the glass behind me, a muffled shout. The door dragged and I turned. It was Josef. Outside, he was all smiles. "You staying here? I thought . . ."

I told him what the storeroom looked like, and about having to wait in the lobby until the sleeping tenant came down.

"I'll fix that. Wait here."

Emerging a few minutes later, he handed Sheila a key. "I know the clerk. The man will be out of your room within the hour. I'm just going to supper. Will you join me? It will be a pleasure eating with you instead of waiting on you. What I mean is that I will enjoy eating and conversing with you," he was quick to add.

Sheila sighed. "Look, Josef, we're only going for a light meal."

"So am I. I have to report for work soon. Allow me."

"No." Sheila was adamant. "We are indebted to you as it is. You will be our guest."

"I can't do that. Suppose we each pay our own way. Then no one is obligated. I know a small family restaurant only a few squares from here, and it's on the way to the Romany."

Over an inexpensive glass of wine, and in the face of Sheila's obvious displeasure, I found myself telling him all about me. His eyes flickered when I spoke about the highwaymen.

"You're a brave girl, Sara. I certainly can't picture any of the girls I know doing that."

"A child her age shouldn't have to go through such experiences!" exclaimed Sheila. "That's why I'm trying to convince her we should go to America."

Josef had a faraway look in his eyes. "These are difficult times, but I believe we're all capable of doing many things that surprise us. I guess it has to do with the price we're willing to pay for survival."

I thought of Carmen's caustic remarks about gigolos and Madame Adrienne. "And who is to say another's price is too high?"

Josef looked up in surprise. "For a little girl, Sara, that is a very wise observation. You have a lot of insight for someone your age. I'm sure your mother is very proud of you."

Sheila, fixing him with a long stare, cleared her throat. "I'm sure you know she is not really my daughter, Josef."

"Mrs. Stern, I guessed it from the beginning."

"How?" I asked.

He grinned. "Little things you both said that didn't add up. Don't worry, your secret is safe with me. I have a few of my own, as you might guess." He sipped his wine.

Sheila put her fork down with deliberate care. "Is being Jewish one of them?"

Josef concentrated on carefully slicing his boiled potato into little wedges. He spoke softly. "My mother was Jewish . . . a ballet dancer. She ran off to marry my father . . . a Gypsy fiddler. They're both dead a very long time. I am 19, and I make good money as a waiter to pay for university. Sometimes I am paid to escort unattached ladies to social affairs." He speared a potato wedge. "Aside from that, I do not accept money from them under any conditions. I don't know why I tell you all this—I tell no one else. Actually, I do know . . . I want you to trust me, so I tell you my own secrets. What more do you want to know?"

I said nothing. Sheila stared at him for a moment. "We respect your honesty, Josef. One thing puzzles me. Why are you so interested in us . . . so solicitous about our welfare?"

He hesitated. "Maybe it's because I have no family of my own. You both looked so vulnerable and . . . please don't be insulted . . . so ill at ease the other evening, I felt you needed protection." He looked away, slightly embarrassed.

"You were right," I said. "And that was kind of you, Josef."

"Yes it was." Sheila said in a low voice. "Now, I'll tell you my story." She left nothing out, reiterating her conviction that we should leave for America as quickly as possible.

"I'm still not sure, Sheila," I said. "Hungary has always been my dream. It may be dangerous here, but so was Poland . . . and Russia. Some of the wonderful things I've heard about Hungary must be true. Aren't they, Josef?"

He pushed his plate away. Satisfied the surrounding tables were deserted, he continued. "Listen carefully, Sara. Jewish professors are being discharged from the university. Jewish students are restricted to a new five-percent quota. Jewish civil servants are being thrown out of their jobs. The 'wonderful things' you mention were true only during the Jewish Emancipation from 1867 to 1914. This is ironic— when the Jewish religion was officially recognized in 1895, like the Catholics and Protestants, Orthodox Jews worried assimilation would destroy us. Now, Horthy won't even allow us to assimilate! Many of my classmates were killed in the recent riots—and that is just the beginning."

"But I always heard how Jews lived like kings here."

"Only until the war, Sara. In 1919, Bela Kun and the Communists took power and a few Jews held important posts in that government. When Horthy was appointed regent just a few months ago, he started taking revenge—murdering his enemies and making all Jews pay the price. Want to hear more?"

"Do you think we should go to America?"

"There is a better place," he said softly. "Palestine!" Now his eyes were blazing.

Sheila drew back. "That is going from the frying pan into the fire! All that sand, swamps, and malaria? And I read the Arabs rioted in Tel Aviv and murdered a lot of Jews."

"At least they died defending their own land! Here, or anywhere else in this world, no matter how long we've lived in a country, we are always outsiders."

"That's true, Josef. Papa told me no matter how many generations of his family lived in Russia he is considered a Jew, not a Russian. We don't belong anywhere."

"Wrong, Sara. You belong in Palestine!"

"Listen," exclaimed Sheila fiercely, "it's one thing to cross the ocean to America where no one waits to kill you—but another to cross an ocean, even if it's a much smaller one, to face murderous Arabs! Would you honestly want to do that, Josef?"

"That's exactly what I intend to do!"

CHAPTER

30

Sonia was in charge of new girls. "Sara, today you work only with the seamstresses. It's Friday and they're rushing alterations on gowns to be worn tonight. Whatever they need you get . . . scissors, thread, needles, shoulder pads . . . whatever. Don't let Madame Olga see you standing around. Idle hands make her nervous, especially when too many gowns are promised for the same time."

I could feel the tension as soon as I entered the room. Needles flashed and tongues wagged faster than I could follow. The dressmakers, buried in fabrics from the waist down, seemed to be treading water furiously in a sea of brightly colored evening gowns.

Madame Olga was like a bee gathering pollen. Pushing against the tide of material, she darted from one gown to another. "Less talk, ladies. These gowns will dazzle at the ball tonight, so time is precious. Smaller stitches, Theresa— the countess has eyes like a hawk. Remember, we are the *crème de la crème* of Budapest—of all Hungary—so work with pride!"

She thrust a broom into my hands. "Don't stand there, girl. This floor must be spotless!"

Madame Olga was like a general on the battlefield, seemingly every place she was needed to exhort and cajole her employees to greater heights. Her loyal . . . and intimidated . . . troops responded without fail. And so it went, day after day without letup.

Weeks passed, and soon it was like I had worked there forever. One afternoon, Sonia collared me. "Madame Olga just discharged the inventory woman, and you are taking her place. You told her you could read and write?"

"What's wrong with that?"

"I see you're not accustomed to dealing with aristocracy. They feel threatened when common folk know too much. You must never let on that you have a brain . . . it makes them nervous. Now, they'll watch you closely."

"But I have nothing to hide."

"No matter. Better get a move on, she's waiting for you in the storeroom."

"That awful room with remnants all over the floor?"

"Wrong room. The inventory storeroom is on the third floor. Remember—volunteer nothing. Just answer whatever she asks."

Bolts of material, lined up like soldiers, encircled the spacious room where Madame Olga waited behind a desk. "I don't see any cots in here, Sara, where do you sleep?"

"In a rooming house down the street."

"I see. Well, you are now in charge here. Sit, and learn from the story I am about to tell you." She polished her wire frame glasses. "I discharged the last clerk because we almost lost a client over a bolt of material that was short three yards. The clerk swore someone else cut it off without advising her or deducting it from the ticket. Our designer is the only other person with a key. He denies doing it." She paused for effect. "I distinctly remember a crisis with the same material about two weeks earlier. It was late, and only he and I were here to placate another distraught client. She decided to add a jacket to her dress and questioned whether we had sufficient material. The designer personally cut the material from the bolt and brought it to her. He claims he told the clerk the next day, but I do not believe him. That clerk was meticulous. Her records always balanced to the meter."

I looked at her blankly. "If you believed her, why did you discharge her?"

"I discharged a clerk to keep a designer." Her eyes met mine. "Business is business. Think—who is more important? See how fast you take her place!"

"But, Madame—how will . . . what if he does that again?"

She shrugged. "You said you kept inventory before. You will be earning more. With more money comes more responsibility. And more risk."

At the hotel that evening, a note from Josef in our mailbox said he had the next night off, and if we'd like a short tour of the neighborhood, to meet him in the coffee shop right after work. "Let's do it, Sheila," I said. "It's summer and it doesn't get dark until late."

Josef was waiting for us when we got there. "Sara got a promotion yesterday, so we are paying," Sheila announced as we slid into a booth.

"Since I haven't seen you in some time, I accept. I'm ordering a chocolate croissant in her honor. At this rate, there's no telling where she'll wind up at Olga's. What's the secret of your success, Sara?"

"Being nearby when the previous clerk gets discharged." I repeated the story. "I couldn't believe she could hurt an innocent person like that. Madame Olga said 'business is business,' but I don't think it has to be like that, do you?"

"No, it shouldn't. However, like going to America, some people lose their souls when it comes to money. You don't have to be like her. As long as you are forewarned you can't be taken by surprise." He paused. "Tell me, has she ever said anything about me?"

I nibbled at the croissant. "Well, now that you mention it, a few strange things from time to time."

"Such as?"

"She heard we'd been seen with you. She said we should be careful. Especially Sheila. It seems you have . . . an 'unsavory reputation,' as she put it. Also, you're a troublemaker."

"Troublemaker? Is that the word she used?"

"Actually, she called you 'a Bolshevik and an anarchist.'" I laughed. "But that was after she said you were a handsome young man and people are gossiping—she worries that Madame Adrienne might hear of it. Sometimes, she asks if you ever speak against the authorities. I told her we never discuss politics." I sipped my hot chocolate. "Now why would she ask that?"

"Well, it sounds like she discussed me in great detail! First of all, I'm not a Bolshevik."

Sheila grinned. "An anarchist?"

"Not even that. With her crowd of White Russians, anyone who ran from the czar would fit that description. Therefore, both of you are Bolsheviks in their eyes. Be careful around Madame Olga."

Sheila frowned. "Originally, when I mentioned running from Cossacks I remember her being extremely sympathetic."

"She has a purpose in mind, Mrs. Stern. Olga and her White Russian friends have close ties to Horthy. They are obsessed with restoring the nobility. Everyone else is the enemy. Especially students and Jews. Police are constantly harassing us. At Madame Adrienne's private dinner parties I've had many heated political discussions; fortunately, she has well-connected friends and I do not have to worry about repercussions."

"What has all that to do with Olga and us and Cossacks?"

"I'll explain as we walk. I'm glad you could make it, for it's a beautiful time of the day to see the fashionable Castle Hill district."

"On one condition, Josef," exclaimed Sheila. "No talk about Palestine today."

The sight of so many well-dressed, laughing couples parading up and down the boulevard was in sharp contrast to Josef's words. "If you think about it, Mrs. Stern, who did Cossacks hunt down? Aristocrats? No! Pogroms targeted Jews and Gypsies. So, running from Cossacks marked you as one of the inferior masses . . . and you don't look like Gypsies.

"And your friends," he continued, "are people like yourself. So, if you happen to mention what you do in your spare time, it could give Olga valuable information, which she would then dutifully passes on to the secret police. Yes. Don't look so surprised! The police are anxious for advance knowledge of protest meetings and marches."

"I never thought of that. But if she hates Jews, why would she give me an important job keeping inventory?"

"Children are more open and innocent of guile than their elders. Besides using your inventory ability to her advantage, perhaps you'll happen to disclose what you hear in the streets, or what your fellow immigrants are thinking and doing."

"But that works both ways, Josef . . . if I were so inclined."

His eyebrows shot up. "Would you really do that?"

"You mean spy on her? For what? I was only saying Olga runs the same risk."

"And I'm saying . . . would you spy on her if you believed in the reasons?"

Sheila drew me closer. "She's a child! How could you think of putting her in such danger?"

I slipped out of her grasp. "In the first place, I'm not a child . . . and he didn't ask me anything. Besides, I'm not afraid of her!"

Josef nodded. "Mrs. Stern, that 'child' admitted she shot a man who was trying to kill her." He made a face. "Anyhow, it was a rhetorical question. Forget it." He pointed down the street. "See that magnificent palace? It's hundreds of years old. Makes the others look like carriage houses. We're on Castle Hill, which stretches for one mile. The grand mansions and stone buildings made this a natural bastion against river marauders in the early days. And here in front of you is the famous Siklo—the funicular to Pest. Ever been on one?"

"No, and I'm not interested in going on this one! Wait a moment." Sheila, still plainly upset, stopped to rest on a bench.

Placing my hands on the stone wall, I studied the soaring steel structure. "I'd love to take a ride on it some day. I'm sure you would find it exciting, too. Come on, Sheila, Josef told you he wasn't serious about spying." I coaxed her to her feet. "Everything is so magnificent—I just love all this!" I turned to Josef. "Now tell us all about university life. It must be wonderful."

"Wonderful?" He exhaled sharply. "I'm studying archeology . . . a field that depends upon the largesse and favors of wealthy people. Architecture—poor people don't need architects. And who else but wealthy people concern themselves with economics? Isn't that ironic?" He laughed bitterly. "Wonderful? It's terrible!" He shook his head in frustration.

Sheila relented. "Don't be discouraged. It's to your credit that you care so deeply about things, Josef. You're aiming high and trying to make a better life and a better world. We admire that. It will get better before you know it. You'll see."

He cleared his throat. "I didn't mean to burden you with my troubles. It's just that a lot of things suddenly converged. Seeing you enjoying sights that remind me of how things used to be, well . . ." He squared his shoulders. "Thanks for the sympathy."

By the time we returned to the Magyar, Josef brightened considerably. "I have an idea. Life in Budapest is not complete without a picnic in the park. If you're free Sunday and you fix sandwiches, I'll bring a basket, a blanket, and a bottle of wine."

My heart bounded at the prospect. I'd never been on a picnic and it sounded like the perfect way to enjoy a day off in Budapest . . . until I remembered Sheila's feelings about spending time with the moody Josef. I looked at her.

She didn't hesitate. "I hope you like egg salad."

31

Josef bit into his sandwich even before the blanket settled to the ground. "The most amazing egg salad I ever had. It tastes like salami. Make it yourself, Mrs. Stern?"

She laughed. "I changed my mind. I sliced the salami; Sara spread the mustard and relish according to a secret family formula. You can pour the wine."

Josef passed the cups around. "The cheapest wine of preference for poor students. *Nazdarovya! . . . L'chaim!*" As we touched cups, a kite suddenly dipped wildly overhead, heading straight for our blanket. Jumping up, I seized the tail before it landed in the potato salad. A young man rushed over, breathless. "Excuse me, ladies. I'm sorry to . . . Josef? I didn't realize it was you." He bowed. "I beg your pardon again, ladies. I hope I didn't spoil your lunch."

Josef sprang to his feet. "Mrs. Stern. Sara. This is my friend, Franz. As you can see, he is not very good at steering kites."

Acknowledging us with a polite nod, Franz kept his eyes on Josef. "I want you to know how sorry I am that you resigned. Can you think it over? You know we'll never win without you."

"It's over, Franz, but I appreciate your saying this. It makes me feel better." Josef seemed uncomfortable.

"It's a disgrace! You know I do not feel like they do. There are more like me, but . . ."

"But they're afraid to speak out. I know. Thank you for your support, Franz. I'll see you in class."

I couldn't wait for his friend to leave. "Resigned from what, Josef? What was he talking about?"

He grimaced. "I've been on the fencing team a long time without any problems, but Horthy's campaign has finally penetrated us. Because most fencing clubs will not compete against a team with Jewish members, every one of my teammates—except Franz—refused to practice with me last week and threatened to resign if I remained on the team. So, I resigned."

"I wouldn't give them the satisfaction of resigning!" exclaimed Sheila.

"If it concerned only me, neither would I. Our coach, whom I admire, said he'd stand with me in a showdown; but he is a good man, and I will not put him in jeopardy. If all the others resign he has no team and no job. No other university or club would hire him under such circumstances." He shrugged. "What's the sense? I know it's only a sport, but . . ."

"That's why you were upset the other night." Sheila studied the wine in her cup. "It's their loss."

"Sheila's right. I certainly wouldn't want to be with people who didn't want to be with me."

"Neither do I. Anti-Semitism from strangers is one thing, but to hear it suddenly from teammates I considered friends—well, that *is* a shock." His voice thickened. "I'd like to kill them."

"Me, too. But not literally, because then we'd have to kill the entire world."

"It would stop anti-Semitism, wouldn't it? Just line them up against a wall and shoot every last one of them," he said bitterly. "A reverse pogrom—without Cossacks and horses. When you killed the highwayman it put an end to his anti-Semitism, didn't it?"

"Yes, it did," said Sheila softly. "But that was not in cold blood, Josef. It was her life or theirs. Your fencing friends aren't trying to kill you."

"Not just yet, but for how much longer? Why shouldn't we beat them to it?"

"Because that is murder. Do you understand the difference, Sara?"

"I do, but somehow, that doesn't sound fair." Remembering past terrors, I shivered. "Are you saying it's permissible for them, but not for us?"

She pondered the notion. "No . . . and yes. Our religion and our morality are what separate us from animals. You're an educated man, Josef, you should know that."

"I know you're right, logically." He sighed, then raised his cup. His eyes were blazing. "You know the real answer, don't you? *Eretz Yisra'el!*"

"Palestine again?" Sheila frowned.

"Every Passover for thousands of years we've been wishing that."

"Sara, the wishing days are over!" Josef inhaled sharply. "I think it's time to tell you the whole story. My friends and I are preparing *now*! Each of us is studying specific areas—agriculture, mechanics, construction, government, and finance—skills to build an independent community in Palestine. We can live peacefully with the Arabs because

221

we're paying for the land. To be on the safe side, we have been drilling with hunting rifles in small groups for some time. What do you think of that?"

"I think that's exciting! I read Theodore Herzl's pamphlet. Do you think a Jewish state is possible, Josef?"

"Without a doubt—if we all learn our parts well. That's why I'm taking those classes at university."

Sheila shook her head. "University classes are one thing. Making it work in the desert is another. How can you survive there when even Arabs can't make things grow?"

"Our engineers are confident that irrigation will allow us to grow whatever we need. All it takes is determination and hard work, and we're not afraid. We need a land of our own as a haven when Jewish life is threatened anywhere. Then safe in our own country, we can thumb our noses at the rest of the world and tell it to go to hell!" He lowered his voice. "I have to swear you both to silence because the secret police are everywhere. One innocent slip and we're done for. Not even a good man like Sandor can know."

"I understand." I turned to Sheila. "Every night I thank God for helping me escape to Hungary. Now, I do not know. In Russia it was easy to recognize the enemy. Here, it is puzzling. Everyone appears to be so nice, but Josef says it is dangerous. I believe him. The idea of our own country sounds wonderful! A place where I won't be an outsider anymore. That, I would fight for. I think we should go to Palestine, Sheila."

"I'm not your mother, Sara, but you are still a child and I feel responsible to say what I think is best for you. I agree it is dangerous to stay. But no one waits to kill you in America, and you can live in a big city rather than in a desert that is too hot to grow anything green. America is safe. Palestine is not."

I shook my head. "Without being disrespectful, Sheila, I'll be 13 soon. If we were not together, Palestine is where I would go. Please try to understand. I can take care of myself and I'm not afraid. Can we talk about this again before you decide?"

Sheila sighed. "Of course. We're not deciding anything definitely, not right now."

"Enough serious talk for one day," said Josef. "Like the rabbis say, freedom and assimilation can be dangerous to life and soul." He stretched out on his back. "Just look at the sky. Only in Budapest can you see such beautiful clouds."

I rested my head on the picnic basket, closing my eyes against the bright sun. I heard Sheila ask, "When are you planning to leave?"

Hearing no response, I opened my eyes. Josef, sitting with hands around his knees, was staring into space. "I'm sorry. That is a secret I cannot tell."

"I love this job, Sara, because the gossip is so delicious!" Sonia and I met accidentally in the finishing department. "It's amazing how people in this room are up-to-the-minute with the latest gossip about the nobility. You know how? Foolish society women chatter in the fitting room in front of us as though we are invisible. And when their maids come to pick up their gowns, they fill in every private detail of their mistresses' lives. Listen to the story Sophie is telling now."

Sophie clearly enjoyed being the center of attraction. It seems that a titled widow was being jilted by a suitor who suddenly decided that America offered better prospects. "He is a phony prince," said the seamstress, with obvious relish, "and deeply in debt. So he sells himself to an American heiress who lives in a place that sounds like Transylvania. She owns a big estate in Filla Delfia, and all she cares is that he has a title. Bogus and broke he is—and the stupid American. They deserve each other! I always said rich people have no morals."

"And you'll have no job," Sonia snapped, "if Madame Olga hears you cackling about clients like that. Get a move on. Remember, the Markova gown and the dress for Fedorovich are promised for this afternoon!"

I couldn't believe my ears! I waited for Sonia at the door. "Did you say Fedorovich? The wife of Count Peter Fedorovich?"

"You know her?"

"I know *him*—if he's dark-haired, good-looking, and about Josef's age."

"That's him. How do you come to know a count?"

"Oh, I met him once or twice, long ago in Russia. Is she pretty—his wife?"

"Very pretty. A little older, I think. I don't know if they will come in person or send a maid today, but come to the pickup counter at five o'clock, if you're interested."

"Not really. I was just curious whether it was the same family I knew in Dreska."

At a few minutes to five I made it my business to check some records in the room next to the pickup counter. Hearing Josef's voice, I poked my head out the door. "Hello. What brings you here this afternoon?"

"Just picking up something for a friend. I'm going past the Magyar, if you can leave now."

I looked at the wall clock. "Let me just tell Sheila I'll meet her at the hotel. She's working late today."

I said goodbye to Sheila and met Josef, who was waiting outside, package in hand.

"Do you deliver all of Madame Olga's gowns?"

He chuckled. "No, Sara. Only for good friends. This one is for Count Fedorovich's wife. Everyone knows I live nearby, so it's no trouble dropping off a package on my way to work."

"That's certainly very nice of you. How do you know the count?"

"He's a frequent guest at Adrienne's parties. Also, he and his friends occasionally fenced with our team at university."

"I thought you detested aristocrats?"

"I do. Peter is different."

"Does he fence with you now?"

"No."

I felt my stomach drop. "Because you're Jewish? Then he's just as bad as the others!" I held my breath.

"That's not the reason—he travels a lot. Count Peter isn't like the others. He's really a decent fellow."

I felt better. "Then he's never changed. He was that way when I was growing up in Dreska. Like a big brother." I told Josef how he came to befriend my father and me, and how we chanced to meet again at the inn.

"A remarkable story, Sara. But then, Peter is a remarkable man. Someday, I'll tell you more things about him that will make you proud."

CHAPTER

32

Yad Mordechai, soon-to-be State of Israel. May 13, 1948, 2130 hours –

One more day and the British leave forever. I can hardly wait for the 15th! My work on Mother's manuscript is keeping pace, for I should be finished with everything tomorrow night. I hope that, somehow, I'll be able to meet up with Mother and Father on the 19th and hand them the completed work. I know they will be surprised.

The other night I mentioned that our unit leader, Ari, is a young veteran Palmachnik who is admired by everyone. He and I had been talking, and, up close, he is not so young after all. To my surprise it turned out that he knew Michael, my older brother who was killed in a shootout with the British in 1932. It is difficult to believe that 16 years have flown by. What is more difficult to comprehend is that we are still fighting the British, despite the short truce when Jewish soldiers fought alongside them against the Nazis. Thanks to God only one more day of British rule . . . and then freedom!

Michael was the best big brother a girl could have. He was 17 years older than I was—more like a combination uncle-brother—but I could talk to him about anything. He was serious about everything and excelled in whatever he set his mind to. He taught me so many things, especially about loyalty and putting your trust in people you loved. I remember being afraid of the water as a child and his telling me to trust him not to let me drown when he taught me to swim. Well, I almost *did* drown, but it was really not his fault. I hate the British army for so many things, but mostly for taking his life. Having written all that, I feel better. I was not looking forward to writing about Michael because it hurts so much to remember, but, strangely enough, I do feel better now.

Ari also told me something I hadn't known before. He said that earlier this year my other brother, Aaron, had been involved in Haganah's secret negotiations to purchase arms from Czechoslovakia. Joel Aaronson's unit distributed them after the first planeload of weapons landed in March.

When I saw Joel earlier and told him what Ari said, he made light of it. The more I see of him, the more I realize what an admirable, modest man he is. There is an intensity about him that reminds me of Mother's description of Josef. Both are ardent Zionists. I think Mother and Father would approve of Joel; now all I have to do is come to terms with myself regarding our religious differences.

How ironic! Reading that last sentence, a stranger would think we are Jew and gentile! I told Joel I would give him an answer tomorrow night. As of now, I am fairly certain we can make a go of it. I am trying hard not to allow the war to influence me.

Speaking of that, my conversation with Ari was most interesting. He has been a soldier for most of his life and is not optimistic about achieving lasting peace with the Arabs. He is confident we will ultimately be victorious but worries the Arab leaders will not allow their people to accept us. They will keep the population uneducated and uninformed. Our open society threatens them. I told Ari that although he is the one who has fought the battles and has the experience, Joel and I, and others like us, are determined to do whatever we can—once the war is over—to work for better relations with the Arabs.

Ari listened carefully and wished me luck.

In my heart, I know a better day is coming. With that thought, I'm off to sleep. I'm sure tomorrow will see a lot of last-minute activity, although I cannot imagine what more we can accomplish.

33

Budapest, Hungary. Summer 1920.

It was exciting to know that Count Peter was still in Budapest. I wondered how his aristocratic wife would greet a lowly Jewish peasant girl from the shtetl. The thought of seeing his father again reawakened old terrors, and suddenly the idea lost its appeal.

Sheila and I had endless discussions trying to decide upon the best place to go. "I know I said you were a big girl and could do whatever you wish, but I really believe America is best for both of us, Sara. Palestine sounds like an adventure to you, but it's dangerous! Josef is a good man—an idealist—but we can't allow him to influence us in such a big decision. Let's not rush into anything."

The more I thought about it, the more confused I became. People lost their souls in America . . . that I knew.

"But," Sheila emphasized over and over, "isn't it better to lose your soul and be alive, than . . . than the other way 'round?"

I wasn't sure I agreed with that argument. The promise of a land where Jews would be free from hate and persecution stirred my imagination. Josef said we would be building a new land for everyone—making history, he said. That I could possibly play a small part in such an undertaking took

231

my breath away. I didn't know what I would do if Sheila did not change her mind.

We had just returned to our room after a light supper when the telephone rang. I picked it up. "Yes. What is it, Josef? Where are you?"

"In my room. I've been ringing you every 10 minutes. It's urgent I talk to you and Sheila."

"You want to come here right now?" I repeated for Sheila's benefit.

She shook her head vigorously.

Covering the receiver with my hand, I whispered, "He says it's urgent. I can't say no."

Within seconds, there was a light tapping on our door. Josef was breathless. "I ran down the stairs—couldn't wait for the elevator. I'm glad you're here, Sheila."

He drew a deep breath. "I have a sudden crisis, so I must tell you everything! Our Palestine plans are in danger. The bigger secret is that Peter Fedorovich and his friends are helping us buy land in Palestine. Messages and cash are hidden in gowns I carry back and forth from Madame Olga's."

I was speechless. Sheila paced up and down, finally stopping in front of him. "Why are you telling us this? We don't want to know those details."

"This is an emergency. We need a new courier, quickly! I'm being watched constantly and must find another place to live. We're so close to success and we're desperate. You two are the only ones . . . actually, Sara is the best choice, but I could not ask her without your approval, Mrs. Stern." He gave her a searching look. "They wouldn't suspect a girl her age."

My heart pounded. "I . . . I . . ."

"No!" Sheila was having difficulty controlling herself. "You must be crazy to even think of putting her in such danger! I'm not her mother and I said she could decide for herself; however, I love her too much to allow her to get involved. There must be someone else you can send instead of a child. Besides, Sara's not good at hiding her feelings . . . or pretending."

"That's the very best reason why she would not be in any danger. And the fact that she works in the salon makes her the perfect courier. That she knows Count Peter is the best reason of all! She would immediately have his trust . . . we have to think of him, too. His life is also in jeopardy." Josef glanced in my direction. "You would be helping to save a lot of Jews, but think it over carefully, Sara."

One thing was clear. Over time, I had come to understand Peter's part in Papa's death as an act of love and mercy. He helped our shtetl in Dreska, and now he was helping the cause of all Jews. There was nothing for me to think about. "I'm the most logical one, Sheila, and I'm not afraid. I'll do it, Josef!"

Sheila threw up her hands. "When she talks like that, there is no changing her mind. God help us!"

"Who hides the money or messages in the gowns?" I asked. "Sonia?"

"No. The person who tells you to make the delivery or hands you the package will not be aware of what's inside. Don't try to figure it out." Josef kissed me on the forehead. "That is for your courage and the hope it gives us." He reached for the doorknob.

"Wait a minute. Isn't there something more I should know? A password? An idea as to when this is going to happen?"

He grinned. "That's the beauty of it. Act naturally and go along with whatever occurs. It will happen in the ordinary course of the day, with nothing to cause undue attention. That way, nothing can go wrong. Everything is well planned, believe me."

Sheila took my hand. "Just tell me when you go so I won't worry. And don't try to be a hero, and don't tell me you're almost 13. You're still 12! I'm going to be a nervous wreck before this is over!"

I expected Josef's accomplice to make himself, or herself, known. I stared into every face. Not a single untoward look. Not a single sign. The nice people continued to be pleasant; the rude ones, still ill-mannered. Olga was seldom around, but whenever our paths crossed she was polite, sometimes even complimentary. No one asked me to deliver a package. I heard nothing from Josef. It was all so disappointing.

One afternoon when a duplicate order crossed my desk, I ventured cautiously into the designer's domain. Pompous and short-tempered, the slender Austrian spoke only to those who addressed him as Herr Designer.

"Can't you see I'm busy!" He slammed his heavy cutting shears on the table. "If my initials are on it don't question the order. Enter it! I do not duplicate orders."

"But Herr Designer, the same fabric was ordered last week, and I am responsible for inventory. Please look at these two forms."

His face turned crimson. "That's the trouble with you people—you think you know more than your betters!" Picking up a steel-tipped yardstick, he raised it as though to strike.

My betters? Was "you people" another name for Jews? I grabbed his shears. For a few seconds, we confronted each other. I stared at him until a hint of uncertainty appeared in his eyes.

The designer took a step back. "You dare threaten me? I'll have you discharged for insolence!"

Suddenly, I realized what I had done. How could I be a courier if I no longer worked here? "Please, Herr Designer, I asked a question and you raised that stick. I'm sorry." I placed the heavy shears carefully on top of his patterns. "These are not the scissors I was looking for after all."

"Girl, you do not fool me for one minute—I am not so dumb like the others." His face still red, he struggled to keep his rage under control.

"Please, sir," I handed him the papers, "tell me if the top order is correct. I don't want to make a mistake."

He made a show of studying the initials and date. "It does not look like my handwriting. Cancel it."

Back at my desk, I waited for the trembling to subside. My first encounter with polite anti-Semitism had me questioning myself. Perhaps "you people" meant inventory clerks and I was super-sensitive? Could it mean foreigners . . . or Russians? How could he know I was Jewish?

No, my instinct told me his slur was intentional. I felt inadequate . . . and guilty for not acquitting myself better. But I had to put Josef's plan ahead of everything else. The knot in my stomach would not go away.

It was still there when Madame Olga appeared at my desk just before it was time to go home. "I was coming to see you for another reason, Sara, but suddenly the designer wants me to discharge you. Immediately. What happened?"

"I have nothing to add to whatever he's told you, Madame."

"He's told me nothing, child. Use your head. Despite what the Bible says, the meek and the poor are too stupid to inherit the earth. The Bolsheviks think they have inherited the earth but they are godless—they will never succeed!"

Madame Olga drew up a chair. "Sara, you are smart and capable enough to have a future here . . . if you control yourself and keep your place until the proper time. My plan to apprentice you to the designer is now out of the question." She paused. "Do you deserve to be discharged?"

I remembered the story of the woman I replaced. "No. But then, I am only a clerk."

"Is that how you see yourself?"

"Certainly not, Madame!"

"Spoken with such conviction! Tell me, Sara, just how *do* you see yourself?"

I hesitated.

"Don't be afraid," she said softly. "The truth. It is only between the two of us."

"Well, Madame, I see myself as deserving to be treated fairly and with respect. I am as good a person as Herr Designer . . . or the ladies who come here. I see myself in fine clothes and living like they do, someday."

"Very interesting," she mused. "You know, people pay with their lives for saying such things. And how would you accomplish that? By killing them and stealing their possessions?"

"I am not a Bolshevik, Madame. I want to go to university and better myself."

She looked at me a long time without saying a word. I feared I had gone too far.

"You are a strange girl, Sara, but you are honest. I admire that trait in people." She moistened her lips. "Let me give you some advice. You have ambition and that is good. And you have spirit, too. That is also good, but you must learn to keep it under control."

She polished her eyeglasses. "Perhaps Herr Designer has overstepped himself this time. You will stay." She handed me a slip of paper. "Would you please deliver a gown to this address on your way home? Students usually do that, but today no one showed up."

I was sure she could hear the beating of my heart. I felt myself turning red. Josef said Madame Olga was definitely not a friend, so this couldn't possibly be about Palestine. I relaxed. "Certainly, Madame."

"Pick it up at the counter downstairs."

CHAPTER

34

"Tell my mother where I'm going, please." I took the large package from Sonia and glanced at the label. If I were lucky today, I might see Peter or his wife when I made this delivery! What would I say if she came to the door? Walking at a brisk pace toward the Castle Hill district, I wondered what was hidden in the gown, and who put it there. Suddenly, I was aware of being jostled on both sides.

"Hello, Sara!" Greeting me like a long-lost cousin, the blond young man on my right threw his arm around my shoulder. It was not a friendly grip. "It's good to see you. That's a bulky package—let me carry it."

I tightened my hold on the parcel. "I don't know you! Who are you?"

"Friends." The stocky youth on my left smiled, hooking his arm in mine. "Keep walking, Sara."

Passersby might easily take us for students out for an early supper. Sandwiched between a pair of husky young men, all I could think of was how angry Madame Olga would be that thieves stole a client's gown. Her reputation with the aristocracy would be ruined . . . and it was entirely my fault! I slowed my pace. Then I came to an abrupt halt. My muscular friends did not miss a step. "This is a mistake. It's only a dress I'm carrying. Who are you?"

"It's no mistake. Keep smiling at us, Sara. And keep walking."

"No. I'm not taking another step. And if I'm not back soon, my mother will call the police and come looking for me. She knows exactly where I'm going."

"Josef sent us. Don't be afraid." The blond one laughed, but his eyes were as cold as steel. His thumb dug into my arm.

"Prove it, or I'll scream at the top of my voice!"

"Keep your voice down and don't be such a hero. Listen to me!" He kissed me on the cheek. "That kiss is for your courage and the hope it gives us." His eyes bore into mine.

Josef's exact words the other night! "What . . . ?"

"I told you Josef sent us. Now, let's all act like old friends and stroll into that pastry shop across the street."

Pastry shop? The baker's mysterious behavior the last time was beginning to make sense, but the familiar jangling of overhead bells did nothing to relieve the tension. A solitary customer was paying her bill at the cash register. The proprietor bristled when he saw us. "Take any table," he growled. "I'll be with you in a moment." He glared at me.

I struggled to control my emotions. Realizing we were all somewhat on the same side, my initial fright slowly gave way to anger. I turned to my companions. "I'm in no mood for pastry."

"Neither are we, but study the menu until the customer leaves." The one who kissed me was no longer smiling.

The baker hung a "Closed" sign on the door and drew the shades. "Hurry," he ordered the blond one. "Check that package in the back and see if it's in there." He glared at his companion. "Why did you bring her here? Are you crazy?"

"She was about to make a big scene on the street and we had no choice. This is Sara, Josef's friend. The shipment came in unexpectedly at the last minute and . . ."

"I don't like the way this is going. A complete stranger has no business in this!" The baker whirled around. "I remember you, girl. First you came with Josef. Then you came with that woman asking directions. Now you are here a third time. A real coincidence, I'd say. All of a sudden you are one of us? What kind of game are you playing?"

"Game? They kidnap me and *you* are angry? I am *not* one of you. I promised Josef I'd be a courier only if he was in trouble. You're mistaken about this package, though. Madame Olga herself asked me to deliver it, and I was there purely by accident. I'm sure whatever you are expecting is not inside."

An excited shout came from the back. "It's all here!" The student emerged, waving a bulky manila envelope. "I just called his house and . . ."

"Shut up!" The baker grabbed the envelope. "Let's not go into details—she's not one of us." He shoved me toward the door. "Thank you for your help, Sara. Now leave!"

"I'm supposed to deliver that dress," I said. "And by the way, you put the bow back in the wrong place—it goes in the corner."

"Very observant," the baker muttered. He turned to the students. "Change it, and get moving! Sara, go home. We'll make the delivery."

I stood my ground. "Just a minute, please. Josef said something about being watched. If I don't deliver the package personally, you are all in trouble." I picked up the parcel. "How do I get in touch with Josef?"

"She makes sense," the blond one remarked, looking to the baker.

With a grim expression on his face, the baker opened the door. "Go, then. Take the next left; it's a shortcut to Castle Hill. The Fedorovich mansion is on the river side."

"The third mansion," advised the blond student. "Be sure to use the tradesmen's entrance on the side. And you can't call Josef; he'll contact you."

I continued on alone, my mind in a jumble. This incident was like a silly schoolboys' conspiracy. And I resented the reminder to keep my place by using the tradesmen's entrance. Olga had promised to promote me if I can remember that fact. She and her titled friends would like nothing better than to keep Hungary in the Old World forever. Count Peter's father saw his Old World collapse in Russia, so he came to Budapest. And all the time, I believed that a Jew could live like a king here! Freedom here was a mirage! But it was the impetus that pushed me to leave Russia, and I was grateful for that. Now, I couldn't wait to leave this land of pampered ex-royalty, secret police, conspiracies, and two-faced people like Madame Olga and her despotic designer!

By the time I reached the imposing Fedorovich mansion, I had calmed down. I caught a quick glimpse of manicured hedges and a wide cobblestone driveway before taking the narrow gravel path to the tradesmen's entrance. A young girl wearing a maid's cap answered the bell.

"I have a gown for Countess Fedorovich." I had one foot on the threshold when the girl slammed the door against my toe. As I tried to keep my dignity and balance, it occurred to me that there was something to be said about this servant knowing her place. The door reopened. A kindly, older maid in uniform peered out. "Please forgive the little one, she's pretending to be a maid. Might you be Miss Sara?"

"I am."

"I have a message for you." She touched a finger to her forehead. "Give me a moment so I can repeat it exactly: 'Romany Café tomorrow night. Six-thirty.'"

"The countess or the count will meet me there tomorrow night at six-thirty?"

"I don't know, Miss Sara. That's all I've been insrcuted to say."

CHAPTER

35

"Carmen, I'm meeting someone here at six-thirty. Did Count Fedorovich make a reservation for that time?"

"Sara, I don't even have to look. Royalty never dines before eight." She consulted her book. "There's one for a small, private dining room at six-thirty, but no name. First door on the right. Josef is the waiter."

"I didn't think he worked here anymore."

"He hasn't shown up the last few days, but I'm still using the old schedule."

To my surprise, Josef opened the door when I knocked, a broad smile on his face. "Good to see you, Sara. I have an hour before I go to work, so we can talk while we eat."

"I thought . . ."

He grinned. "The count? Sorry to disappoint you—this was the safest way to contact you. Under the circumstances, I couldn't include Sheila, so please explain that to her." He was in high spirits. "Thanks to you, Sara, the final exchange came off without a hitch! My group is ready to move out now."

A light knock sounded and a waiter entered with our food.

"I took the liberty of ordering goulash for both of us." Josef waited for him to serve and leave the room. "My friends must have taken you by surprise. I'm sorry, but the last six passports we needed were in that package. They were smuggled into Olga's late in the day, ahead of schedule. We couldn't risk leaving them overnight, and our contact on the inside wasn't sure you were available. To make matters worse, Madame Adrienne was out of town, and Count Fedorovich was not going to be home to receive the package.

"A decision was made to intercept the package from whoever made the delivery—risky business in broad daylight on a crowded street. Then, a miracle! Your talk with Olga kept you later than usual . . . and you know the rest."

"But only she and the designer were in the shop. You mean, one of them is part of your group?"

Peppering his goulash, he smiled. "There were three others; a shipping clerk, the cleaning woman, and Sonia. But let's not discuss that any further." His eyes shone with excitement. "Fourteen of us are ready to leave within the next two weeks—we're the advance group of a larger contingent. And it's none too soon. Orchestrated attacks are increasing; a Jewish bookstore near university was totally destroyed last week, the owner badly beaten. The pastry shop was supposed to be next, but Madame Adrienne—who knows nothing about our activities—is pulling strings to keep the baker safe. Any problems at the salon, Sara? Madame Olga treats you well?"

I shrugged. "She's difficult to work for, but I have no complaints."

"She must really like you, because she's outspoken in her feelings about Jews and foreigners. I don't want to come between you and Sheila, but you both can still change your minds and come with us. However, I would not advise it if there is the slightest doubt in your minds."

I sighed. "It's complicated. I would love to go, because I now believe that without our own land, Jews will never be safe anywhere. Sheila is wavering; she does not share your passion, but I believe that down deep inside she sees the logic of a Jewish homeland. She says she is frightened for me and I've had enough danger for one person. I can argue that, but when she says she's too old to be a pioneer, what can I say? Sheila has no one else in this world, and I will not leave her. She has had so little personal happiness, what with Uncle dying only weeks after they were married. No, I will go wherever she decides."

"I understand, and that's very commendable." He gave a wry smile. "You are correct about me, Sara. Palestine *is* my passion. I've planned and dreamed this for a long time!"

"I know how you feel. Hungary has always been my dream . . . until now. Are all of you leaving together?"

"No. Each travels alone to different cities. We leave from different ports and wait for each other in Haifa."

"When does your ship sail?"

"Maybe four, six weeks. When do you leave for America?"

"Sheila said something about four or five weeks from now; I'm not positive."

The next morning, Sheila went directly to her office while I had coffee in the galley with Sonia. She thought I had lost my mind. "Why would you want to go to America when you have America right here? They are wild and godless over there; in Budapest, you are safe and free. What more could you want?"

I held my tongue. How could I tell her what was happening to Jews without giving myself away?

Sonia sipped her coffee. "You have a mother who doesn't boss you around or try to run your life—I can't wait to get married and leave home. You're too young for a sweetheart yet, but that will happen in due time. Have you and your mother thought it out carefully?"

"There's so much more opportunity in America, Sonia. Everyone is equal, everyone is free. No royalty to keep you in your place."

"Maybe not royalty, Sara, but rich people are just as bad. They will lord it over poor people no matter where we live. Money makes them aristocrats, you'll see. Is it so bad here? You have a steady job and Madame Olga likes you. Times will be good again, you'll see, now that we're getting Jews out of government. Always conspiring to take over the world."

That was the last straw. "I am Jewish, Sonia."

She looked at me blankly. "Are you joking?"

"No."

"You don't look Jewish."

"How many Jews do you know, Sonia?"

"A lot." She paused. "Really just a few, I guess. They say one of the seamstresses upstairs, Ida, is Jewish. And," she thought a moment, "there's the greengrocer in my neighborhood. He's Jewish. And now, you . . . and your mother."

"You really think we're conspiring to take over the world?"

"I don't know. I never thought about it before." She brightened. "But you're different. You and your mother . . . you're not like the rest."

"How am I different, Sonia? How?"

"I . . . I can't put my finger on it, but you are. Believe me—if all Jews were like you, we wouldn't have all these problems!"

248

"What problems?"

"You know. Not enough jobs, for one. And our money doesn't buy what it used to. I don't have to list everything; you know perfectly well what I mean." Sonia stood up. "We'd better get to work. Herr Designer is threatening to move to Paris again, but this time I heard Madame Olga say she'd pay for his ticket. Listen, Sara, I'm truly sorry you're going. I'll miss you." She ran off without looking at me.

I couldn't remain angry with her because she was only repeating the slanderous stories newspapers had been printing lately. No mention of the sporadic hoodlum attacks in Jewish neighborhoods, only caricatures and articles to feed the ever-present anti-Semitism that was always a part of my life. Lately, however, there were increasing reports of harassment and broken windows in Jewish establishments in other areas of the city. Josef wasn't the only one sounding the alarm.

Back at my desk, I gazed at the pile of orders, my mind elsewhere. No question now . . . it was only a matter of *where* we should flee to. Would it never end? Maybe Palestine was the answer, after all. But Sheila was right—there are no pogroms and no angry Arabs in America. In any event, I would never leave her, especially at her age. I picked up the papers and began entering orders.

Reflecting upon my conversation with Sonia, I suddenly realized the enormity of what I had just done. Our decision to leave was to be a secret until the last moment, and here I had just told Sonia . . . before telling Madame Olga! I rushed upstairs.

Madame Olga had the bearing of a Prussian officer. She looked up from the piece of lace in front of her. "Yes, girl, what is it?"

"I want to tell you I'm . . . my mother and I . . . are going to America. I want to thank you for giving us jobs here."

She stared at me. "Your mother should have been the one to tell me. So be it." She turned her attention back to the lace.

I turned to go.

"I'm still talking, Sara. You are smart for your age and will go far . . . if you control your temper and your tongue. Sonia tells me you are Jewish." She pursed her lips. "Take some advice from an old lady. Raw courage is for fighting Cossacks. In the business world, biding your time is wiser than confrontation." She peered over her glasses at me. "Remember that, when you get to America. You will find they are not as forgiving as Madame Olga."

Humbled, I could only nod my understanding.

She resumed her lecture. "There is a way to accept the unacceptable without losing your soul, Sara. Find it, and you will be successful."

"I know you are correct, Madame, but sometimes it is difficult."

"Think first, Sara, and don't be foolhardy. Also, my child, you must learn the world is not simply black or white." She sounded wistful. "I suspected you might be Jewish or German when we first met. Now that I know, I'm afraid you and your mother will have to leave.

"Sonia is not vicious," she went on, "and neither am I. However, one Jewish employee is enough. Three is too much. I cannot afford to be known as a Jewish salon. You and your mother will leave tomorrow. You will be paid for another week. I do not harbor ill feelings for you, but business is business." She held out her hand.

250

I could not look at her or take her hand.

"Accept what you cannot change, Sara. Sometimes," she added softly, "it is not as unacceptable as you think."

Slowly, I reached for her hand. Why did I feel so sad?

"Sheila, I feel so bad! It was stupid of me to tell Sonia before we told Madame Olga. Now we're both out of a job."

"Never mind, Sara, it's only a question of another week or two. But I've learned this: When one door closes, another opens. It will all work out fine, you'll see. Let's go get something sweet at the pastry shop to cheer us up. Something creamy and rich."

The bakery was in total darkness. Two girls blocked the doorway, their eyes pressed against the window for a better view of the interior. I had a terrible premonition.

When the girls walked away, it was easy to read the sign on the door: CLOSED PERMANENTLY BY HEALTH INSPECTOR.

36

Sheila looked exhausted. "I finally reserved passage for us on a ship to America that leaves in five weeks. Now, all we need are passports and visas. The passport office sent me from one department to another. They don't seem anxious to issue papers to Jews, Sara."

"Maybe Josef can help. Let's go to the Romany and see if he's there yet."

Window-shopping along the way, I was suddenly aware that the same two reflections were appearing behind us each time I looked in a window.

Nudging Sheila, I drew her casually to the next window. Exasperated, I turned to confront them. "Stop following us. We've been through all this before and I have nothing of value. I'm meeting Josef shortly, so there's no need to . . ."

"We're also meeting him at the Romany. Mind if we accompany you?"

"If you wish."

"Who are they?" whispered Sheila.

"Some of his friends. Don't worry."

In the lobby, Carmen acknowledged us with a wave of her hand. "Sandor is waiting in his office."

I turned to our escorts. "Josef is coming later. Please excuse us. We have private business with Sandor."

"So do we." They pushed past me into his office.

"Good afternoon, everyone." Sandor was his usual jovial self. He pointed toward the main dining room. "Sometimes he comes in for an early supper before work, gentlemen. He might be in the kitchen right now, or upstairs changing clothes."

The men rushed out. Sandor pulled us into a corner. "Secret police," he whispered. "Speak only if your are spoken to. One will act stern; the other, friendly . . . it is how they pry information. Answer only what they ask—take your lead from me." Smiling, he handed us cups of coffee. "Now we will talk as though everything is normal."

These two were *not* more of Josef's friends! Inwardly cursing my stupidity, I sank into an armchair. I looked at my hand holding the cup. How could it be so steady when I felt so shaky inside?

Sheila, sitting stiffly in her chair, forced a smile. "We haven't seen you in a long time, Sandor. We reserved tickets for America. How is business?"

"Not good, but it is temporary. Everything will . . ."

The door burst open. "He's not there!" The first policeman scowled.

Sandor calmly consulted his watch. "He doesn't start until seven, so there's still time. He might even be eating at home tonight, right ladies?"

We nodded. "Sometimes he does that," I said, studying the two strangers. I finally realized what was so frightening about them. Their faces were devoid of expression, as smooth and bland as a store mannequin . . . lifeless eyes. My stomach felt queasy.

"And exactly where is home for him? I'm talking to you, girl!"

I turned to Sandor.

"Don't be frightened, Sara. Leonid and Paul are detectives, and you do not have to worry about telling them whatever you know. I told them you both lived at the Magyar, but Josef . . ."

Leonid interrupted. "I asked her, not you. Now tell me where he lives, Miss."

Sheila leaned forward, smiling innocently. "He used to . . ."

"Not you," growled the other one. "Let the girl talk. Your turn will come."

"He . . . he used to live at the Magyar. I do not know where he lives now."

"Now, Missus, it's your turn. Where is he now? You're his sweetheart."

"Sweetheart?" Sheila laughed. "He's young enough to be my son. We only know him as a waiter here."

"So what? He has a reputation for liking older women." He whispered something to his partner. They both smirked.

Sheila turned crimson.

I jumped up. "Stop making fun of my mother!"

Leonid gently pushed me back. "Sit down, girl. We were joking about something else."

Whirling around, he pointed an accusing finger at Sheila. "Now, listen here, woman, I'm losing patience. Tell me where he is, or it will go hard with both of you."

"Excuse me, sir. I do not mean to be impolite, but where we come from we do not ask men where they live if they do not tell us."

"Where do you come from?"

"Drohobych. It is now Poland."

The two men conferred in whispers.

"Listen, Paul," Sandor said, "I already told you they are innocents from a small town. They know nothing about this playboy or what he does on the outside. They are strangers to Budapest and only met him here by chance. My niece told them to look me up—you know how close we Gypsies are."

Paul whirled to confront him. "They're Jews, not Gypsies. Do not try your sly Gypsy ways with us, my friend. And why are you volunteering information all the time?"

"I am a law-abiding citizen. I have always cooperated with the police. Ask your chief."

Leonid was the calmer one. "We know how civic-minded you are, Sandor. And we do appreciate all the information you give us."

A slightly more restrained Paul turned his attention back to me. "Now tell me, girl, where does your mother's sweetheart live? We're not going to harm you."

"Please, sir, he is not her sweetheart. I do not know where he went after he left the Magyar."

The detectives exchanged looks. "If that's the way it's going to be, bring your papers to my office tomorrow morning at nine o'clock. Room 35." He handed Sheila his card.

"The census bureau?"

"Yes, Mrs. Stern. We keep track of people." Paul chuckled at his own joke. "Come Leonid, we'll wait inside for him."

Leonid checked his watch. He made a half-bow. "Thank you both for your information. Sandor, for your own good, I trust Josef remembers to show up for work tonight."

When the door closed behind them, I turned to Sandor. "How could you betray him like that?"

Chapter 36

Placing a finger to his lips, he motioned us to the farthest corner. "He's long gone. In two hours I will tell them Josef just called in sick. That should buy him another day."

"Where is he now?"

"Far from here, Sheila. Don't worry; he can take care of himself. Now we only concern ourselves with you, because the authorities seem to be cracking down. Tomorrow, go to the passport office and try to get American visas and passports."

"I've already done that, but they are sending me in circles."

He exhaled. "I was afraid of that. But go back, anyway. Let everything look normal. Who else do we know who might help? I don't want to use my source except as a last resort."

"Sheila, do you think Madame Olga . . . ?"

"She's no friend, Sara. I don't care what she told you. Remember, we were out of a job the moment she learned we were Jewish."

"With an extra week's pay, don't forget. I just have this good feeling about her."

Sandor shrugged. "It's worth a try. If Olga can help, you'll get papers quickly. If not, let me know. In any event, be ready to leave Hungary quickly. If I can get you the papers, I'll have visas for England, and the American visa should be waiting for you in London."

Sheila looked at the detective's card again. "Census bureau, indeed! That's scary, Sandor. Tomorrow we have to show our papers to those men, and now I remember Josef once telling us they were forgeries. What should we do?"

He looked thoughtful. "I doubt they'll study them that closely. They're not that knowledgeable, but if they

257

say anything, tell them it's what you've always had. Plead ignorance . . . and above all, both of you should act like country peasants. I can always convince them about the papers; after all, 95 percent of the émigrés are here on forged papers . . . and titles."

"We'll be careful," I said. "Now, will you please tell us about Josef. Where is he?"

Sandor looked pleased with himself. "I, too, have influential friends, but the less you know, the better. Josef told me about Madame Adrienne and his dealings with Count Fedorovich. For your information, Josef is no stranger to the secret police, and you've been seen with him a number of times. My sources inform me Olga is the one who told the police you were Jewish."

"You said she was your friend!"

"No, Sara. I said I knew her. Not everyone I know is a friend. For instance, the chief of detectives knows me . . . just as he knows everyone else willing to pay bribes for information. Drinking with me last night, he let slip that a waiter of mine was about to be arrested. It took until midnight and a bottle of wine before he named Josef. I immediately went to Josef's apartment. I must say, this Palestine business is a side of him I never knew."

"I told you he was a good person."

"Yes, you did, Sara. Anyhow, last night he assured me he'd be out of the city in an hour or so. He's very professional, ladies, so don't worry. To give him more time, at nine this morning I called the chief to assure him Josef is working tonight. You know the rest. Don't be frightened by tomorrow's meeting—if it were serious, they would have brought you in this afternoon. Remember—you are simple, country Jews visiting a big city."

CHAPTER

37

Room 35 of the census bureau was in the basement. Mannequin-face sat behind a scarred wooden desk, his back to us. His wrinkled shirt looked like he'd slept in it. A floor fan pushed stale cigarette smells in all directions. An old file cabinet tilted precariously against a water cooler.

The policeman swiveled around and pointed to the worn, wooden chairs facing his desk. "Sit, if you don't mind a few splinters."

My stomach was churning as I carefully sat on the edge of the chair, but I'd gladly settle for a dozen splinters if our forged papers passed inspection. Sheila placed them gingerly in front of him. She kept her eyes down.

"I am Paul, in case you forgot." He glanced briefly at the wrinkled documents before tossing them back. "You are planning to leave Hungary?"

"Yes," she answered meekly.

"For Palestine?"

"No, sir."

"Why not? You belong to that same group of student agitators."

"Please, sir, we're not students, and we don't know anything about agitators. We're not interested in Palestine. I am too old, and she is too young. We're going to America."

"Hungary is better than America. Why are you leaving?"

"Like I said before, sir, I am old, but my daughter is only 12. There is much opportunity for her in America. We have reservations to leave . . ."

"We know all about your reservations," he said disdainfully, "so don't try to hide anything from us. What we don't know is why a handsome young nobleman, the son of a respected cavalry officer, wants an old Jewish mother as a sweetheart. Enlighten me, please, Mrs. Stern."

How had they connected us to Count Peter? I shivered inwardly, afraid to look at Sheila. I squirmed as the rough edges of the chair pricked my leg.

Sheila seemed not to have heard the question. "Also, I am applying for passports and visas again right after we leave here." She was still properly submissive.

"We were past that point, Mrs. Stern. Answer my question!"

"I am trying, sir. You said not to hide anything and I . . ."

"Get on with it!"

"You want to know why he . . . ?"

"Yes. Tell me why a handsome university student bothers with a Jewish woman your age . . . with a 12-year-old child?"

I gasped. They were talking about Josef, not Peter!

"What's wrong with you, girl?" The detective glared at me.

"Nothing, sir. I'm sorry. I just got another splinter." I scratched my leg furiously.

Sheila gave him a sad smile. "Sweetheart, sir? At my age, I don't think so. He was the waiter for our table at the

Romany. We never saw him before. Respecting my age, he helped us move our clothes to the Magyar. That is all, sir."

The detective turned his attention to me. "What is the waiters name . . . his full name."

"Josef, sir. I think he said his last name is Alexandrov . . . at least it . . ."

"Who arranged your meeting?"

"No one. A Gypsy girl I once . . ."

"Skip that—I know how you got to the Romany. Tell me, what did Josef Alexandrov say he does for a living?"

"He's a student who pays for university by . . ."

"What did he say about going to Palestine?" His voice was loud and threatening.

"He never . . ."

"What do you know about Palestine?" he shouted.

"Please, sir," I whined, "give me a chance to finish. You are talking too quickly for me. I know nothing about Palestine."

"Do you own a gun?"

Sheila answered for me. "No!"

"I asked the girl, not you!"

"No, sir."

"No?" He consulted a notepad. "What else do you know about Josef Alexandrov?"

"He said he was a Gypsy . . . actually, I think he said half-Gypsy. Isn't that right, Mother?"

"If you please, sir, that's what I remember, too, sir."

The detective snorted. "Half-Gypsy, indeed! His father was Baron Yulanov, a brilliant Cossack officer who performed with other trick riders in New York City years ago. He remained there, abandoning his wife and their baby, Josef, who were back in Russia. The grown son is ashamed of his father and will not use his name. He became a revolutionary—an agitator!" Paul bared his teeth in a wolfish grin. "Do you also believe Josef is a Gypsy, Mrs. Stern? Don't even bother to answer. He has a way with women. What else did he tell you that you believe? I'm talking to you, Mrs. Stern."

"He said he was on the fencing team at university . . ."

"What else?"

Sheila hesitated. "He said he was half-Jewish."

Paul snickered. "Half-Jewish? Like he's half-Gypsy!"

"Why would we doubt him?" Sheila said innocently.

His blank stare returned. "A man who renounces his father's good name? You really are a pair of country Jews. Why are you no longer working for Madame Olga?"

"Because we're Jewish."

"That's true," I added weakly. "When I told her we were Jewish, she discharged us immediately."

"Who else in authority can vouch for you besides Sandor and Madame Olga?"

"No one," said Sheila.

"You can try the designer there, but I tell you now, sir, he does not like me."

He left the room abruptly.

Sheila turned to me, put a finger to her lips and stared straight ahead.

It seemed like an eternity before he returned. "I just spoke to Madame Olga. She said you were fired because you are a stupid girl. Herr Designer, who is very testy about titles, says you are impertinent and given to lying. According to them, you are a pair of gullible country bumpkins. The mother is inept—that's what Madame Olga told me—and the daughter, he looked down at his notepad, 'knows figures but can only add simple sums.' Both of you, according to them, are too ignorant to know anything about politics or Palestine. My advice to you is never again lie to officials who are only trying to find the truth. If you are innocent you have nothing to fear."

He seemed disgusted with us. Just when I thought our questioning was over, he pulled a bag out of his desk drawer and turned it upside down. "We found these in your room...a fancy lady's pistol, a pamphlet about a Jewish State, a dress with gold coins sewn in the hem, and this knotted handkerchief. All contrary to what you've both told me. Explain, either of you!" His fingers drummed the desktop.

I caught my breath. They had searched our room and we never noticed! I fidgeted, sending another sliver into my leg. The policeman cast a furious look my way.

Sheila held out her hands in supplication. "You know how old-fashioned grandmothers are. Back in Drohobych, Tanta Hanna sewed a few coins in my daughter's dress in case we were separated. You can see we never tried to use them. A man on the train coming here gave us that pamphlet, but I never even looked at it."

"Neither did I, sir. And you know we're going to America in five weeks."

"The gun and handkerchief?" reminded Mannequin-face.

Sheila shrugged. "My daughter didn't know anything about the gun, sir. She's deathly afraid of guns so I hid it from her. I lied because I didn't know whether it was against the law here. A retired army officer back home gave it to me for protection against bandits. Remember, sir, we're two females traveling alone."

"Only aristocracy owned such fancy weapons, Mrs. Stern. Your friend was probably a Bolshevik who murdered a countess for it during the revolution. The truth, now!"

"He was not!" I cried. "He was my uncle's friend and he had it for years . . . long before the revolution. I swear it."

Ignoring my outburst, Paul pointed to the knotted handkerchief. "You left the best part for last, I notice."

"That's mine," I said. "A keepsake to honor a loyal friend's memory."

"Keepsake? The last time I looked, it was a gold crucifix. Now, why would a nice Jewish girl hide a crucifix in a dresser drawer?" He smirked. "I never heard of a secret Catholic."

I struggled to keep my voice respectful. "Please sir, I'm telling the truth. My friend gave her life protecting me from bandits in Russia. I feel it protects me . . . brings me luck." I gave him an anxious look. "I don't mean any disrespect by that, sir."

He stood to stretch, then tossed his notepad down on the desk in disgust. "I don't know whether you liars are the dumbest or the smartest suspects I've ever met. You are free to go—both of you. It's your lucky day." He slid the items toward us. "Here—that gun is useless beyond six, seven meters. We confiscated the pamphlet."

Picking up the dress, my fingers caught in the ripped hem. "My gold coins?"

He lit a cigarette and calmly blew smoke rings at us. "What gold coins? I said this is your lucky day. If we found any gold coins we'd be obliged to arrest you both for smuggling!"

CHAPTER

38

While Sheila went back to the passport office, I presented myself to a new girl behind the pickup counter at the salon. "Would you please ask Madame Olga if she can spare a few minutes for Sara Stern?"

Sonia came out from the back room. "I thought I recognized your voice. Why don't you go right up . . . you know she's always in her office at this time."

"I don't work here anymore, Sonia. I don't want to take advantage."

She disappeared. Several minutes went by before a chastened Sonia returned. Her face was flushed. "I was mistaken. Madame Olga is not coming in today. Perhaps you can try another time."

"I understand. I'm sorry to have put you in the middle. Goodbye, Sonia. I wish you luck." I pressed her hand quickly and turned away.

"I don't know what to say, Sara," she whispered, averting her eyes.

So much for my intuition. Madame Olga was no enemy, but she was not quite a friend. It must be difficult to walk a tightrope like that when your livelihood is at stake. But then I thought of Marya Petrovna, Count Peter, and the gruff constable of Drohobych. They had all gone out of their way to help . . . some a little more than others, but they did not turn away. I wondered how I would act under similar circumstances.

Stopping off at a tiny coffee shop, I consoled myself with a hot chocolate and pastry. The ruined baker flashed into my mind and suddenly the pastry tasted like cardboard.

"It's puzzling, Sheila," I remarked that night at supper, "that Madame Olga and Herr Designer could hate us so much, yet lie to the detectives so we go free. When she fired us that day, she said the world is not simply black and white. I guess this is what she was talking about."

"Sara, I never believed she would help, but I *was* surprised that she refused to see you." She shrugged. "Maybe we shouldn't be surprised by anything that happens these days. For instance, whose story do we believe about Josef's parents? Do you think he's telling the truth? I didn't want to discuss this with you earlier because I know how much you think of him."

"Yes, I do like him. First, I considered asking Sandor what he knows about Josef's parents." I sighed. "Maybe it's stupid of me, but I think I'd rather not risk being disappointed in someone I admire. Does that make sense, Sheila?"

She gave me a hug. "You're no different from anyone else. Let's just believe what we wish to believe and forget the rest. We're free of the police so far, but I don't think they are finished with us. Paul and that other policeman could be playing cat and mouse with us—I could have sworn I was being followed today. Anyway, Sandor knows I'm getting nowhere at the passport office, but he wants me to keep going back. In the meantime, he's contacting his source."

266

For the next several days, wherever I went my eyes swept the crowds for those anonymous-looking mannequin faces. Over my shoulder, left to right . . . my neck ached from the strain. Traveling by streetcar one morning, I panicked when I noticed a man staring at me. Casually leaving my seat, I edged toward the door. Heart beating faster, I stood aside to let exiting passengers off at the next stop. At the last second, I jumped. The doors slammed shut behind me. I was far from home and alone in a strange neighborhood, but I had escaped "them." Alone, I waited anxiously for another trolley. Let it come quickly, I prayed, before he comes back. I felt a little foolish after taking my seat in the next streetcar, but I also felt easier.

That afternoon, I accompanied Sheila on another fruitless trip to the passport office. We were waiting for yet another minor bureaucrat to stamp our papers. "It's strange, Sara. For a country anxious to rid itself of Jews, they certainly make it difficult for us to leave."

Wearily we traipsed from building to building. Walking down one of the long halls, I thought I glimpsed Herr Designer entering an office at the far end. Well, he always said Paris would appreciate the talent he was wasting in Budapest. I still hadn't fathomed what had prompted him to lie to the secret police. Sheila said she couldn't be bothered thinking about such people, but it kept nagging at me. Everything that happened seemed like an endless circle leading to the same question: Was *anyone* in Budapest actually the person he or she appeared to be? I decided Sheila was right. Why try to unravel such a mystery? We'd been helped more than hindered by the surprises, except in our efforts to secure official visas.

When we finally returned to the Magyar, the desk clerk handed Sheila an envelope. "A messenger brought this, and," he pointed, "that girl in the armchair is waiting for you, Sara."

"I wonder what Sonia wants with you." Sheila opened the note. "Sandor invites us to dinner tonight. Maybe the passports are in! You go talk to Sonia; I'll be upstairs, changing."

I walked to the far end of the lobby where she was waiting. "Oh, Sara, I worried you were not coming back until late. I think I got you and your mother in trouble!" Her words tumbled out about two strange men snooping around the salon and making a lot of notes. "I don't know why they thought your mother was Josef's sweetheart, but I told them that was ridiculous. I think they're detectives, Sara. They questioned everyone. I hope I didn't say something wrong. That's why I'm here." Clutching her handkerchief, she seemed genuinely upset.

"As long as you told the truth, Sonia, it's all right. What did you say?"

"I told them how students usually made deliveries for us, and that you only made that one delivery to Countess Fedorovich."

I could feel my heart pounding. "So why do you think that was wrong?"

Sonia continued twisting her handkerchief. "Well, a funny look passed between them. I had a terrible feeling they were surprised by what I said. Did I do wrong, Sara? I hope not."

I kissed her on the cheek. "Of course not. It was sweet of you to come tell me. There was nothing wrong in telling the truth."

Bounding to her feet, she breathed a sigh of relief. "I'm so happy. I wouldn't want to hurt you or your mother for all the world!" She shifted from one foot to the other. "I'm sorry about what happened when you came to see Madame Olga the other day. Goodbye, Sara. Good luck to you both!" She hurried away.

I couldn't wait to tell Sheila of our conversation. "Do you think the detectives sent her?"

"It's possible, but she learned nothing from you. You handled it beautifully, Sara. Now let's go see if Sandor has our documents."

39

"They're waiting for you in the private dining room," Carmen said.

Sandor stood in the doorway, blocking our view. "An old friend is here, ladies." He stepped aside.

"Avram!" I screamed, throwing my arms around my old friend. I wondered why he did not seem happy to see me.

Sheila shook his hand warily. "What's wrong?"

I had a premonition. "Someone has died. Is it Tanta Hanna?"

"I'll tell you everything in a moment." He handed Sheila a glass of brandy. "Wine for you, Sara. *L'chaim*," he said softly.

I raised my glass but could not bring myself to drink. I felt like sharp rocks were tumbling over and over inside me. "It's bad news. I know it." I held my breath.

Avram's eyes were dull. "Tanta Hanna and Mrs. Goldschein died of influenza about two weeks ago. Two days later, Frieda and Herman died in a fire at the store. It burned to the ground."

Sheila held me tight. "Oh, my God!" she gasped. "And the boys?"

"Safe and well."

"Thanks to God." She exhaled sharply. "What happened?"

"The boys were sleeping at my house while Frieda, Herman, and I stayed late in the store one night for inventory. Around midnight, I smelled smoke. I didn't see any fire so I grabbed a gun and chased after some men running away. I wounded one, but while I was chasing them the store must have suddenly burst into flames." Avram took a deep breath. "By the time I returned it was a roaring fire and the smell of kerosene was everywhere. The constable and I couldn't get past the flames and heat. We found Frieda's and Herman's bodies in the morning." He paused to steady his voice. "We had warnings—'Poland is for Poles and Jews should get out.' But we'd been through all that before."

I remembered all too well. "Was it the same people, Avram?"

"It was. And more. A riot that started over who knows what. Only this time, eight Jews died in our town. Every Jewish home and business was attacked. I don't know how many injuries." He downed another brandy. "I have the boys at home, Mrs. Stern. A neighbor minds them, but I don't know how to raise children. You are the only one I could turn to."

She rested her hand on his arm. "I understand, Avram."

He breathed a sigh of relief. "You are a wonderful woman, Mrs. Stern. Sandor tells me you and Sara are going to America. You will take them with you?"

Sheila did not answer. There was a distant look in her eyes.

"I'll help you raise them," I said, wondering at her silence.

"Give me a minute, Sara. I'm thinking."

Was she changing her mind? Avram shifted uneasily in his chair. Sandor looked away.

Finally, Sheila spoke up. "I have changed my mind."

I held my breath, afraid to look at Avram or Sandor.

"Yes, I've changed my mind. Sara and Josef have been saying this all along, and now I see they are right. I'm taking them to Palestine with us! If we are going to die for being Jewish, then let's die on our own soil. Sandor, how do we add them to my passport?"

Avram held up his hand. "A minute, please, Mrs. Stern. Mordechai and the grandma wanted the boys to go to America."

Sheila clasped her hands together. "Avram, Mordechai is dead, may he rest in peace. Though we had only a short time together, we actually knew each other since we were children. After all that has happened this past year, I do believe he would come to the same decision. Since I am now responsible, I say we go to Palestine. True, Sara is almost 13 and grown, but all three are my responsibility. In America I would be a widow alone with three children. In Palestine they will have many fathers and mothers . . . an entire community will worry about them."

Avram looked skeptical. "That's a brave decision, Mrs. Stern. Better think it over carefully."

"But it's not foolhardy, Avram," I said. "Our friend Josef originally asked us to join him. He and his comrades will surely look out for us. I'm excited just thinking about it!"

Sandor looked grim. "If I may interrupt . . . you're not their blood mother, Sheila. This is a big undertaking. Are you sure you can manage this?"

"Of course, she can!" I said, putting my arm around her. "I'm practically 13. We'll do whatever we have to. Isn't what's in your heart more important than blood, Sandor? Some real parents treat their children badly. I don't have parents, so I choose *her*. Wherever Sheila goes, I go."

Sheila was near tears. The men cleared their throats. Avram pounded his knee. "Then I am going, also—I owe it to Mordechai. You are the only family I have, so I will be the uncle." He blew loudly into his handkerchief.

"This is all so remarkable!" Sandor passed the brandy glasses around. "Sara, this time it's the real thing for you. How do you say it? . . . 'Lah Hah Yem!'"

Sheila dabbed at her eyes, never letting go of my hand. I had never felt such emotion, and this time I didn't care who saw me cry.

The men tossed down another brandy. "For extra good luck," added Avram, settling back in his chair.

Sandor began pacing the floor. "Now, we have to figure out how to accomplish this. My heart breaks to say it, but if I asked my source for papers to Palestine, not only would he refuse but he'd probably report us all to the authorities. It's sad, but true . . . there is much hate in this world!" He halted his pacing in front of Avram.

"What I could get is travel permits for all of you to London. Now, where do we get passports and visas from London to Palestine?"

Avram squirmed in his chair. "I, too, have a similar situation. An expert forger owes me a favor, but he'll not put himself in danger for one other person. Not even for my wife . . . if I had one. I'm sorry, but that is how it is. Anyhow, at least that makes me one less person to worry about."

"Madame Olga won't see me, and Sheila has not been successful at the municipal offices. Our only hope is Josef,

Sandor, wherever he is. Do you know how to contact him, or the baker?"

"Not a good idea, Sara. We must stay away from them. Do you know who arranged the passports that the group received—was it Fedorovich? Can you contact him?"

Sheila shook her head. "We think we're being followed. If the police connect us to the count and then to Josef, then they're both in danger as well as those of his group still here. In fact, anyone we talk to will be suspect. Sandor, I'm afraid it has to be you."

"I have a thought," Sandor mused. "The count often dines here. I'll call him and say we are verifying a reservation. He's bound to be on his guard. Sara, is there something I can say to convince him this is not a trap . . . that it's really for you?"

I racked my brain. "Tell him . . . you'll have to write this down, Sandor . . . just say, 'Sara remembers your dog's name was Volga, and he died a few days before Ilya, her father, was killed.' Nobody else in this world would know those two things."

"It's complicated, but so much the better. I'll call him right now from my office. Take something to eat, everyone. I'll be right back."

Avram took Sheila aside. "The rabbi and the lawyer are trying to sell whatever property is left. Where should they send the proceeds, Mrs. Stern?"

"First, since we are now one big family, please call me Sheila. Tell them to send whatever there is here, to Sandor. He will always know where we will be. Naturally, I will only use that money for the boys."

A frustrated Sandor returned almost at once. "He was out. I'll just have to keep trying. If I'm lucky, I'll have an answer for you ladies by the time you get back to the hotel. Otherwise, it will have to wait until around noon tomorrow. I will call as soon as I reach him. In the meantime, Avram, you will stay here tonight."

The sleepy-eyed clerk at the Magyar shook his head. "Nothing for either of you. Sorry."

As the elevator cage swayed its way up to our floor, Sheila was unusually quiet. "Don't worry, Sheila. Peter must be out for the evening. We'll just have to wait for tomorrow."

"I hope he's not out of town."

"No matter. I have a good feeling about this, Sheila. We just have to be patient."

I opened the door to our room. "I'm going to wait up for a while longer."

"Me, too." Still fully dressed, Sheila stretched out on the bed. She stared at the ceiling. "I hope I'm doing the right thing about Palestine, Sara. In my heart, I know I am, but raising two boys in a strange land without a father, I . . ."

"I'll help you. I'll do anything you want me to, Sheila. I promise!"

"I know, and I love you for that, Sara. They're really good boys. And well behaved. That part doesn't bother me—it's going to a strange . . . a wilderness . . . that troubles me. I don't think I'm much of a pioneer. What if . . . ?"

"The last thing my father wrote was 'Be bold and be brave.' You are that, Sheila. You've thought it out carefully. Neither Avram nor Sandor felt Palestine was a bad choice, only that Avram remembered Uncle talking about America. I have this good feeling that everything will turn out just fine. Like you said this afternoon, the best part is we have

Josef and his friends to look after us. We'd have no one in America."

Sheila made no comment. Just when I thought she had fallen asleep, she sat upright. "Of course, that's true! I guess I just had to talk it all out, Sara. I honestly do feel good about our plans. And I know how much you wanted it almost from the beginning."

At eight the next morning, I stopped at the front desk. "Maria, I'm waiting for a phone call this morning. I'm going into the coffee shop for breakfast. After that, I'll be on that sofa in the corner. My mother will be coming down shortly."

An excited Sheila joined me at the table a few minutes later. "Sandor called just as I was leaving. He said you should wait in the lobby for someone to contact you. He didn't know who or what time, but that person will mention the dog Volga and your father. I brought your embroidery bag to make the time go faster. I'm returning to the visa offices for another try, just in case we're being watched. I'll tell the desk clerk you're expecting a visitor and will be here, or in the lobby later."

Gulping my breakfast down quickly, I hurried back to the sofa. Resigning myself to keeping busy, I spread out the lopsided canvas I had been struggling with under Sheila's patient guidance. My uneven stitches made the flowers look as wilted as a real bouquet left unwatered too long.

Picking up the needle, I half-heartedly worked it through the canvas, my eyes automatically following every person strolling or rushing through the lobby. To my disappointment, no one appeared to be looking for anyone. The morning dragged. The desk clerk never called my name. Just before noon, an elderly woman who lived on our floor came over to inspect my handiwork. At this point, I was happy to speak to anyone. "Good morning," I said, with a smile.

"You did this by yourself, child? Don't be discouraged. It takes years to learn. Give my regards to your mama." Muttering to herself, she left quickly.

Standing up to stretch my legs, I spotted a stooped, elderly man at the newsstand who seemed to be looking around the room. When he headed straight for me, my heart beat a little faster.

"You do nice work, Miss. My legs hurt, mind if I sit here?" He plopped down on the next cushion. "My wife used to knit a lot. Mind if I watch?"

I nodded, afraid lest I interrupt his train of thought. I searched his face for some sign.

He didn't look like someone Peter or Sandor would send, but Papa always said that messengers seldom resembled the message they carried. I smiled at the old man, regretting I had thought up such complicated passwords. Maybe I could give him a hint. "My last canvas was of my dog. Do you like dogs?"

He became agitated. "I think it's cruel to keep animals cooped up for our own amusement!" He picked himself up and left in a huff.

Discouraged, I stuffed the canvas into my bag and headed for the front desk.

40

I waited for Maria to finish talking to a gangly young man I vaguely recognized as living on one of the upper floors in the hotel. When he left, I leaned across the counter.

"Nothing yet, Sara."

"I know. I'm just going outside for some fresh air but I'll be looking at you through the window. I don't want to miss an important call."

"Very good."

I passed through the revolving door to find the young man waiting.

"Good morning, Sara. I'm Robert. I heard her mention your name. I live on the fifth floor."

"Good morning. Aren't you the medical student?"

"Doctor. I work at the clinic."

I took a closer look. A head taller, he certainly didn't appear that old. "Excuse me, aren't you kind of young to be a doctor?"

He looked down at me. "I'm older than I look. Titles are foolish anyhow, don't you think?"

"It depends. Suppose you were a professor?"

"With a capital *P*? What about butcher?"

"Butcher?"

"Capital *B*," he said seriously.

"Without thinking too deeply about it, Robert, I get your point."

"Would you like to join me for a sandwich and coffee? I'm starved."

"I'm sorry, thank you. Perhaps some other time. I'm waiting for an important call."

He hesitated. "How about the coffee shop inside? They can page you there."

It had been a boring, disappointing morning. "Well . . . only if I buy my own lunch. First, let me tell the desk clerk where I'll be."

I took the seat opposite him in the booth. "I only have a few minutes, Robert. I'm meeting someone in the lobby."

"Feel free to leave any time."

"Separate checks, please," I told the waiter.

Nibbling on my cheese sandwich, I concluded his beard was supposed to make him look older. He had dark brown eyes and pleasant features, but I still found it hard to believe he was a doctor. "How long have you . . . I mean, what kind of doctor are you?"

"Research. I hate to see people suffer, so I do research." He looked at my embroidery bag. "What are you knitting?"

"It's needlepoint. But it's terrible."

"Don't be so modest. Can I see it?"

I put the scraggly canvas on the table.

"You're right. It's awful."

We both laughed.

"By the way, Sara Samovitch, I forgot the name of your dog before your friend Ilya died?"

"My . . . dog?" I couldn't believe he waited this long to make himself known and then bungled so important a message! "Would you repeat that, please?"

"I mean your friend's dog. He was named after a river . . . the dog."

"My friend's dog, *Volga*, died before my *father* Ilya died. Is that what you're trying to tell me?"

Beaming, Robert clasped my hand. "Josef sent me to rescue you."

It was laughable. "Rescue? You are a terrible undercover agent! Couldn't you get simple code words straight?"

"I'm a doctor, Sara, not a spy. And you're only a child. Show respect."

"I'm older than you think. You're lucky you ran into me."

"Luck had nothing to do with it. I knew who you were before today. What's so important about a word here and there, as long as I remembered the river?"

"River? 'Volga the dog' is the key phrase here. Why have passwords in the first place? I see by your expression there's no sense discussing it. Do you have the travel documents for all of us?"

"Not so fast. We have lots to talk about. First, we'll take a little walk. Then sit on a bench for privacy. Take my arm so we look like friends, Sara."

He babbled nonstop until we found an empty bench. Instantly, the bumbling youth underwent an amazing transformation. His eyes bored into mine. "Listen closely. In six days I will have authentic Soviet Socialist Republic of Belarus passports for our family, valid for almost one year. Our visa from the British embassy in Moscow is only good for three months, so we must get to Palestine without delay." He moistened his lips. "This is the meat of it: The passports read that I am Samuel Wiseman, professor of anatomy, age 21. You are Anna Wiseman, my bride, 15."

He scrutinized me closely from head to toe. "You're nowhere near 15! This will never do. How old are you, Sara Samovitch?"

"You don't intimidate me. It's none of your business. Be assured I'll look 15 by the time we get the passports!" I leaned closer. "And you're not 21! Eighteen, 19 at best . . . and you probably know nothing about medicine. How old are you?"

"Old enough," he said gruffly. "For your information, I have a medical diploma and it's authentic."

"What about my mother and two brothers?"

He sounded like he was delivering a lecture. "Your mother is my mother-in-law Sheila Goodman, a widow. She and her two sons, David and Louis, 12 and 10 respectively, are accompanying us to Palestine."

"What a coincidence! Mother's actual name is Sheila."

"That makes it easier to remember. You and I must have a photo taken together. Your mother should take one with the boys. We'll each have to memorize carefully the new facts until we know them backward and forward. And we should start immediately calling each other by our passport names . . . Anna."

"Will you remember that, Samuel? Today's episode was not very reassuring."

"No reason to be so combative. Don't forget, I'm an absent-minded professor of anatomy. It says so on my passport, so I'm right in character."

"Tell me, Robert, I mean Samuel. Are the passports genuine?"

"Genuine. Samuel Wiseman and his entire family are real people. Unfortunately . . . fortunately for us . . . they can't make the journey because they are all dead. No more questions, please."

"Do you want us to book the train and ship passages?"

"Absolutely not!" he snapped. "I'm the husband, Anna, and I take care of such matters. We leave Budapest in 10 days. I'm responsible for your safety. I'm making it your responsibility to ensure everyone is up on his identity and ready in time. You will impress that upon them. Please!"

I gave him a long, hard look. "It's not necessary to speak to me like that. This is all make-believe! Who do you think took care of me before you came?"

"I'm just playing my part."

"Well, not only are you a terrible spy, you're a terrible actor! Married people I know behave kindly toward each other. This is not the old world . . . modern husbands treat their wives with respect. When I am old enough, I will never marry a pompous person like you even if he were as rich . . . if he were the richest man in the world!"

His face turned red but he was unruffled. "I have my orders and I pass them on to you. This is not a pleasure trip." He rose to go. "I am due at the clinic. We will all meet for breakfast tomorrow. Eight o'clock. There is much to discuss."

"We can't. Only Mother is here now . . . don't make a face. My brothers arrive in a few days. Oh, before I forget. An uncle is joining us, but you don't have to concern yourself with him. He's a tough old soldier with his own papers."

Later that day, Sheila and I compared notes. "I can't believe Josef's friend was living here all this time," I said. "He's *very* officious and quite young. Doesn't look at all like I expected."

"People seldom do."

"And I don't like him. He seems impressed with his own importance."

"Sara, he is important to us right now, and we're not taking a pleasure cruise. Just as long as we get our papers and make it safely to Palestine, who cares? Anyway, I had the usual luck at the visa office today. Nothing!"

Sitting on a bench near the ramparts the following morning, Sheila and I shared coffee and sweet rolls with Robert. I kept reassuring him that Avram and the boys would show up as expected and handle their roles properly.

He was uneasy. "Traveling in a group like this, each person depends upon the other to play his part without error. I don't like the idea of them joining us late. If one slips, we all are done for."

Sheila had a few questions of her own. "Sara says—I mean Anna—says you're a real doctor. I believe you. Now, Doctor, since you know all about us, would you mind telling us about yourself?"

"Not at all, Mother. Please don't call me Doctor. I'm Samuel, your son-in-law. In actuality, I'm the medical officer as well as the small-arms officer for our unit, and I'm the last one to leave Hungary. On a personal note, my parents died in a pogrom, and I've been on my own most of my life." He paused. "Do not be fooled by my looks, as your daughter seems to be. I am capable of doing anything necessary to get us safely to Haifa . . . anything!"

He glared at me. "This is a military operation and I am in charge. You will take orders from me until we set foot in Palestine. For the success of our mission, it is important that everyone, especially the old soldier, understands there can be only one person in command. No one questions what I say." His eyes locked with mine.

I bristled. "You can stop worrying about me, Doctor, General, or whatever you want us to call you. I have already used a pistol against bandits. I will obey your every order . . . until we set foot in Haifa."

Sheila squeezed my arm gently. "I think we understand each other. Samuel, I promise you that none of us will slow you down or question your authority. We realize your actions are for our collective good, and we are appreciative. We know what's at stake."

"Spoken like a true mother. You will be a good influence on all of us." He broke into a broad smile. "Now, let's all relax and be ourselves for the moment. Remember, we're one happy family. Any other questions?"

"One, and it's most important to me." Sheila placed her hand on his arm. "I'm the oldest, Samuel. If something happens to me, promise you'll ask Josef to look after Sara and my sons. They have no one else in this world."

I could feel tears welling up. "Please, Sheila, don't talk about such things."

An odd look came over Samuel's face. Suddenly he turned back into Robert, the soldier. I saw the muscles in his jaw tighten. "I promise." He stood up. "Time to return. I'll walk back with you for a few squares and then go to my clinic. I'll be in touch with you, but let's keep checking for messages at the front desk in the event we need to talk."

Exchanging nothing more than polite conversation, the three of us casually strolled up the boulevard. After he left, Sheila and I continued back to the hotel. "It was quite remarkable, Sheila. Did you notice his reaction when you mentioned asking Josef to take care of us if . . . if . . ."

"If something happened to me? You can say the words, Sara. I'm not superstitious and it's natural to discuss such eventualities."

I swallowed hard. "I don't want to think about such things."

"All right then, we won't." She smiled. "Getting back to your question, the answer is no. I didn't notice any unusual reaction on Robert's face. What did you see?"

"I saw an expression on his face that brought back what Tanta Hanna—she should rest in peace—said when she first told me about you. You have a special warmth that invites people to be your friend and encourages them to be protective of you. It's difficult to explain. Josef even said the same thing, if you remember. That's the look I saw on Robert's face."

The color rose in her cheeks. "All of that in 'a look'? I think you're imagining things."

Sheila and I heard nothing further from Robert that evening or the following morning. We were in our room in the late afternoon when the phone rang. It was Robert, asking if he could come up.

Offering him the only chair, Sheila and I sat on the edge of our bed. "Is there anything new?" she asked.

"Not really, but there is something I must talk to you about." Robert cleared his throat. He was having difficulty maintaining his military bearing. "I did not sleep well last night," he said shyly, "because this mission has affected me like no other. Mainly, because I have to break the promise I made you." He looked directly at Sheila.

"I agreed to go to Josef if something should happen to you, God forbid, but I have changed my mind."

Sheila was taken aback. "Why? What is so difficult about that?"

"Because," he said with a catch in his voice, "no one else but me takes care of my mother. My real one is dead a long time, as you know, but meeting you yesterday for the first time—well, I choose you to be my mother. Therefore, it is I, not Josef, who will take care of you and your children, starting immediately. I promise to get all of you safely to Palestine. Thereafter, you and the children will continue to be my responsibility. Forever! That means you, too, Sara." He leaned back in his chair, obviously waiting for our reaction.

I could only look on in amazement. Out of nowhere, a new protector had come into our lives. A very provocative one, indeed.

Sheila's eyes were moist. " I really don't know what to say. I'm honored, Robert, but . . . it is too much to ask of someone we just met. Josef knows Sara and me better than a . . . a comparative stranger."

He continued in a low voice. "I'm positive Josef loves all of you and knows you longer; however, in my heart I am no stranger. You may think I'm odd to say this, but I believe fate led Josef to pick me for this undertaking. I ask you and Sara to try to understand the depth of my feelings. I had no family before yesterday. Suddenly, I have one . . . on paper and in real life for the time being. I want that to be forever."

He took a deep breath. "Josef is my best friend, an honorable man who cannot help the fire within him for a Jewish homeland. He will do anything, fight anyone for you, but his first loyalty will always be to Palestine. And we must thank God for zealots like him."

This was a side of Robert I had not seen yesterday. I regretted the way I spoke to him.

"I will fight like Josef," he continued, "but the greater fire inside me now is for my new family. Nothing will ever come before you. I will never desert you, and no one will ever love you more. I swear it! As sure as I am standing here, I know it is our destiny to be one family."

He paused. "Think of the signs: why was I chosen for this particular mission? Passports arranged by a stranger bring Sara and me together as a married couple; Sheila's real name is on her passport; and she is a widow and she is my mother-in-law. The two boys she loves are listed as her sons. For your information, I do not believe in such a thing as coincidence. It was all predestined—it's *bashert!*" He stood and walked over to Sheila. Robert embraced her, kissing her on both cheeks.

Sheila was transfixed. She alternately dried her eyes and looked in wonder from Robert to me. I knew if I tried to speak I would break into tears.

Robert's voice was husky with emotion. "I can see you both feel the same. We are all meant for each other—so in that way we are each other's *bashert!* Yesterday was a very special day for me. October 29, 1920 was the beginning of my new life!"

The expression on his face was one I will never forget. I swallowed hard.

Sheila looked from him to me. "Do you believe in *bashert*, Sara?"

I didn't hesitate. "Now I do."

CHAPTER

41

Yad Mordechai, soon-to-be State of Israel. May 14, 1948, 0200 hours –

I fell asleep about four hours ago and suddenly I am wide awake. I picked up Mother's manuscript and finally finished it. Reading how Father said they were each other's *bashert* gave me goose bumps! Mother stopped keeping a diary once the decision was made for Palestine. She felt she was then beginning a new life.

In less than 22 hours the British will be pulling out of Palestine for good. We will then begin our new life with a battle we did not want but willingly engage in for survival of our people. We trust in God to deliver us from the Arab armies, but, to be on the safe side, we are as prepared as we can be.

We need good luck, too! I showed Joel the gold crucifix Marya gave Mother before she died. I don't wear it—it's in a little cloth packet inside my footlocker. Joel handled it well, considering his Orthodoxy. He does not approve, but he knows its history as a family keepsake for good luck. Ever considerate of others, he suggested Catholics might feel it sacrilegious of me, but he also knows that is not my intent. In a way, Marya's crucifix served as a catalyst for bringing our sometimes conflicting versions of Judaism together. With scholars unable to agree on "Who is a Jew?," Joel and I have finally concluded that love, common sense, and respect for each other will help us thread our way through our differences. It is such a good feeling!

As long as I can't sleep, these are the updates for Mother's diary. She and Father kept the names on their passports—Anna and Samuel Wiseman. I believe it was their way of starting anew and deceiving the "evil eye." They were married May 19, 1924. She was 17; he was 24. Father has been wounded several times but always bounces back, thank God. I hope he is one of the Palmach fighters Yad Mordechai is buying time for in the race for Jerusalem.

Michael and Aaron Stern, my older brothers, kept their real names in honor of their parents, but also came to love Mother and Father as parents. I think of them as my real brothers and love them dearly.

Uncle Josef Yulanov reverted to his father's name "to restore my family's honor." An ardent Zionist from the very beginning, his photo once appeared alongside Menachem Begin's on British "Wanted" lists. He is Father's best friend. A close aide to Ben Gurion, he is promised an important post in the new government. He jokes about "almost" being my father. When I say he married Israel instead, my parents look at each other and laugh . . . they also laugh and wink about Uncle Josef's parents, but that is a secret no one talks about. He is still single and much sought after by many of the unattached women. Uncle Josef is trying to reconcile the warring factions—Irgun, the Stern Gang, and Haganah. I think it's a sin for Jews to be fighting each other at a time like this!

Aunt Sheila married Avram Berger a year after they came to Palestine. We consider them our grandparents. Although he is close to 80, Avram is forever begging Aaron to take him on his next mission.

Alepa Miklos corresponds with Mother from America. Her husband, Viktor, is a distributor of building materials in Baltimore. Stefan, their son, is a surgeon in Chicago.

Uncle Sandor still has a café in Budapest but no longer performs. He promises to visit and play for us as soon as "the trouble" is over. I can hardly wait for the world to recognize our nation so we can finally have peace.

Peter Fedorovich is a prominent businessman in California. Mother and Father say he has been a loyal friend since she was a child. Joseph and his group owe their lives to him—as we do. I hope the State of Israel will one day recognize all he has done.

I almost forgot the most enigmatic figure of them all— Herr Designer. No one has ever spoken his real name. He came to the house once when I was three or four. I remember being frightened of him. Over the years we saw him two or three more times. Mother and Grandma still argue about him. He writes sporadically, but it is all very mysterious. No one knows his present whereabouts. I have the feeling he is a double agent.

This brings Mother's story up to date. Tomorrow, I will review it one more time . . . and then I have a full week to make final corrections before the 19th.

THE NEW STATE OF ISRAEL!
May 14, 1948, 2100 hours –

We are stunned. . . we are ecstatic! Radio reports said the British evacuated Jerusalem this morning, a day *earlier* than planned. Ben Gurion announced statehood this afternoon! We are overjoyed but sober. Word has it that a large Egyptian army is headed our way. I have been in firefights with Arabs before, but this is the first battle we fight as a nation. I pray we will be victorious and never have to fight again. The surprising news has electrified our community to a greater degree of confidence . . . and it is contagious. We will win because we must!

Joel informed me earlier that we are paired for tonight's sentry duty at the water tower—a strategic post assigned only to the most qualified soldiers. This is another reason I am in such good spirits tonight. We were going to hold off making our engagement public for a few more days, but if the State of Israel can announce its birth a day ahead of time, so can we! One of the women found a bottle of wine, and we celebrated both occasions. Joel and I are anxious to call our families, but, for the moment, our personal good news will have to wait. Not too long, I hope.

I hear Joel's footsteps coming up the walk, so this is all for now.

Editor's Note: Deborah's manuscript ends here. Seven Arab armies attacked the State of Israel. The defenders of Yad Mordechai held off a large Egyptian force until they were overrun on May 18, 1948. They suffered 25 percent casualties. Deborah Wiseman and Joel Aaronson were both wounded.

Her father, Samuel, was with the Palmach fighters who reached Tel Aviv in time to save it from the Arabs. Her brother Aaron and his unit later returned to Yad Mordechai, liberating it on November 6, 1948.

Deborah and Joel married in March, 1949. Joel was wounded again in the 1973 war. They live in Jerusalem, where their oldest child, Hanna Aaronson-Goldman, a peace activist, meets regularly with her Arab counterparts. Their son, Ilya, is a major in the Israeli Air Force, and their second daughter, Sharon, is a senior at Harvard.

Samuel and Anna Wiseman (the former Robert and Sara) settled in Jerusalem. Samuel was wounded in the 1956 Sinai Campaign and died in the 1967 Six-Day War. Their son Aaron died in the 1973 Yom Kippur War. Anna Wiseman continued to live in Jerusalem until her death in 1987.

The Wisemans' eldest daughter, Eelia, married the American bomber pilot Elliot Nathanson, who was a volunteer in the fledgling Israeli Air Force. They and the families of their three children all live today in the seaside city of Natanya.